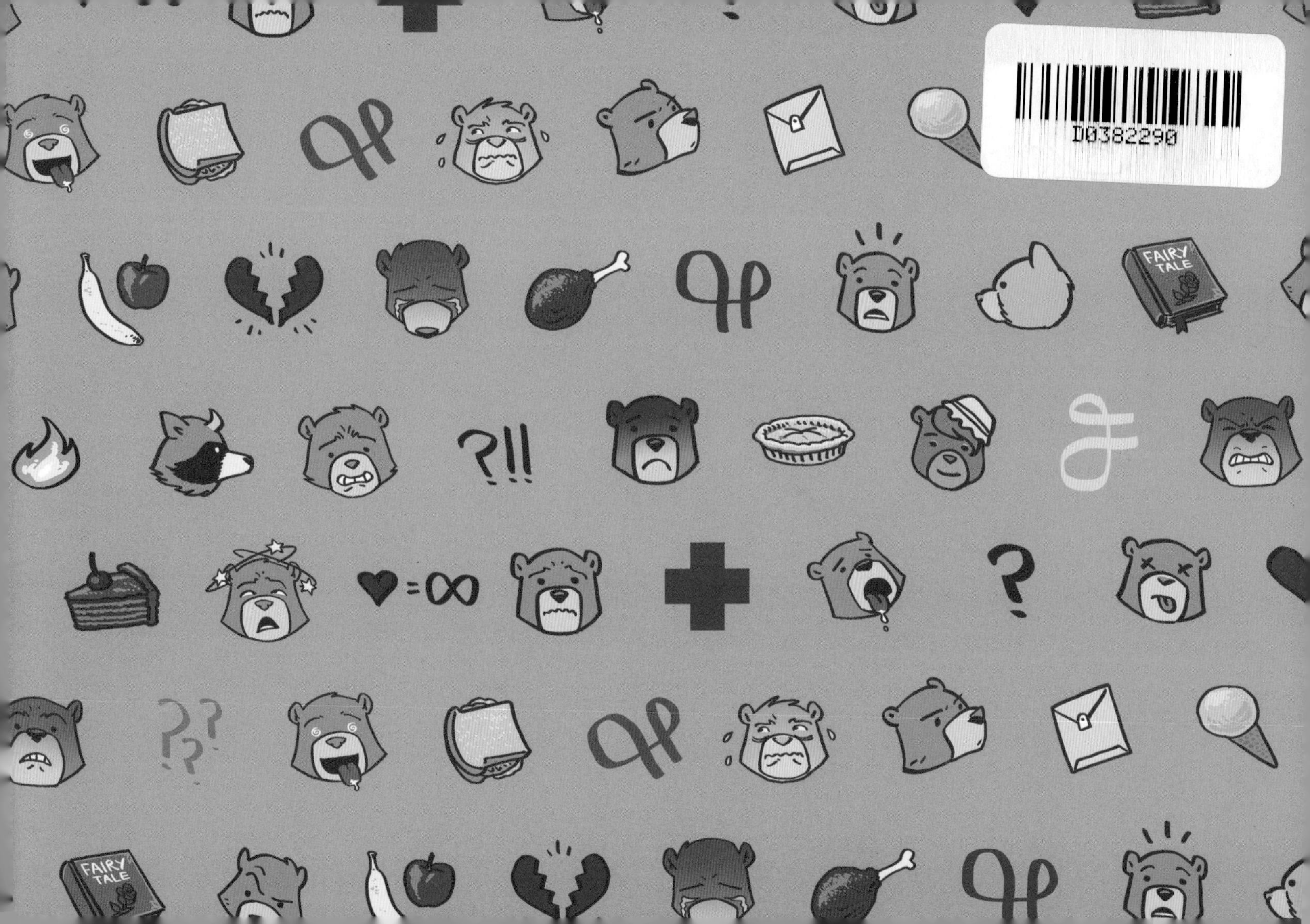
FAIRY TALE
?!!
FAIRY TALE

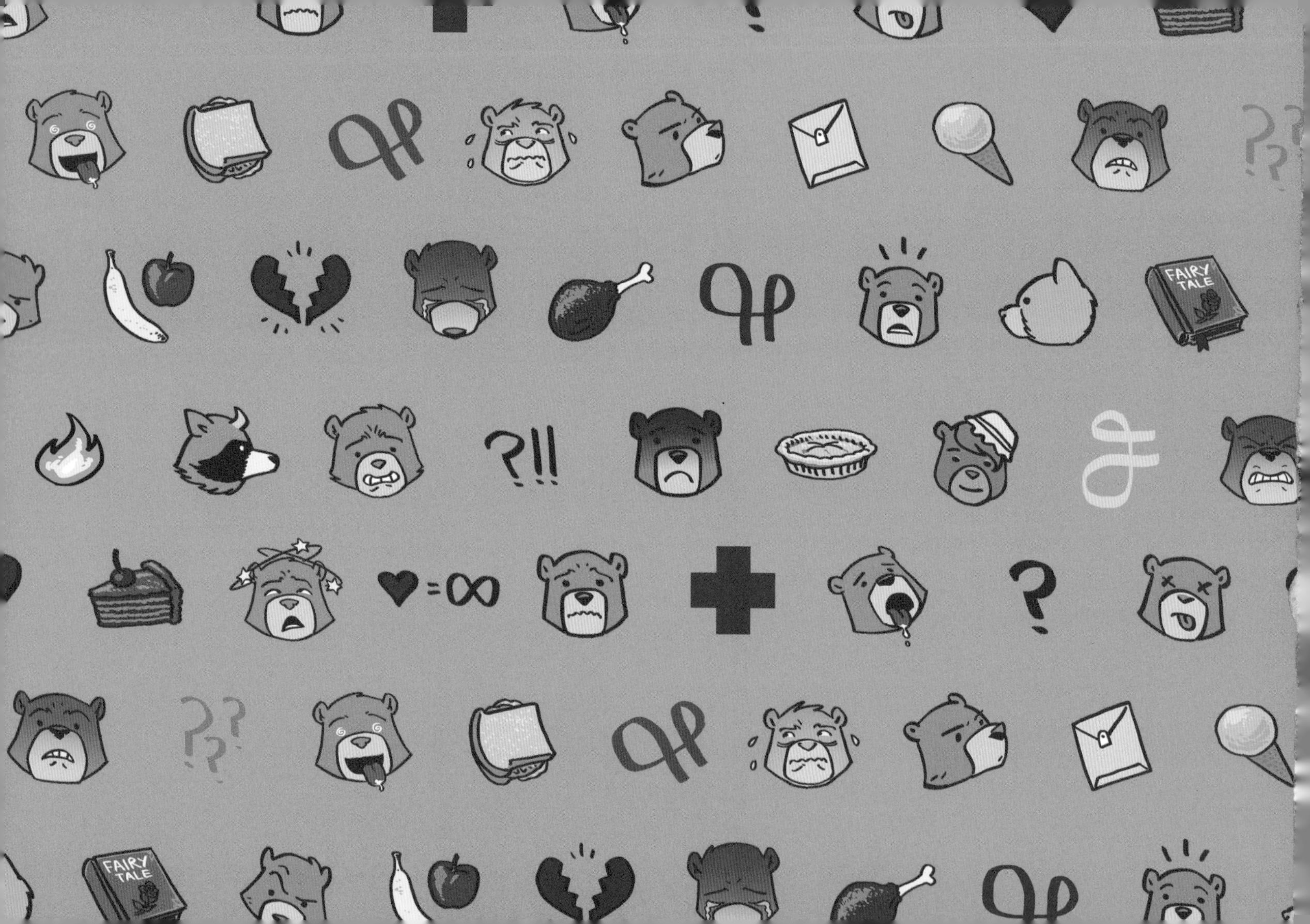
FAIRY TALE
?!!

SPACE BEAR ™

by

ETHAN YOUNG

kaboom! ™

Designer **Jillian Crab**
Original Series Editor **Jim Gibbons**
Editor **Jonathan Manning**
Executive Editor **Sierra Hahn**

Ross Richie CEO & Founder
Joy Huffman CFO
Matt Gagnon Editor-in-Chief
Filip Sablik President, Publishing & Marketing
Stephen Christy President, Development
Lance Kreiter Vice President, Licensing & Merchandising
Arune Singh Vice President, Marketing
Bryce Carlson Vice President, Editorial & Creative Strategy
Kate Henning Director, Operations
Spencer Simpson Director, Sales
Scott Newman Manager, Production Design
Elyse Strandberg Manager, Finance
Sierra Hahn Executive Editor
Jeanine Schaefer Executive Editor
Dafna Pleban Senior Editor
Shannon Watters Senior Editor
Eric Harburn Senior Editor
Matthew Levine Editor
Sophie Philips-Roberts Associate Editor
Amanda LaFranco Associate Editor
Jonathan Manning Associate Editor
Gavin Gronenthal Assistant Editor

Gwen Waller Assistant Editor
Allyson Gronowitz Assistant Editor
Shelby Netschke Editorial Assistant
Jillian Crab Design Coordinator
Michelle Ankley Design Coordinator
Marie Krupina Production Designer
Grace Park Production Designer
Chelsea Roberts Production Designer
Samantha Knapp Production Design Assistant
José Meza Live Events Lead
Stephanie Hocutt Digital Marketing Lead
Esther Kim Marketing Coordinator
Cat O'Grady Digital Marketing Coordinator
Amanda Lawson Marketing Assistant
Holly Aitchison Digital Sales Coordinator
Morgan Perry Retail Sales Coordinator
Megan Christopher Operations Coordinator
Rodrigo Hernandez Operations Coordinator
Zipporah Smith Operations Assistant
Jason Lee Senior Accountant
Sabrina Lesin Accounting Assistant
Breanna Sarpy Executive Assistant

Originally published in digital format as Pilgrim Finch by Stela, LLC. in 2016.

BOOM! Studios, 5670 Wilshire Boulevard, Suite 400, Los Angeles, CA 90036-5679.
Printed in China. First Printing.

ISBN: 978-1-68415-559-0, eISBN: 978-1-64144-725-6

For my son,

Elliott.

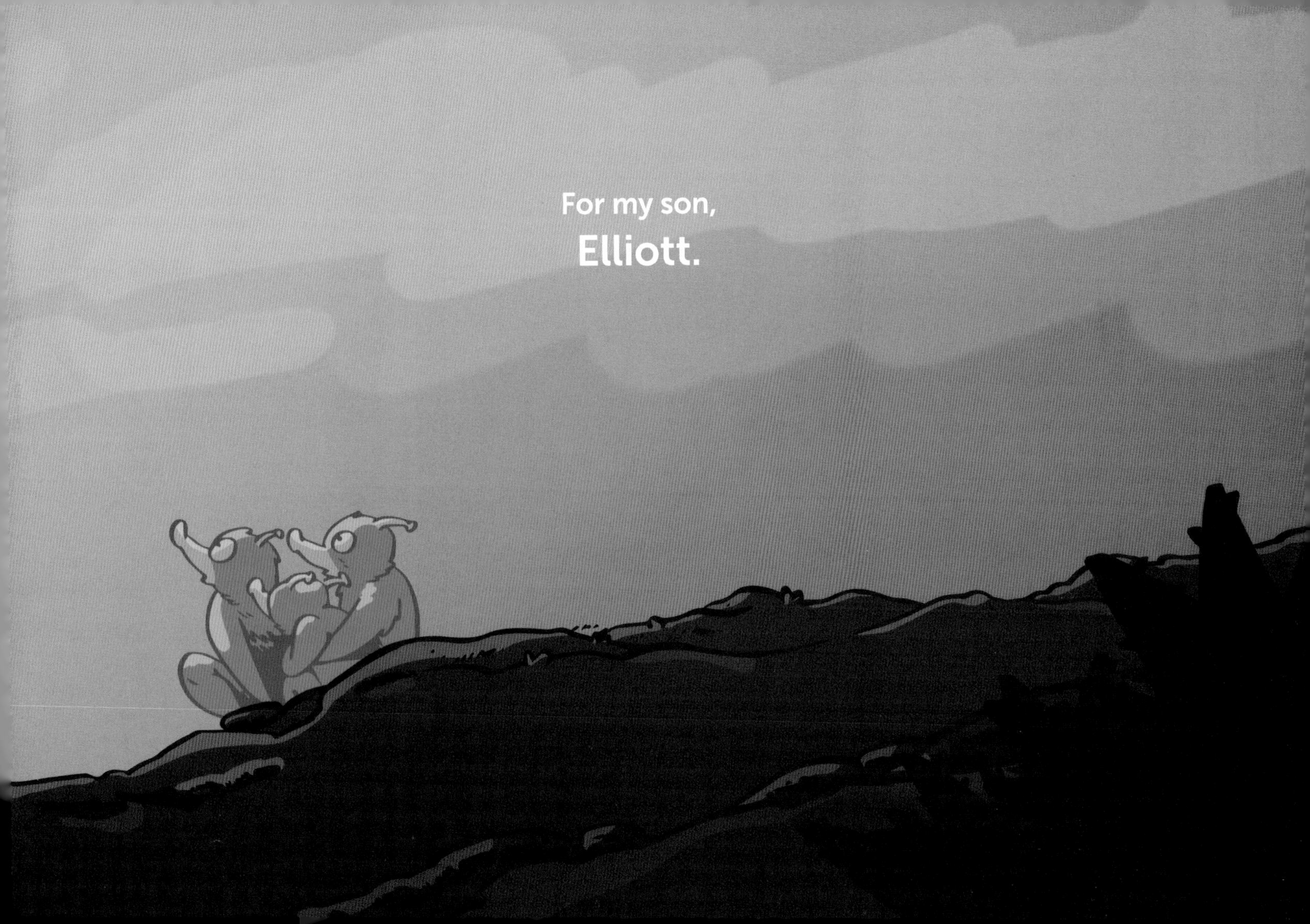

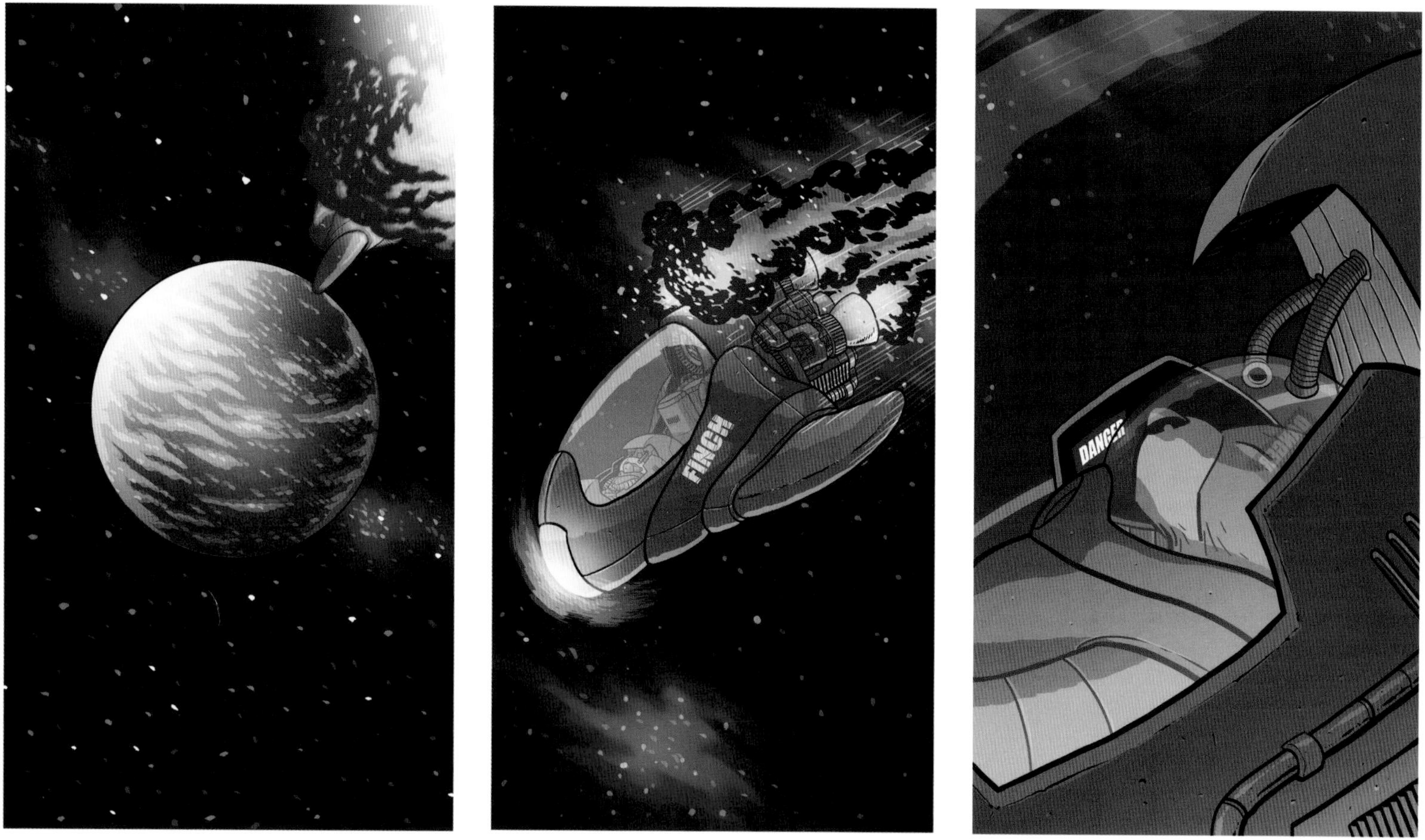
FINCH
DANGER

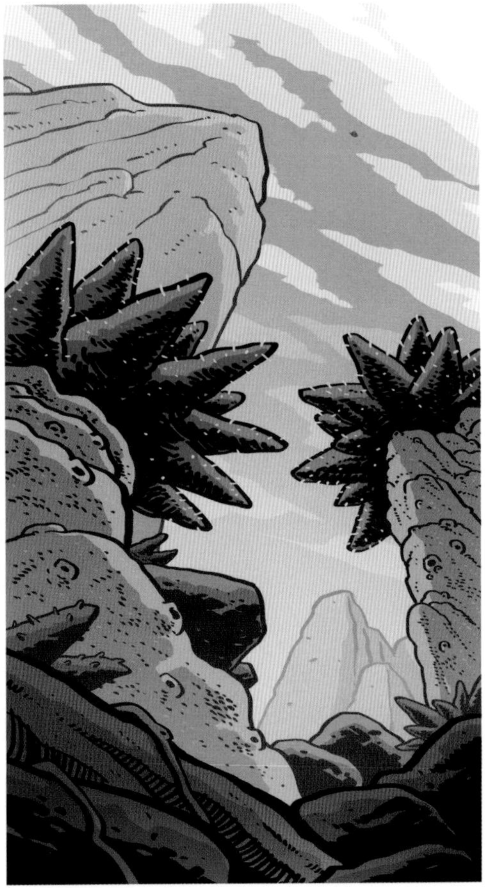

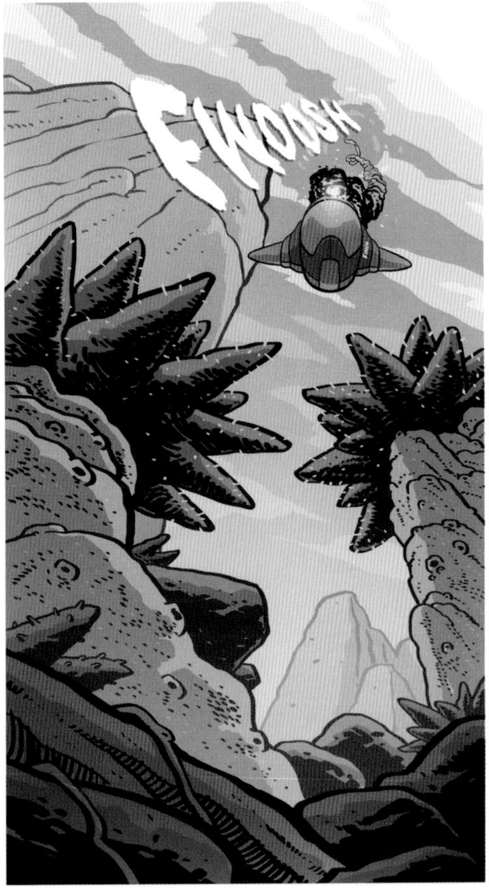
FWOOSH

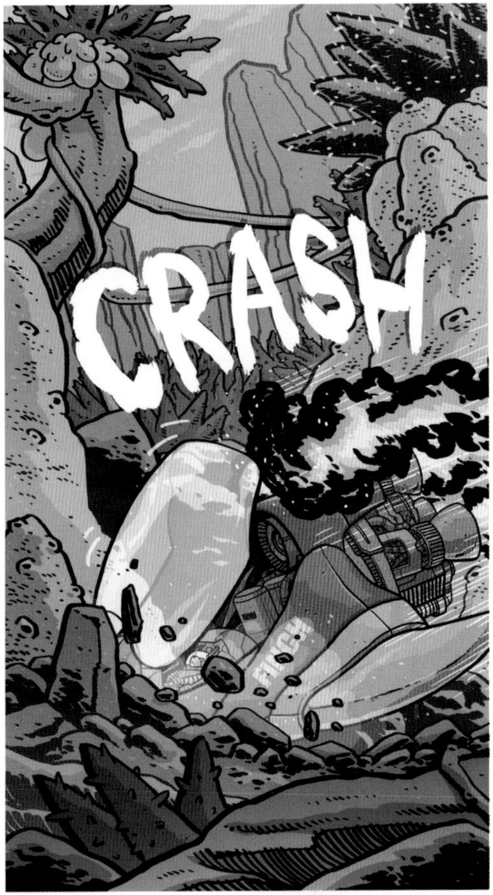
CRASH

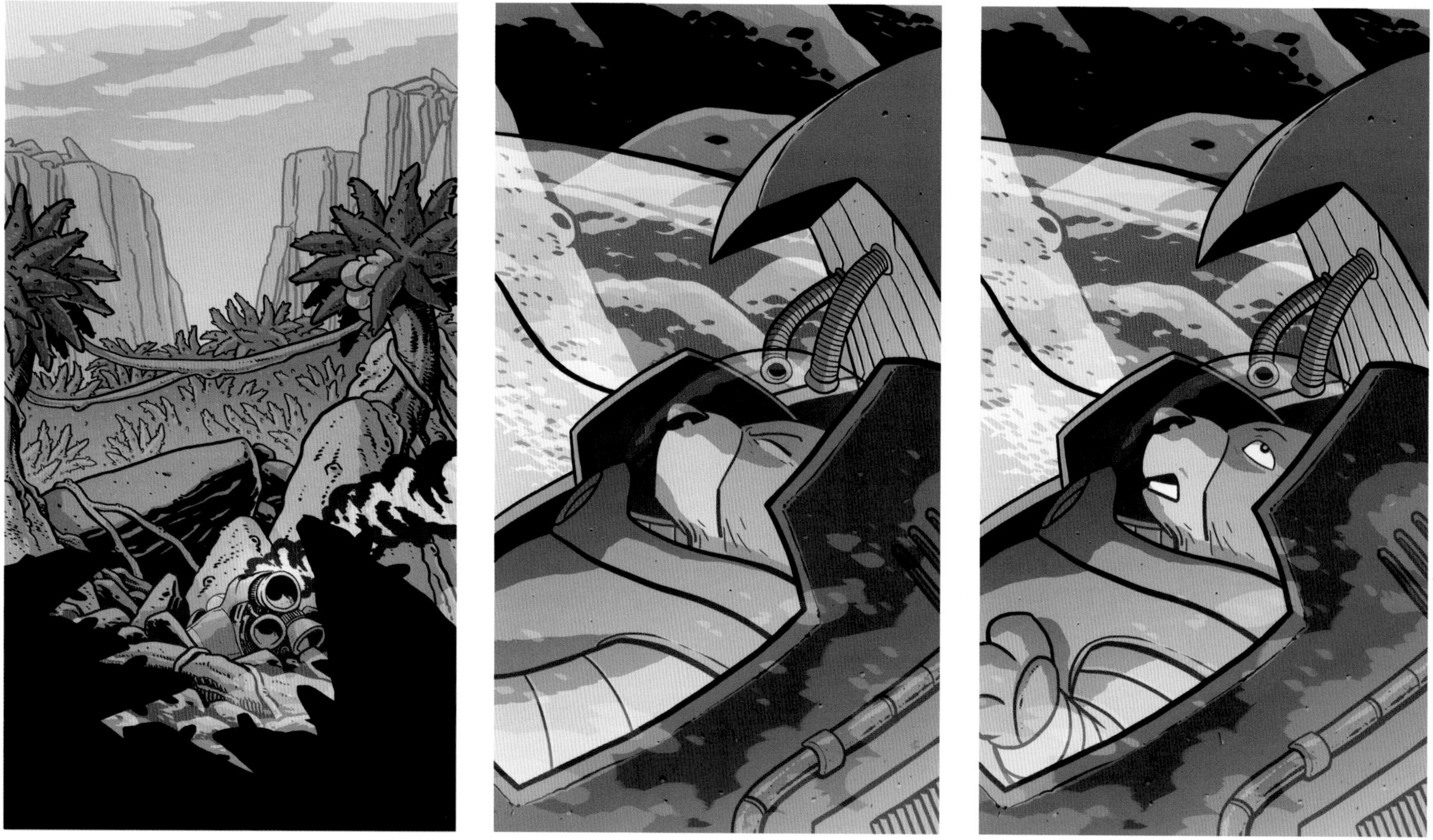

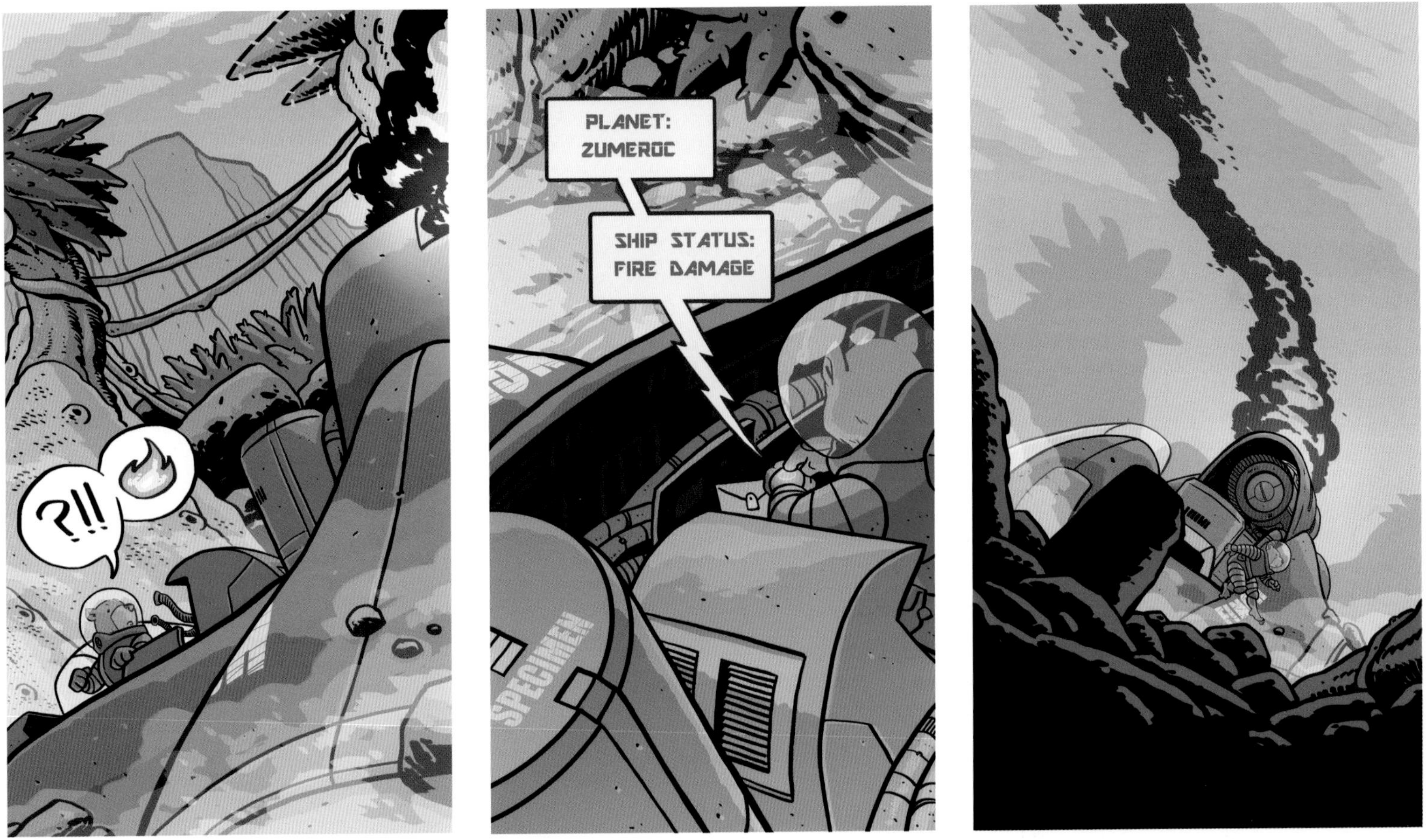
?!!
PLANET: ZUMEROC
SHIP STATUS: FIRE DAMAGE
SPECIMEN
SPECIMEN

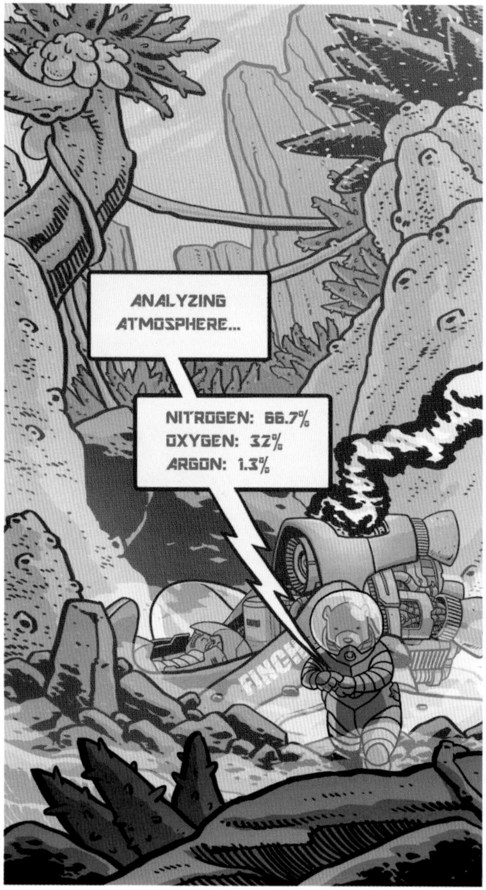
ANALYZING ATMOSPHERE...
NITROGEN: 66.7%
OXYGEN: 32%
ARGON: 1.3%

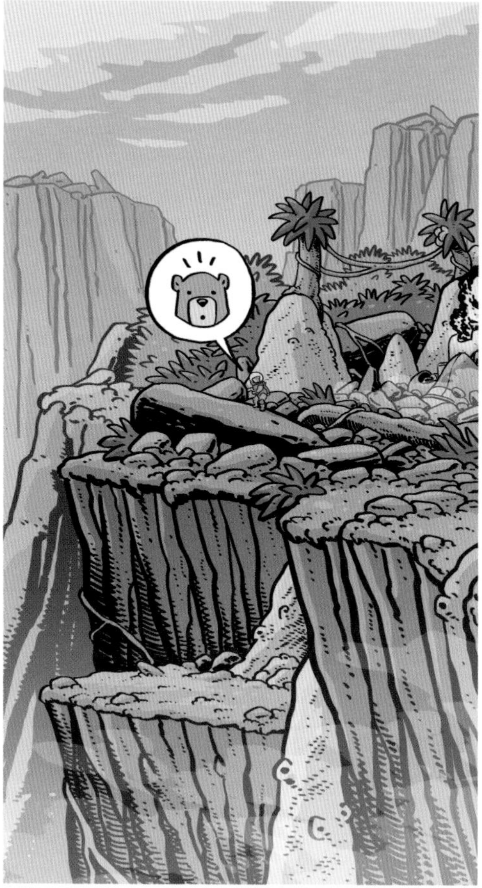

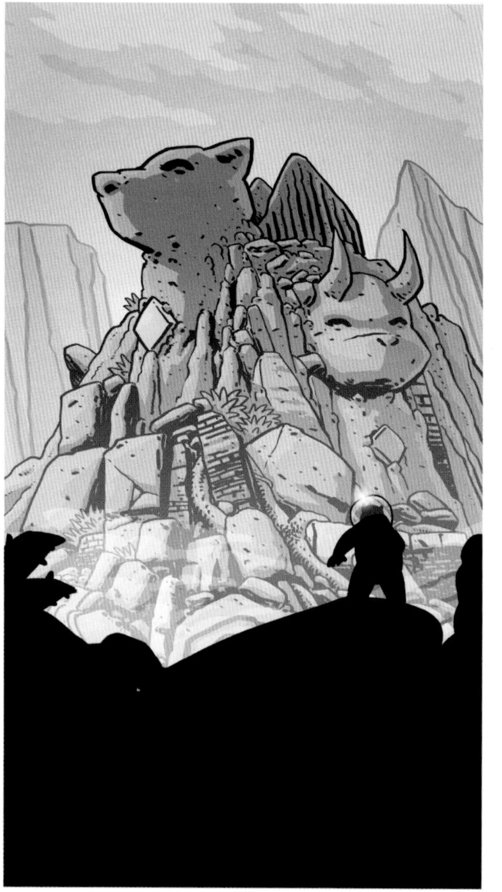

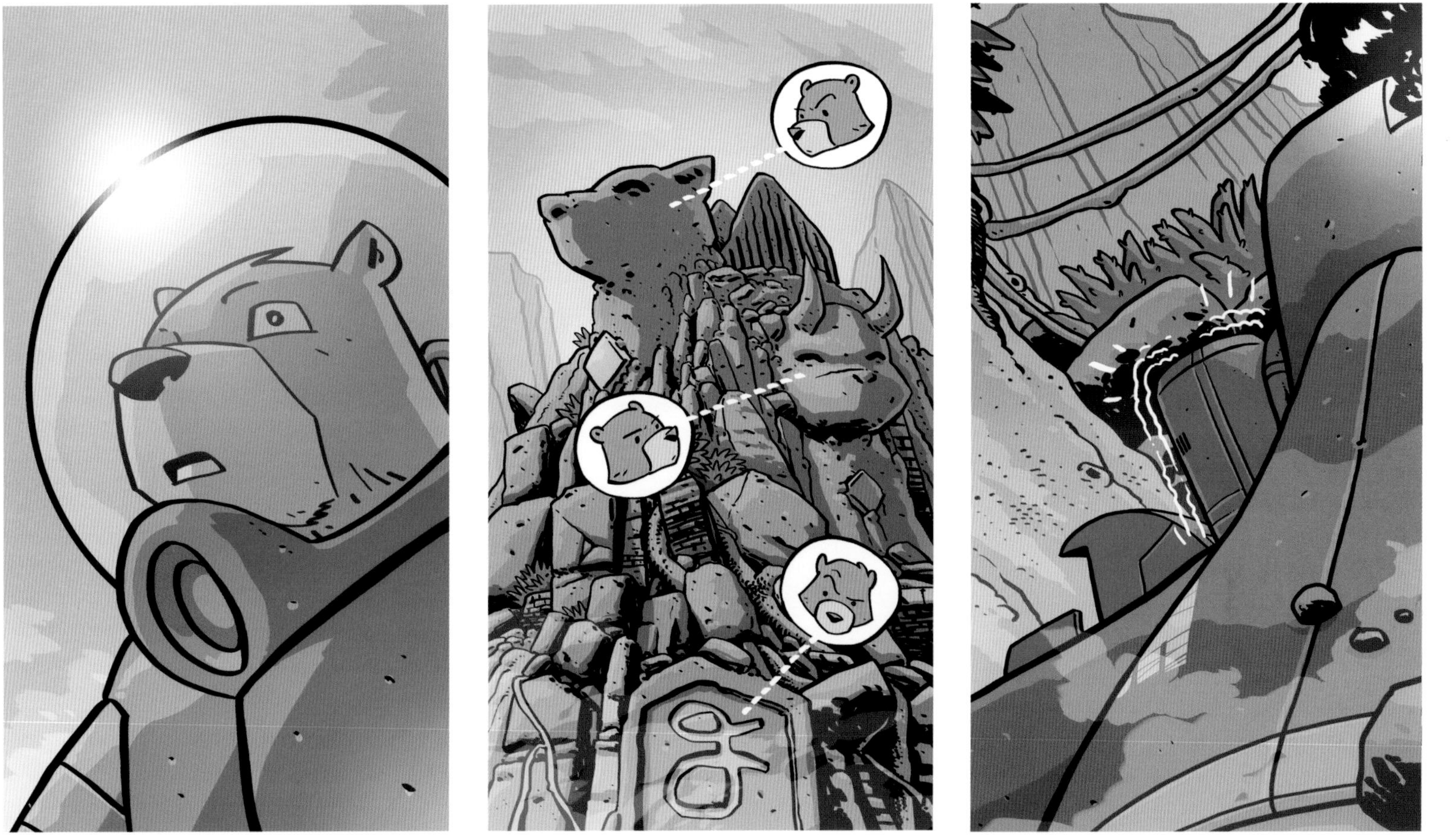

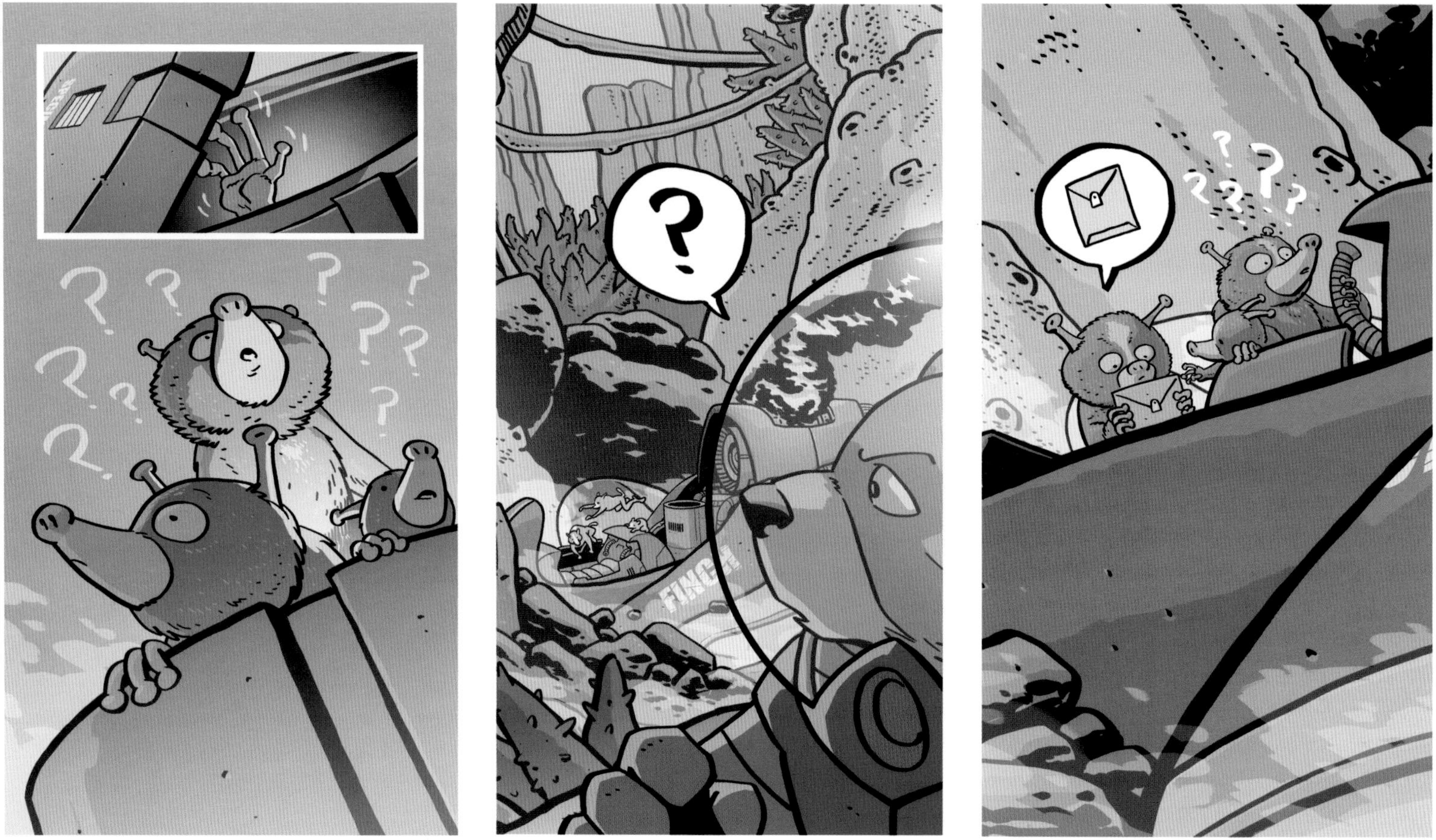
?
FINCH

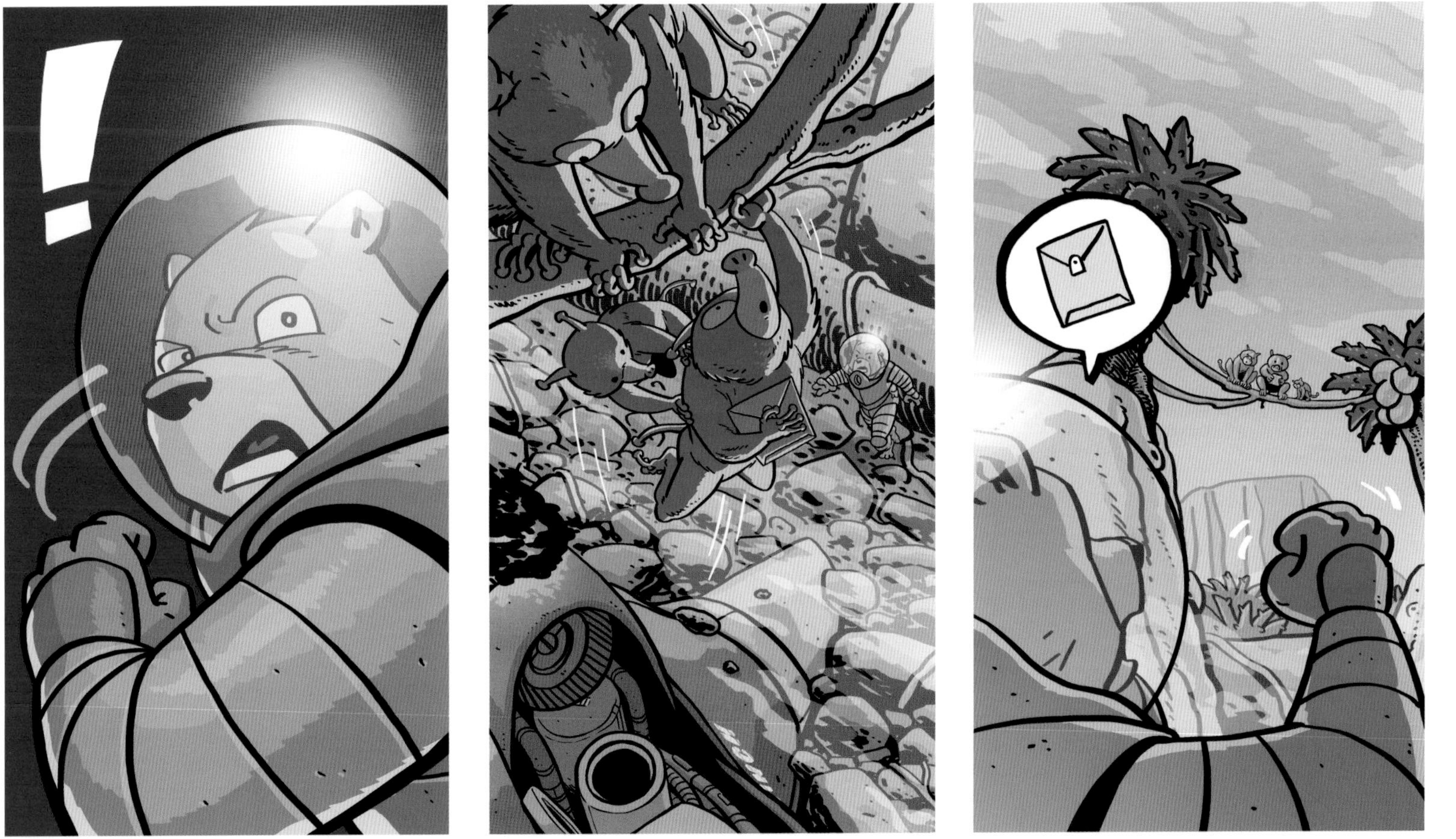
!

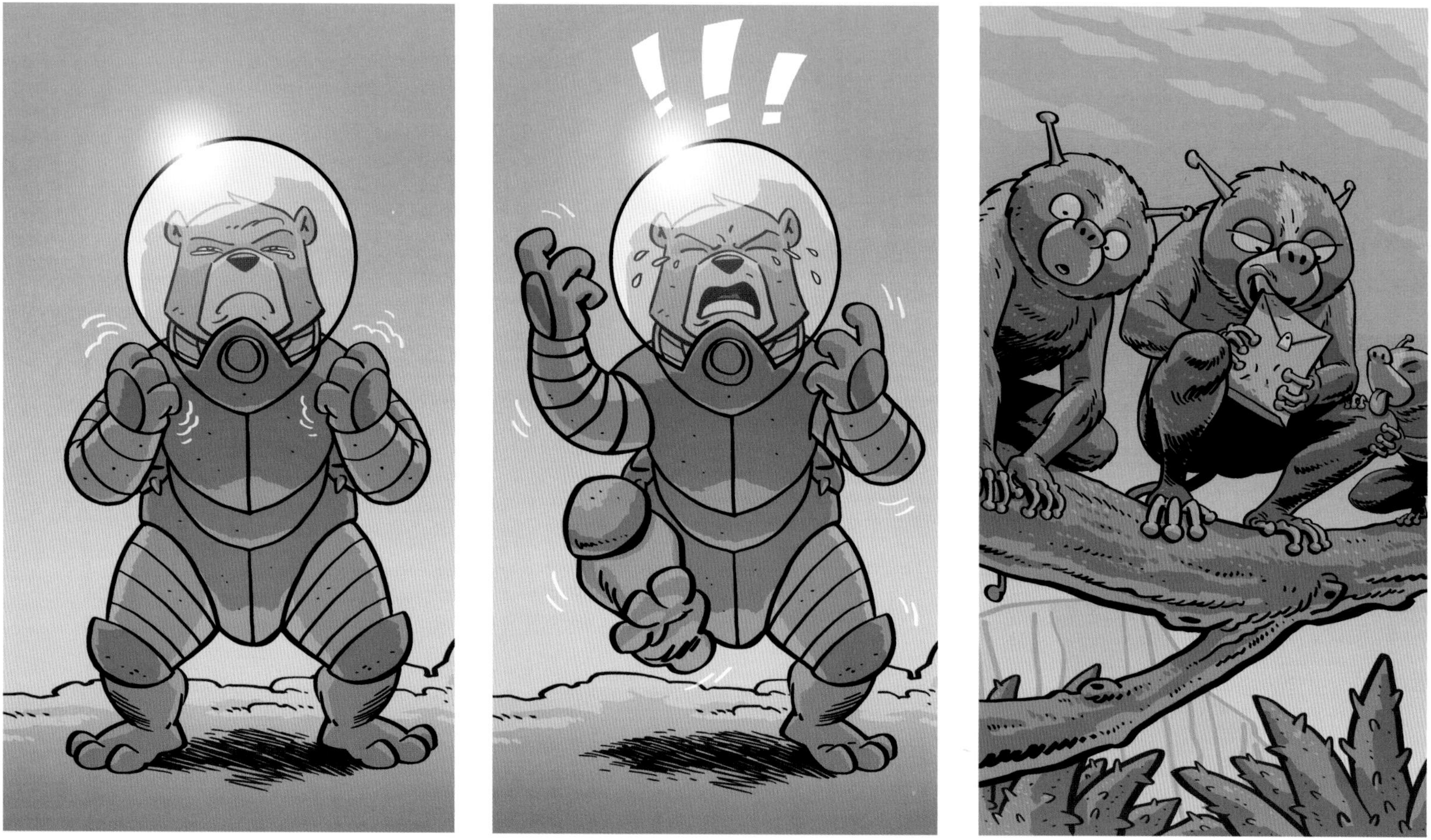
!!!

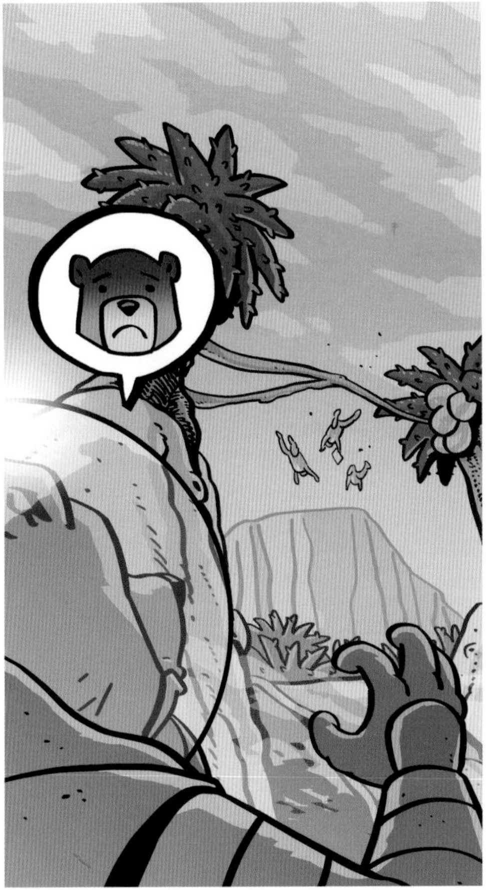
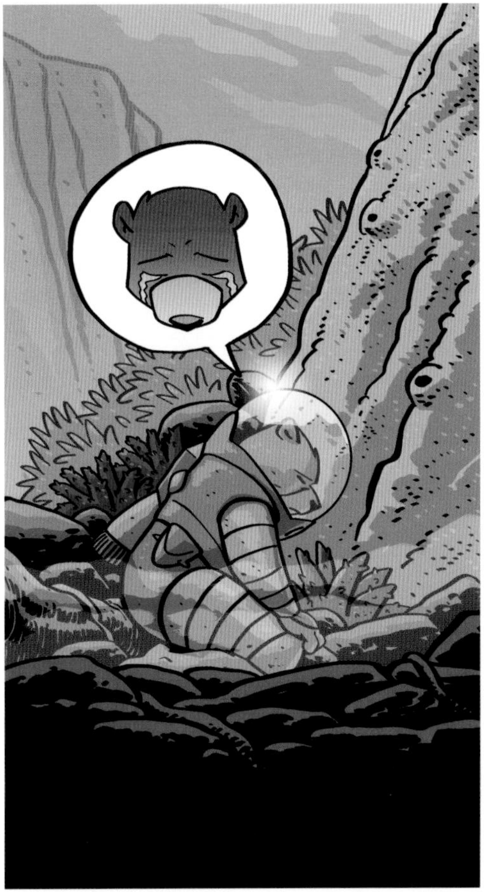
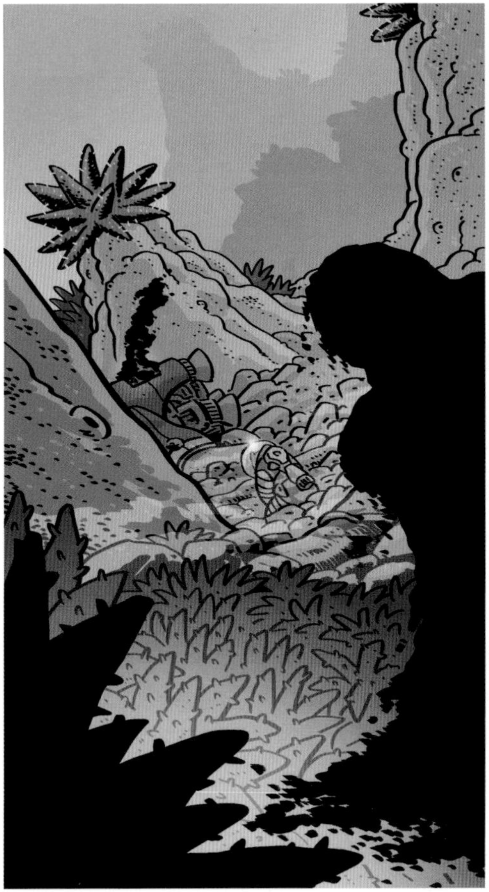

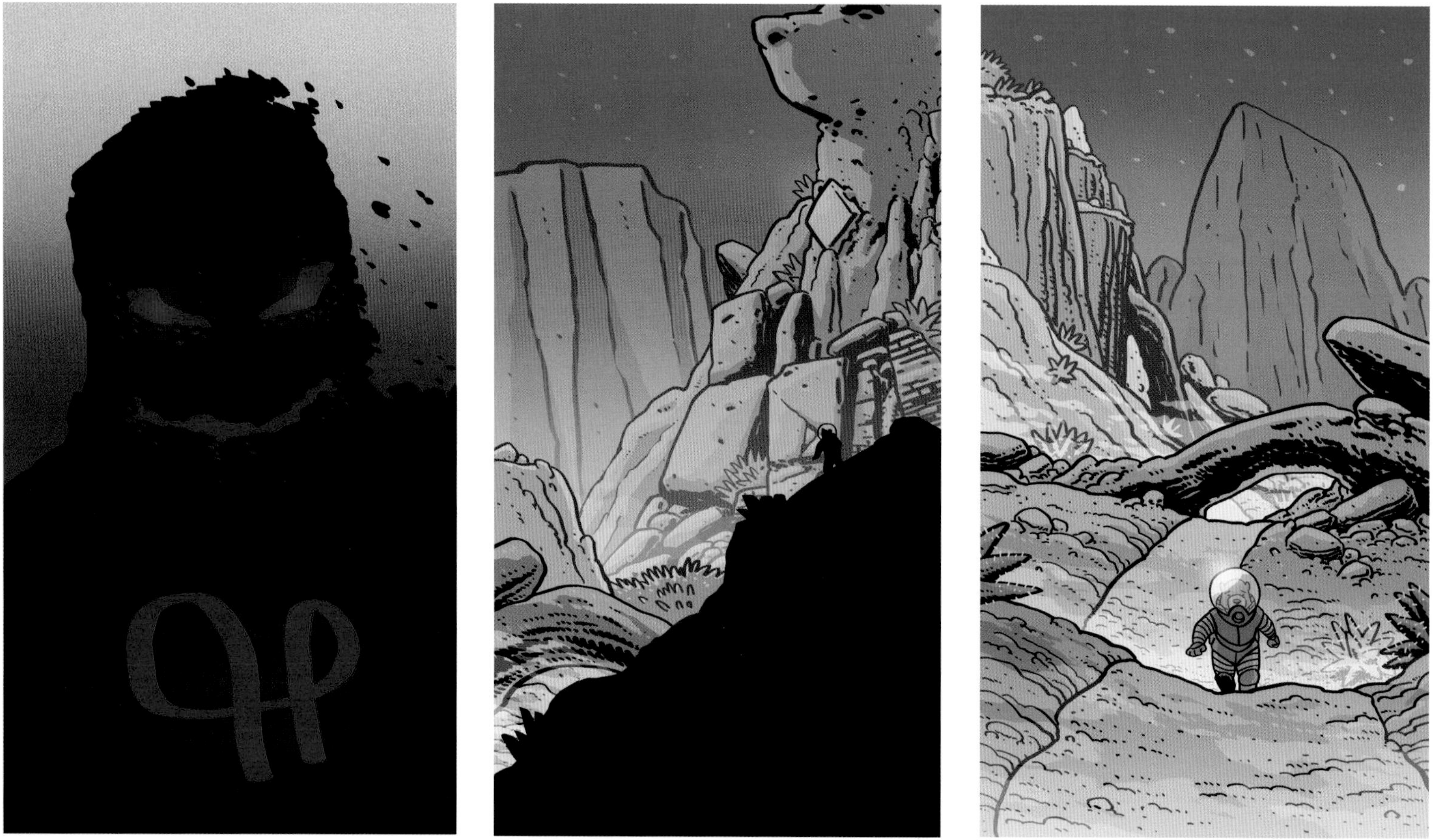

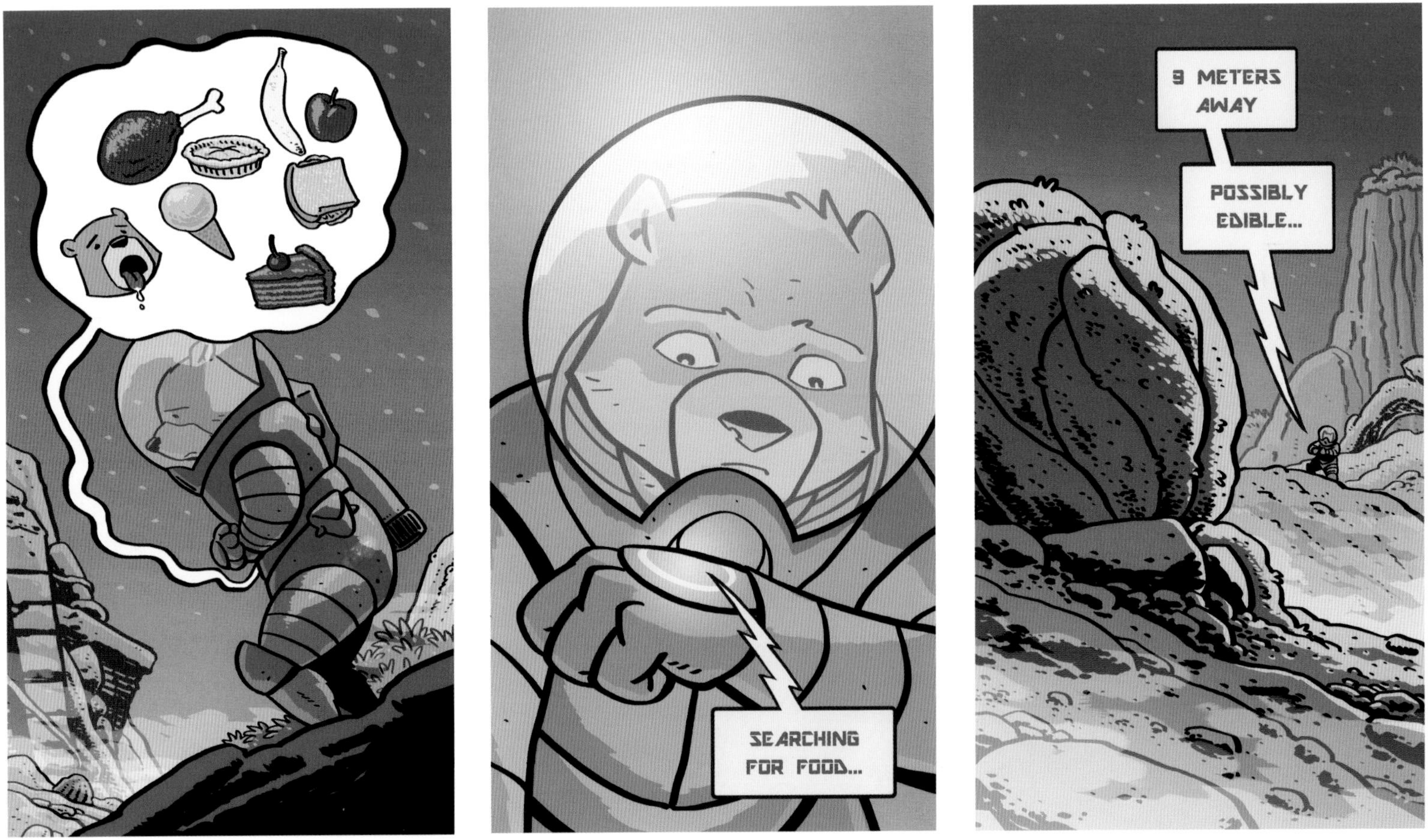
SEARCHING
FOR FOOD...
9 METERS
AWAY
POSSIBLY
EDIBLE...

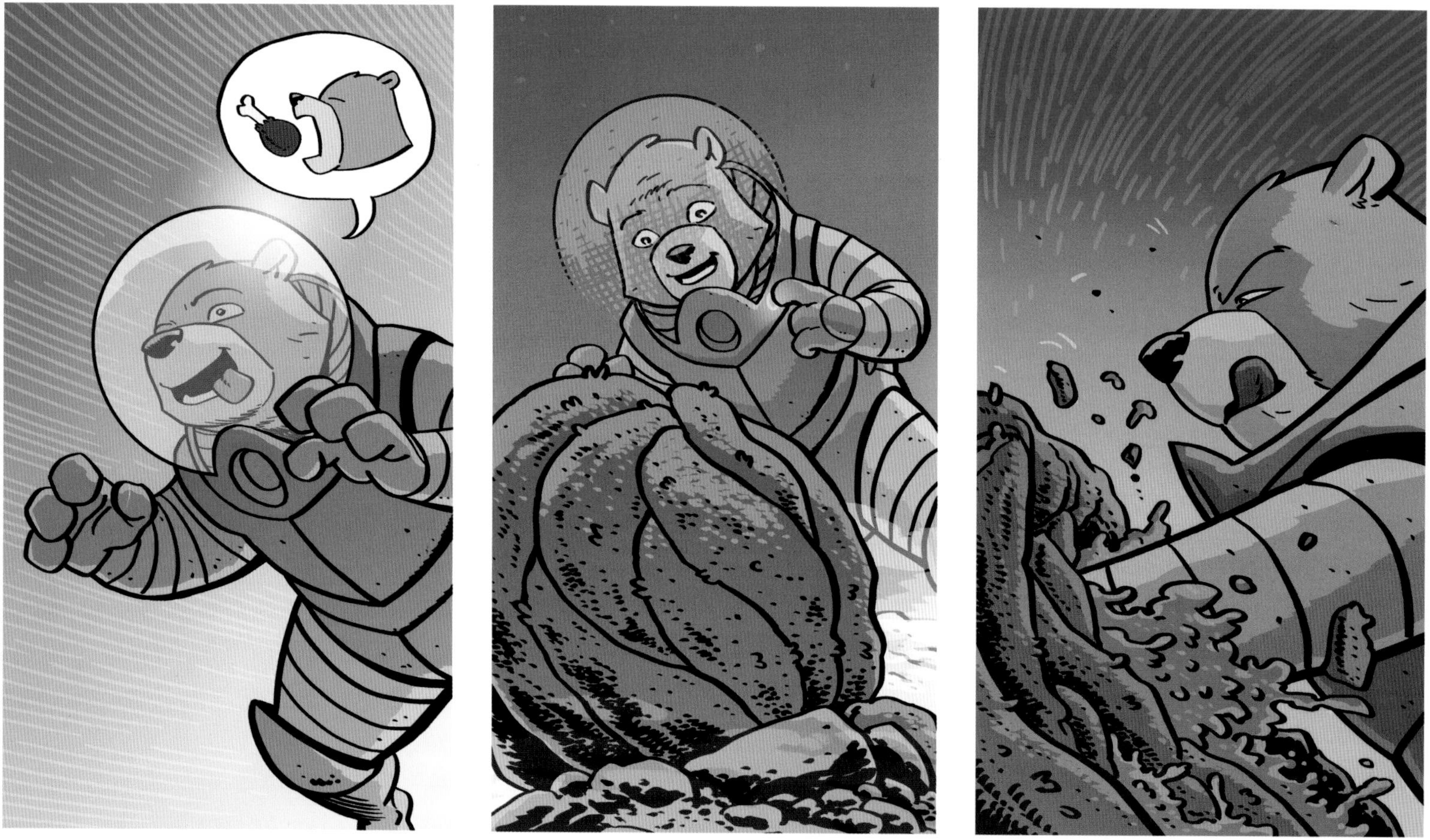

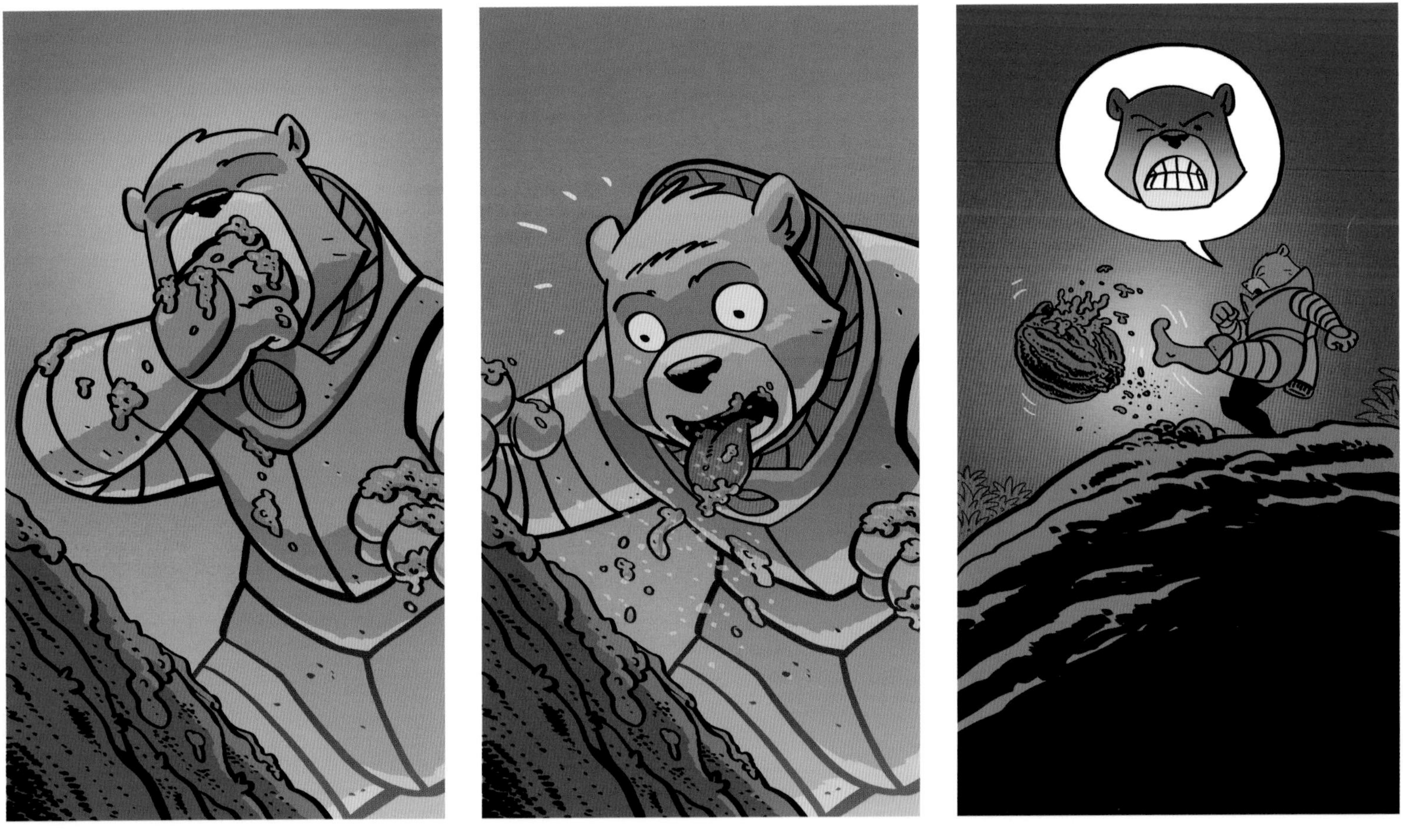

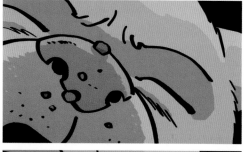

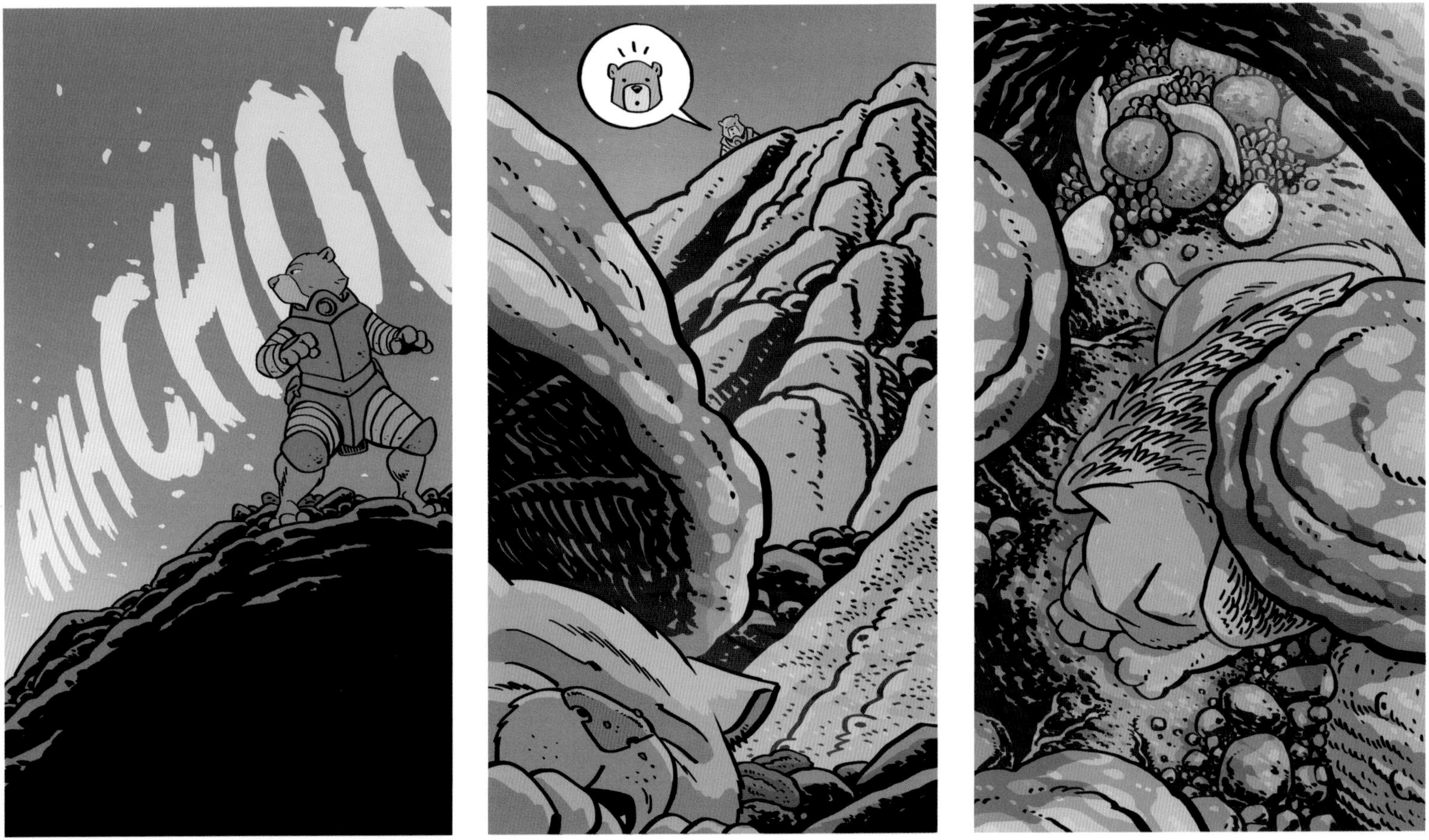
AHHCHOO

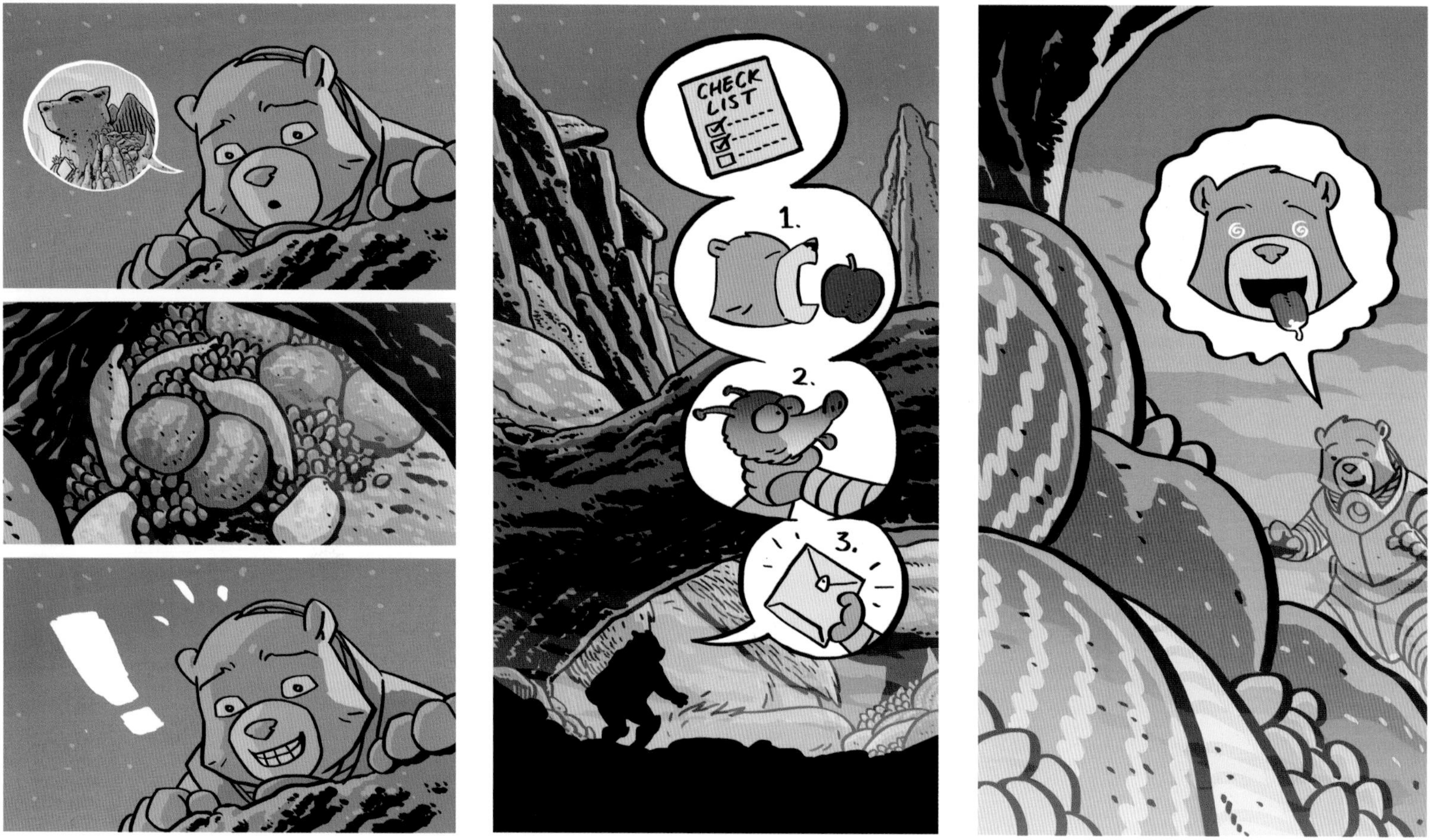
CHECK LIST
1.
2.
3.

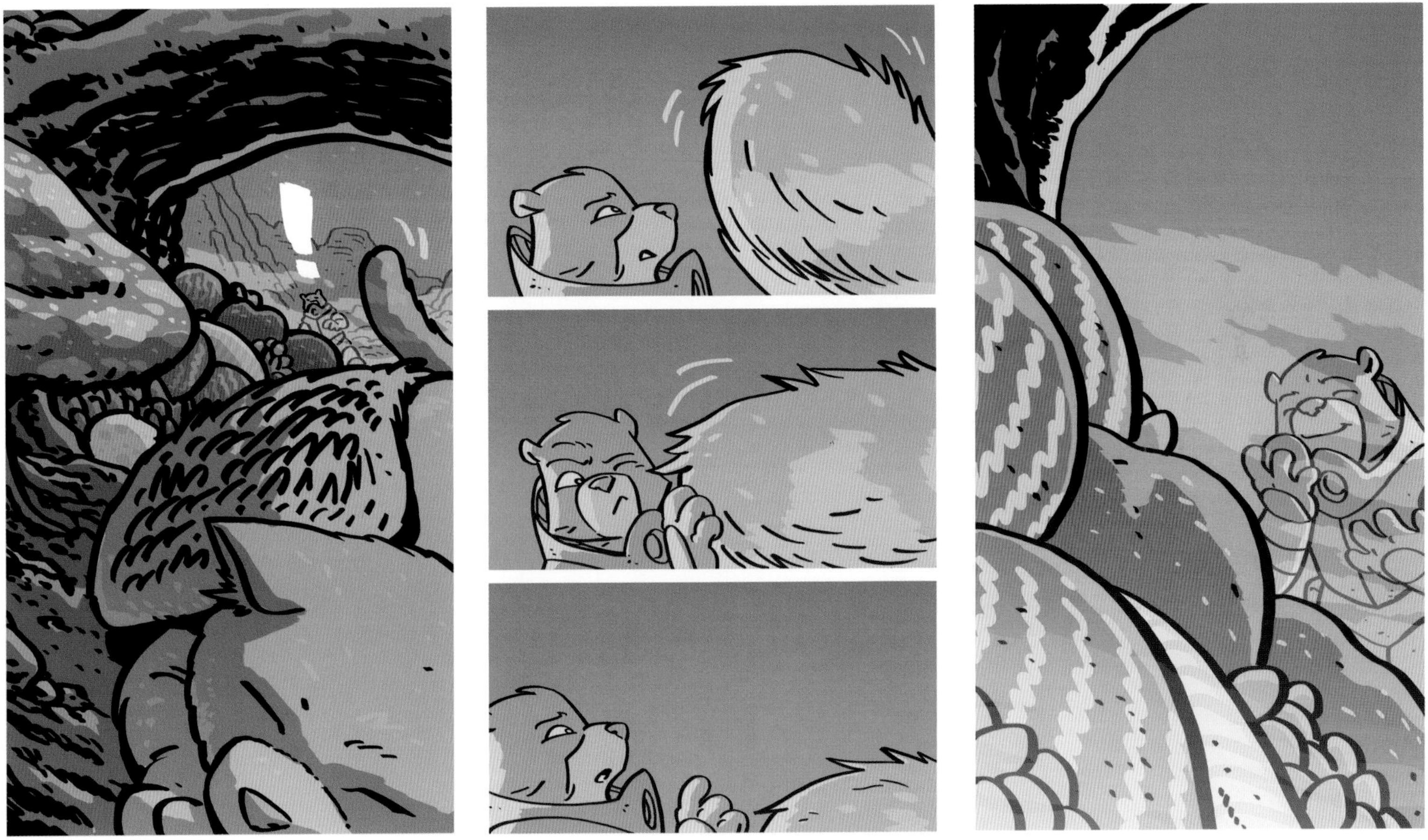

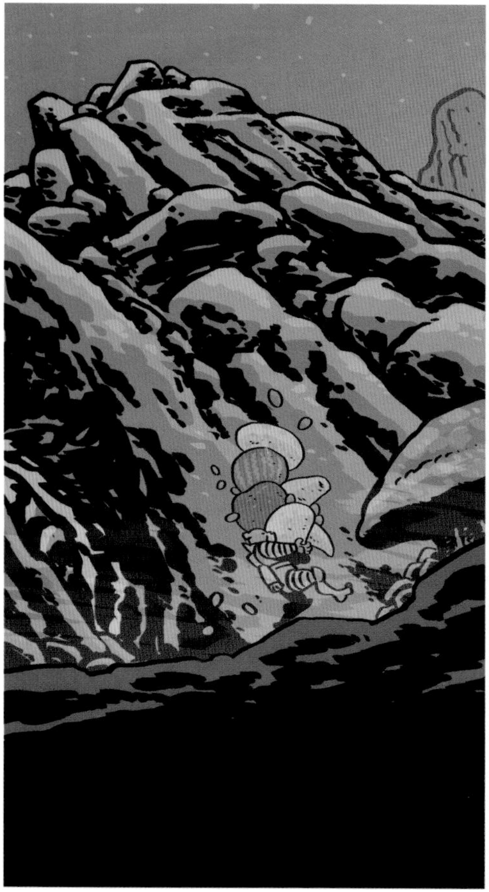
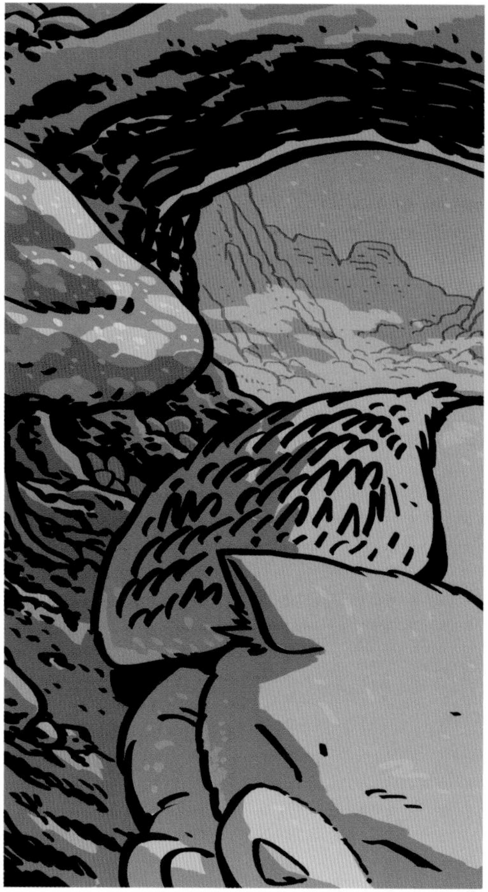
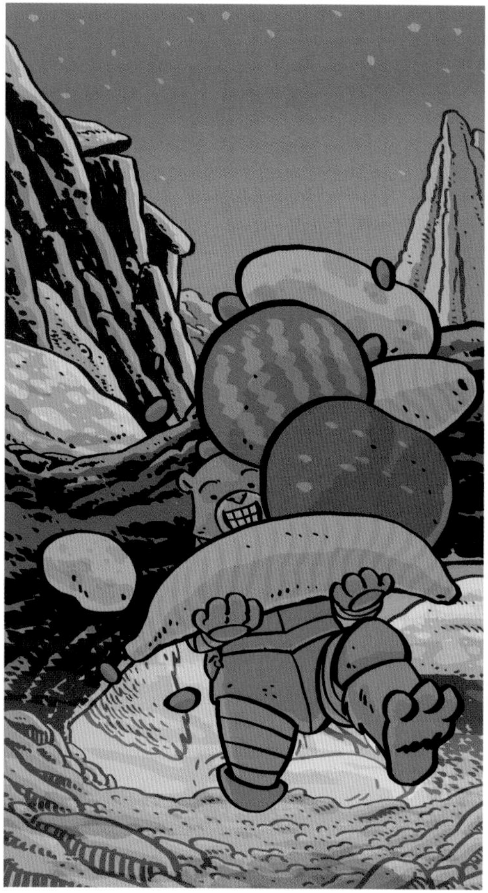

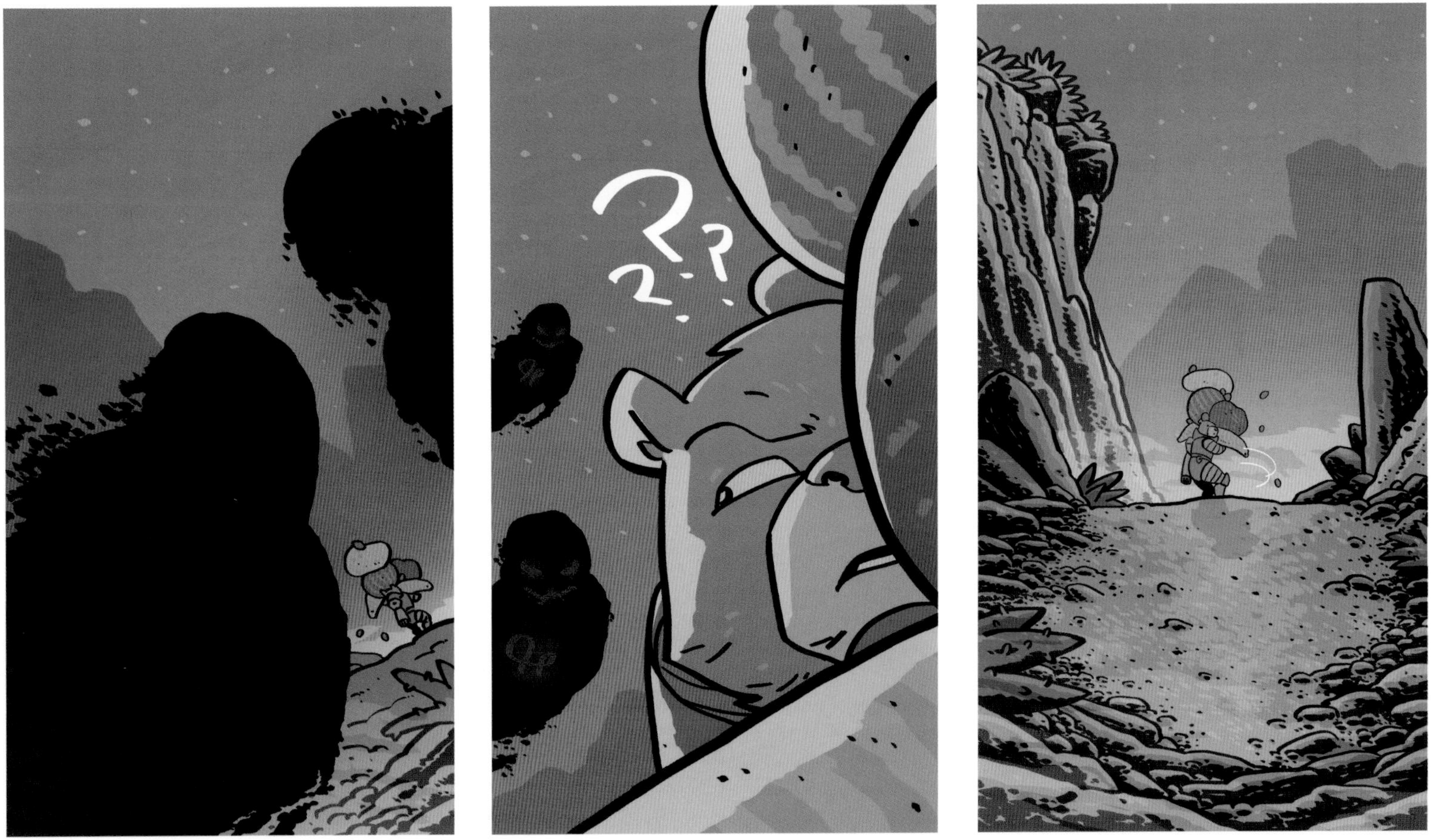
???

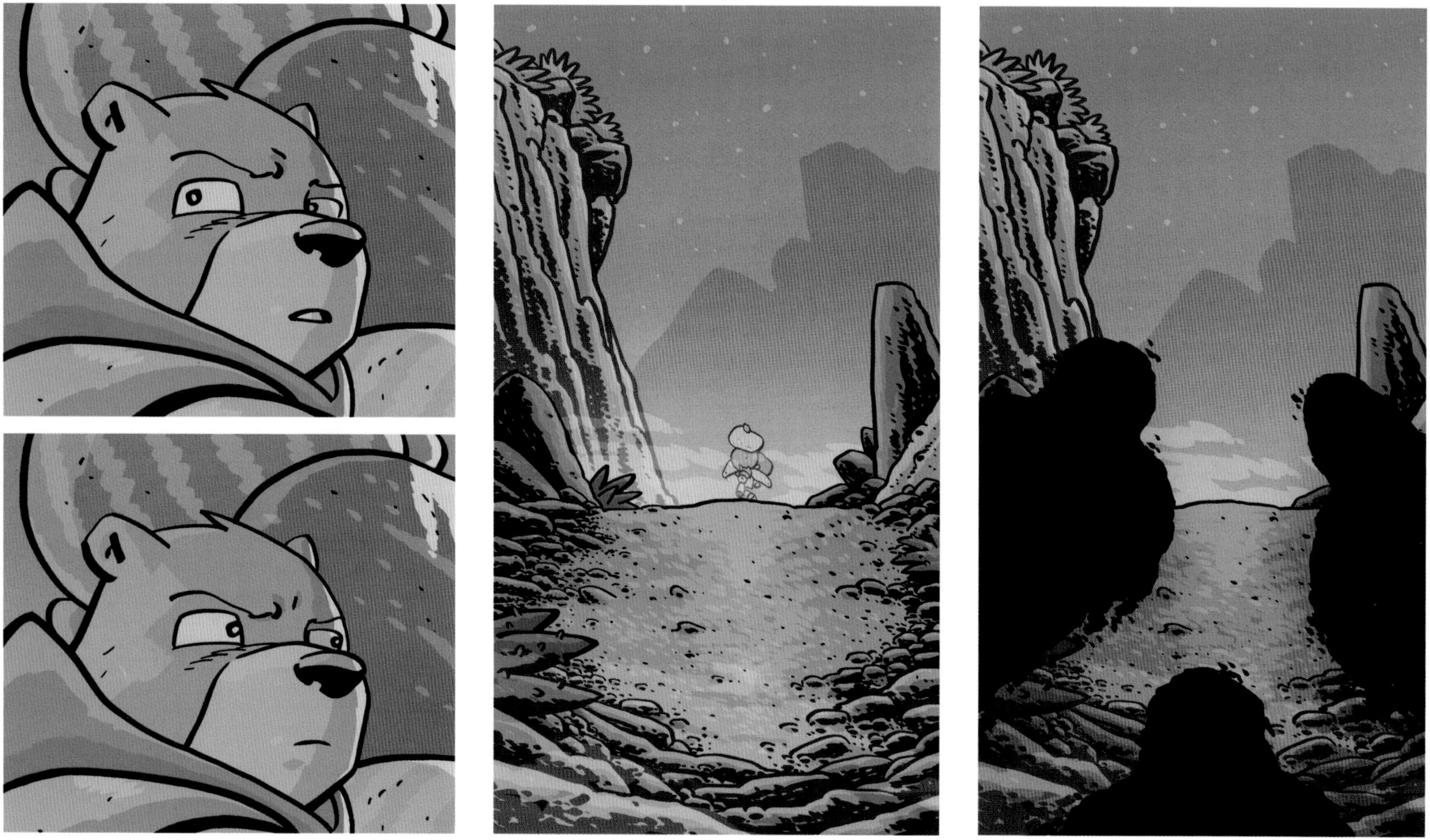

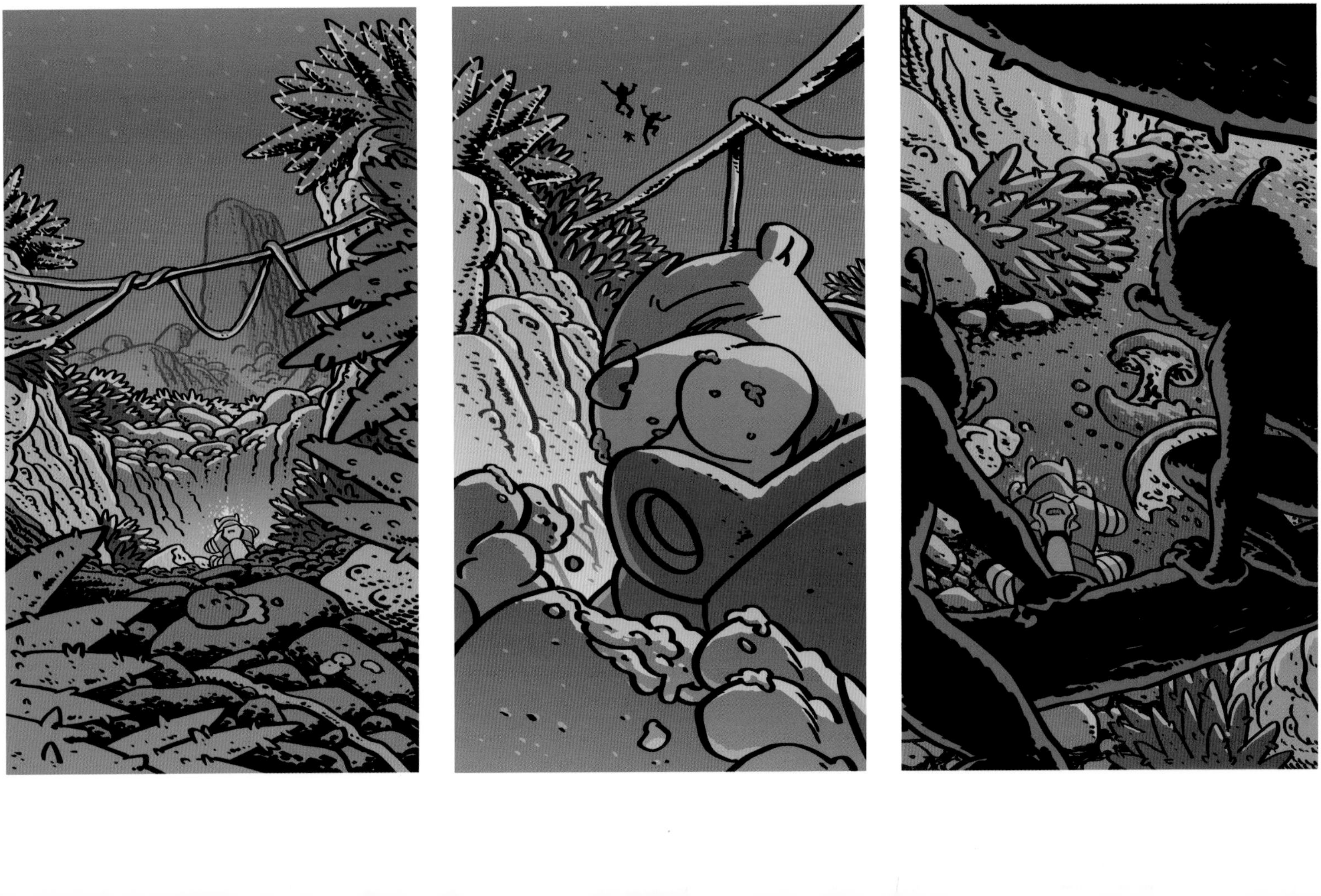

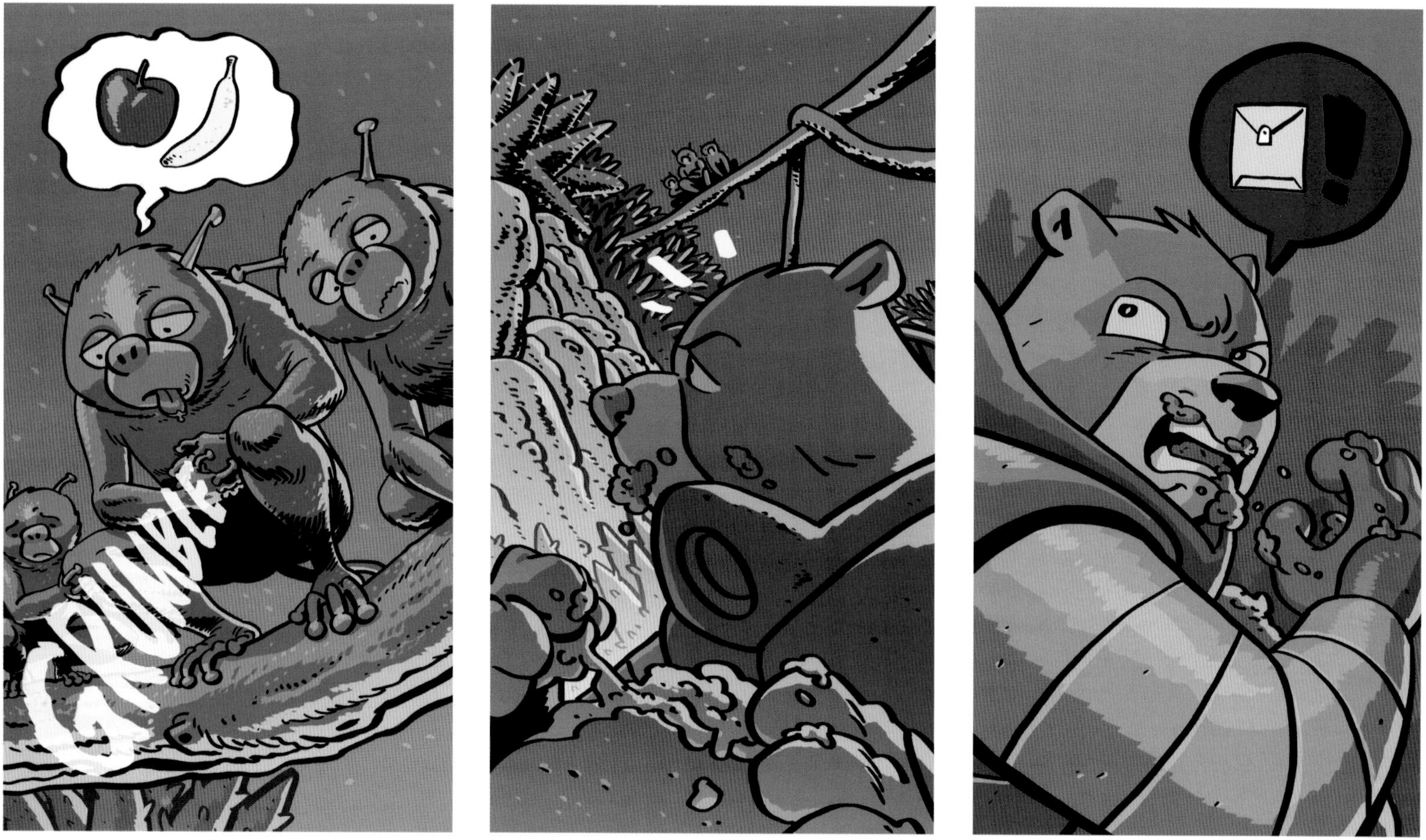
CRUMBLE

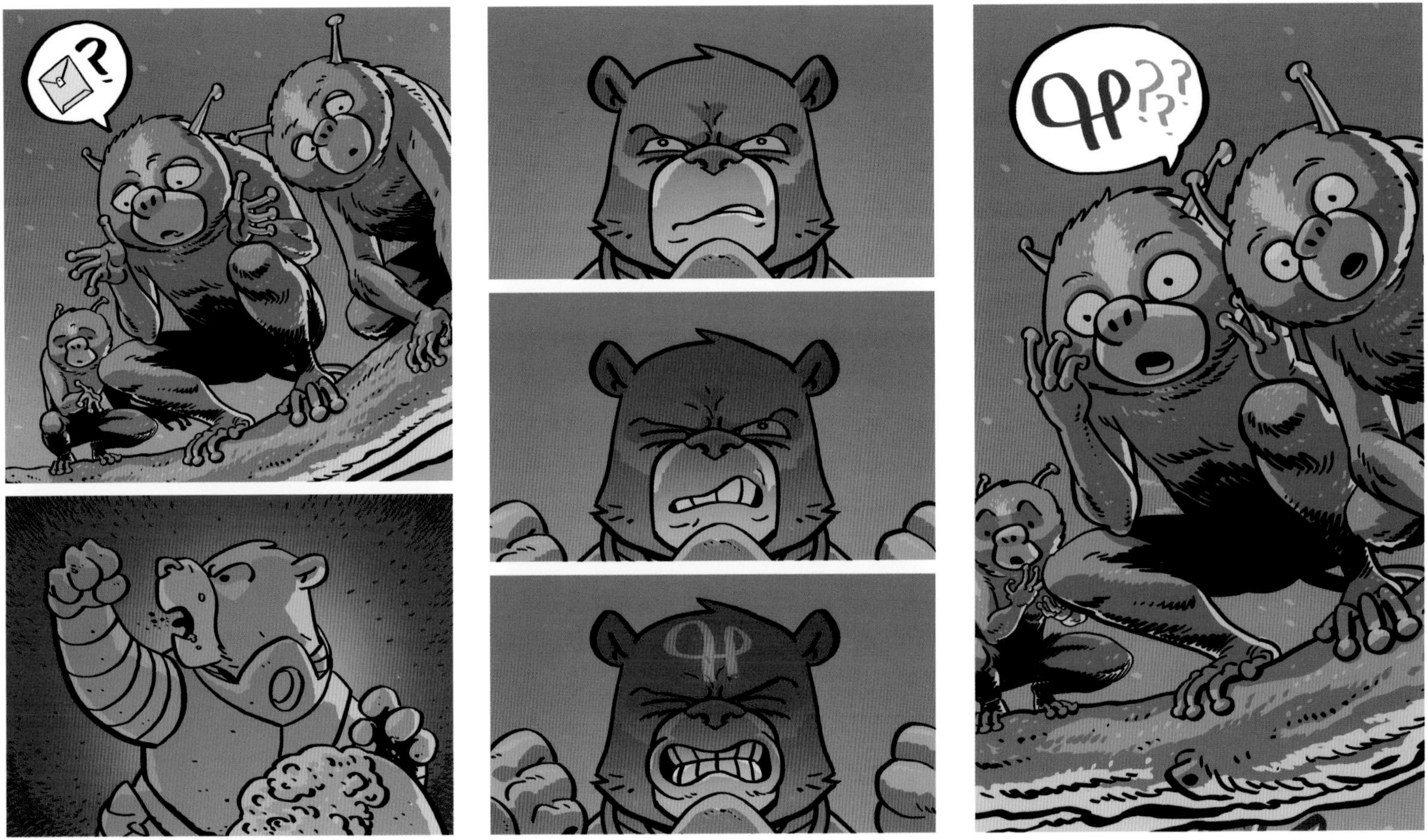
?
???

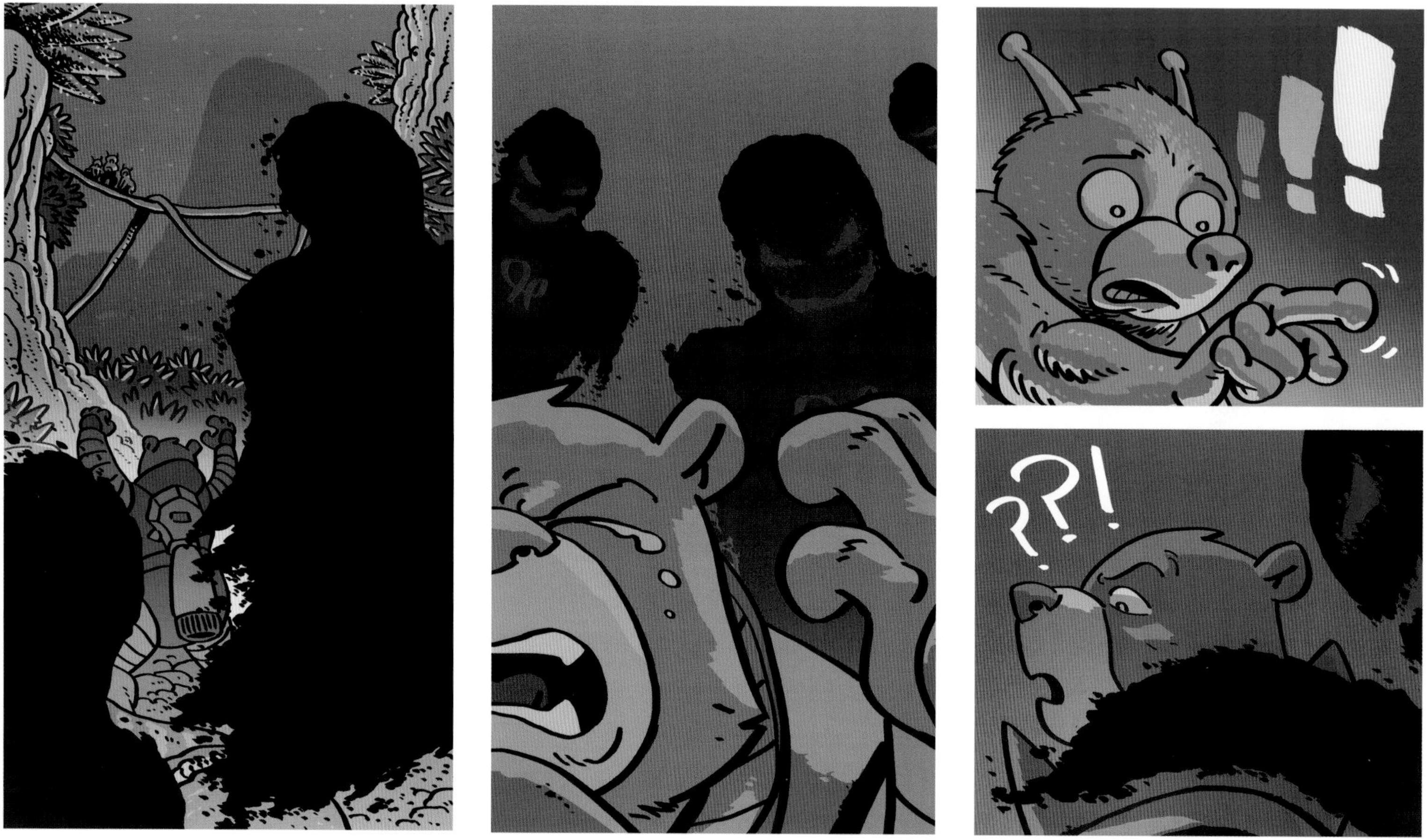
!!!
??!

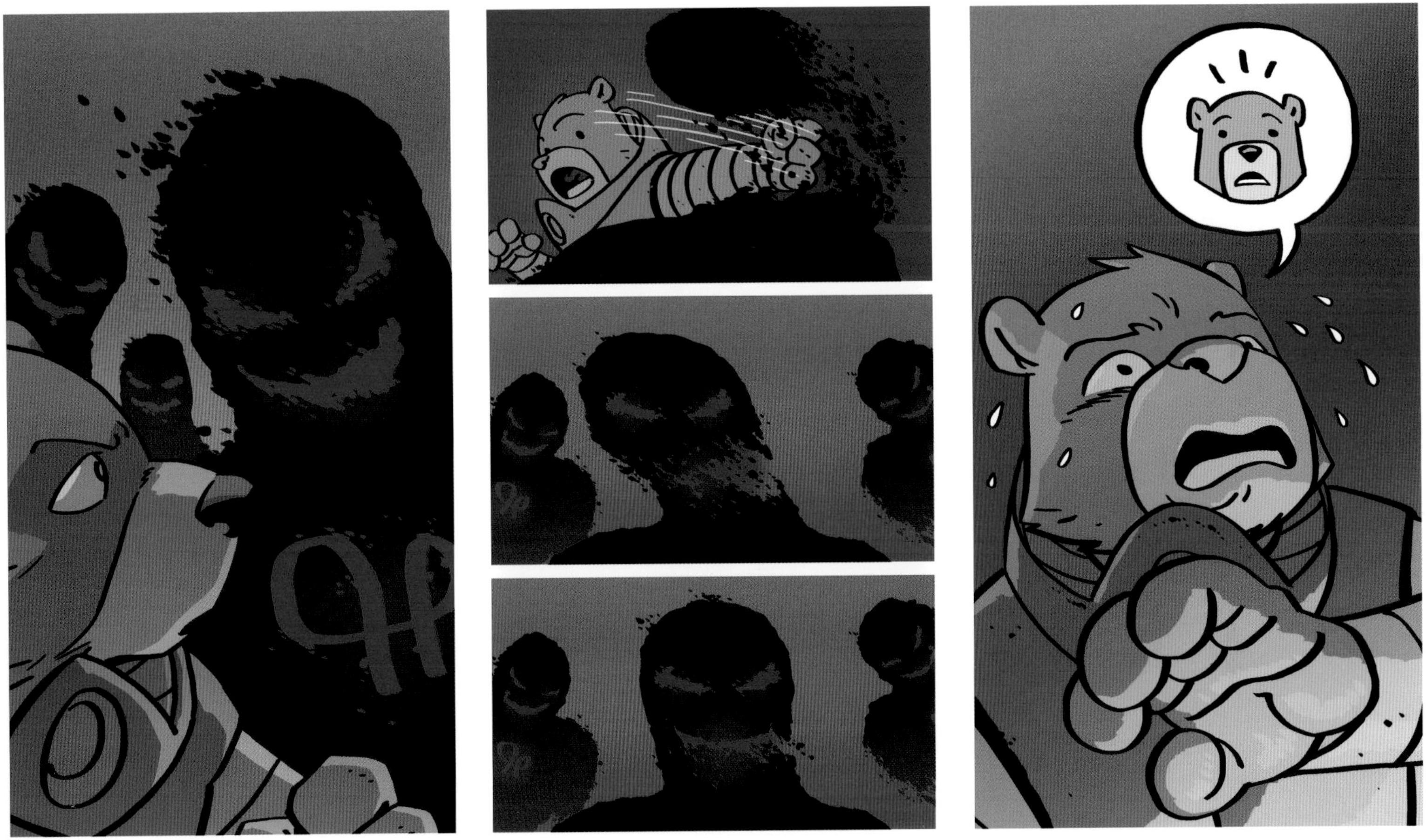

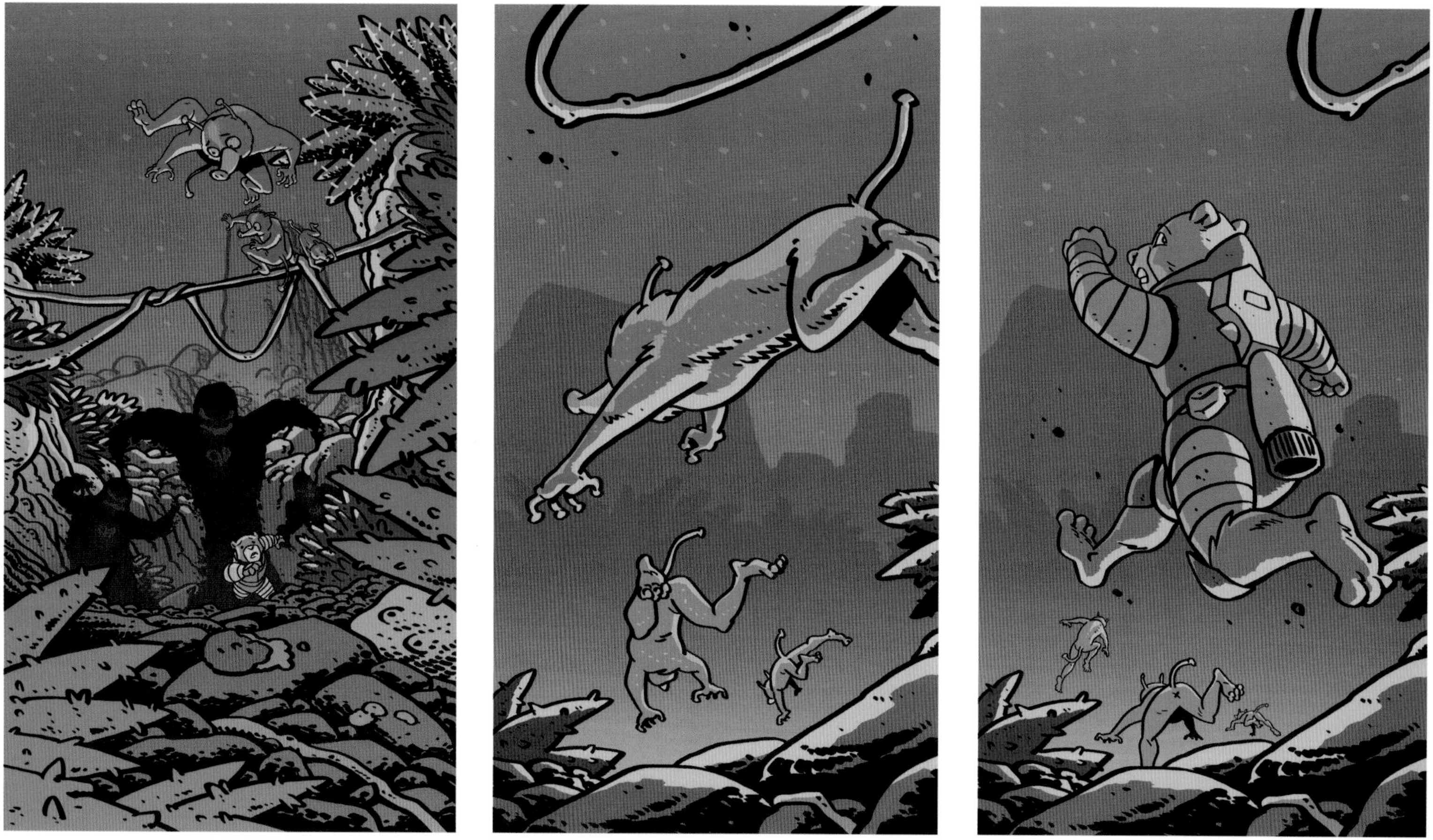

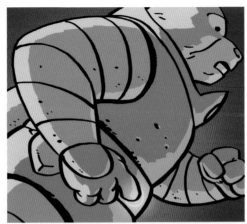

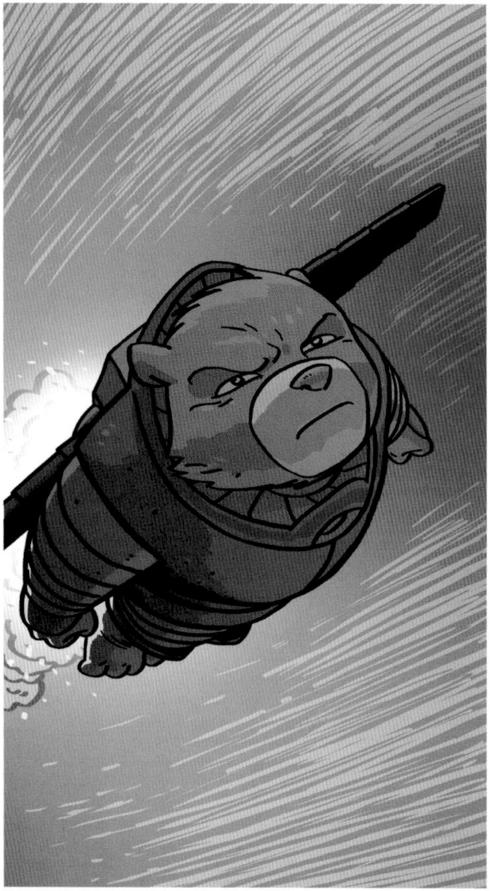
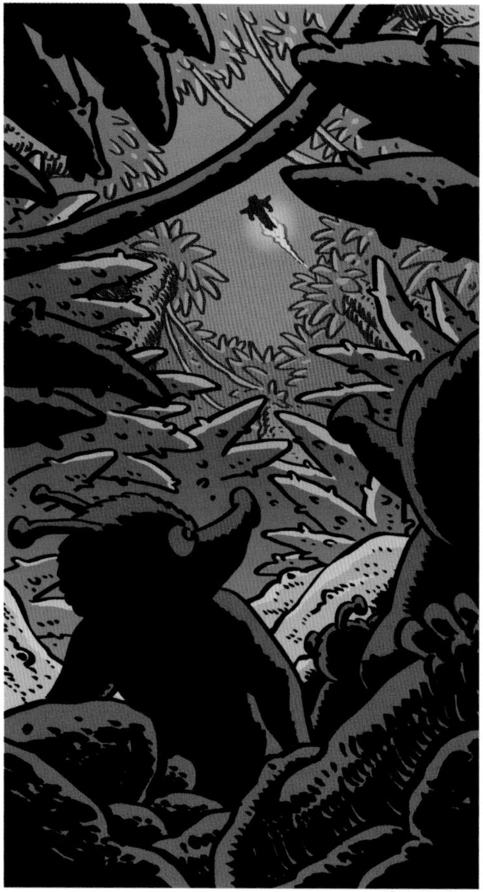
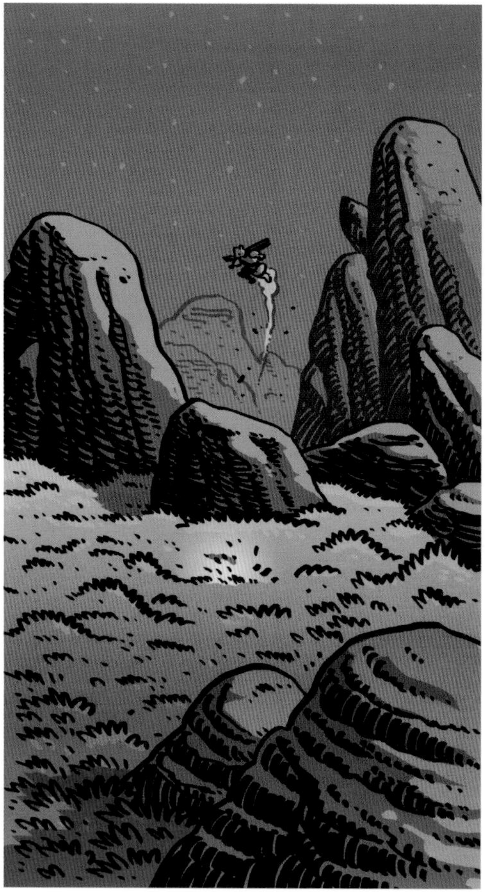

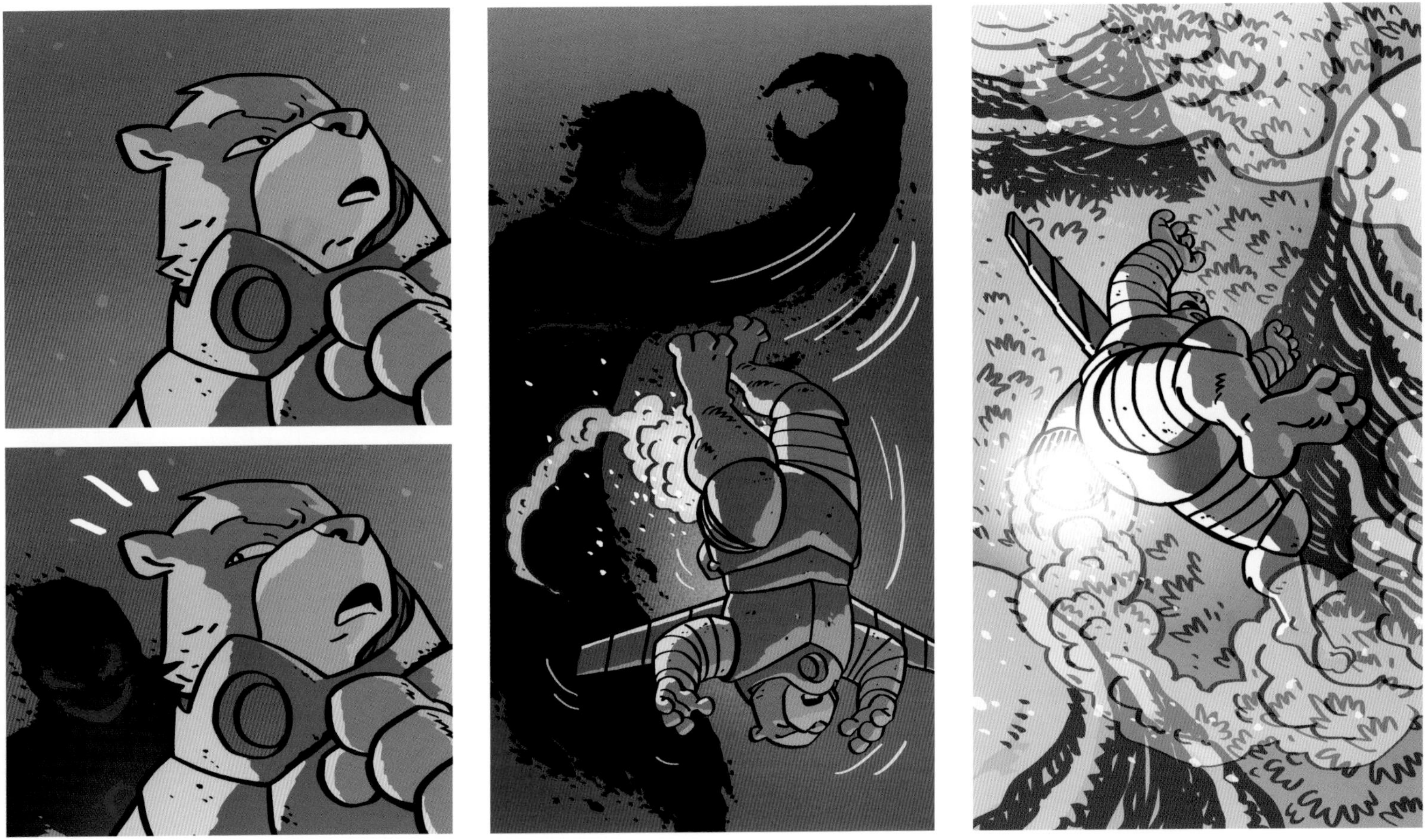

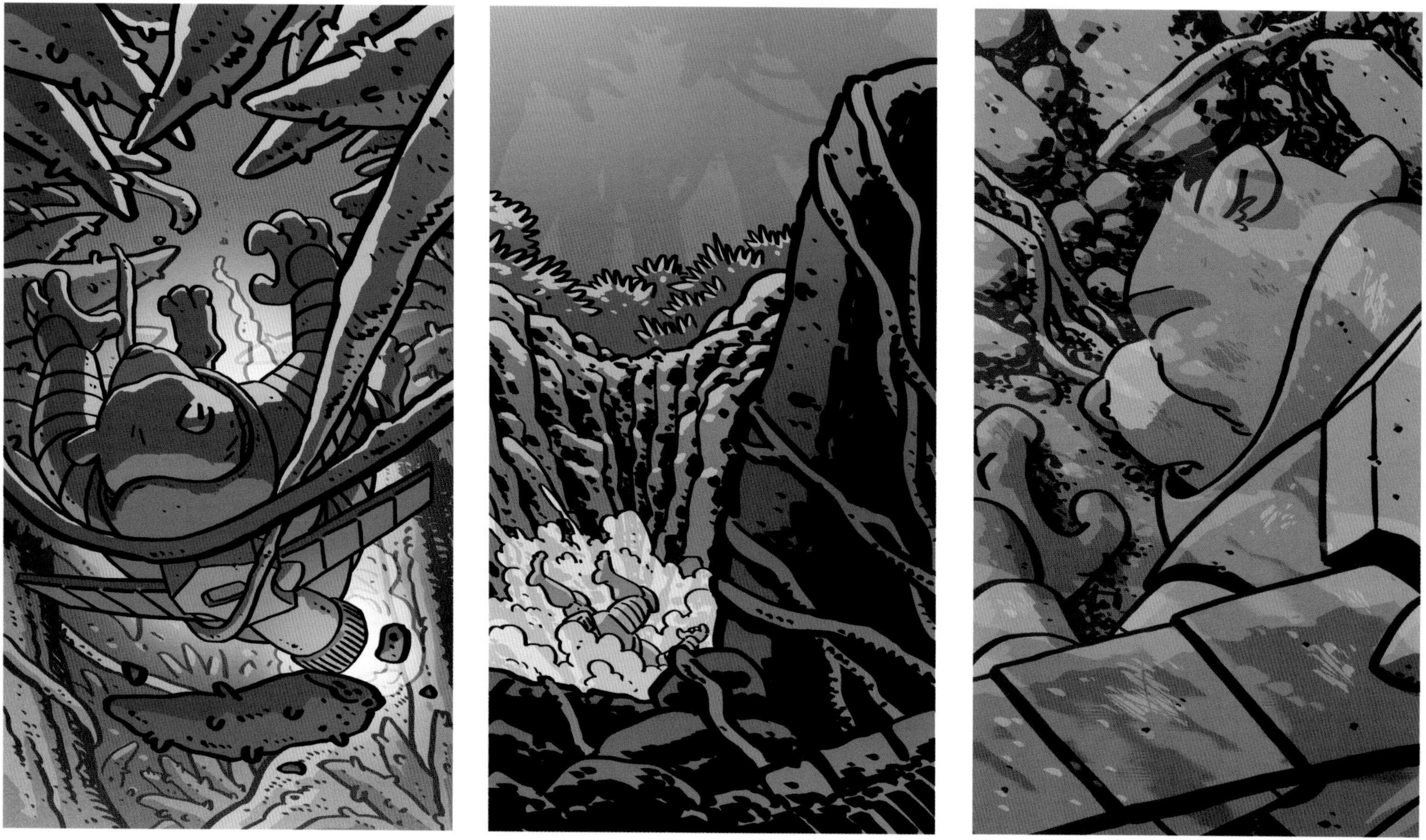

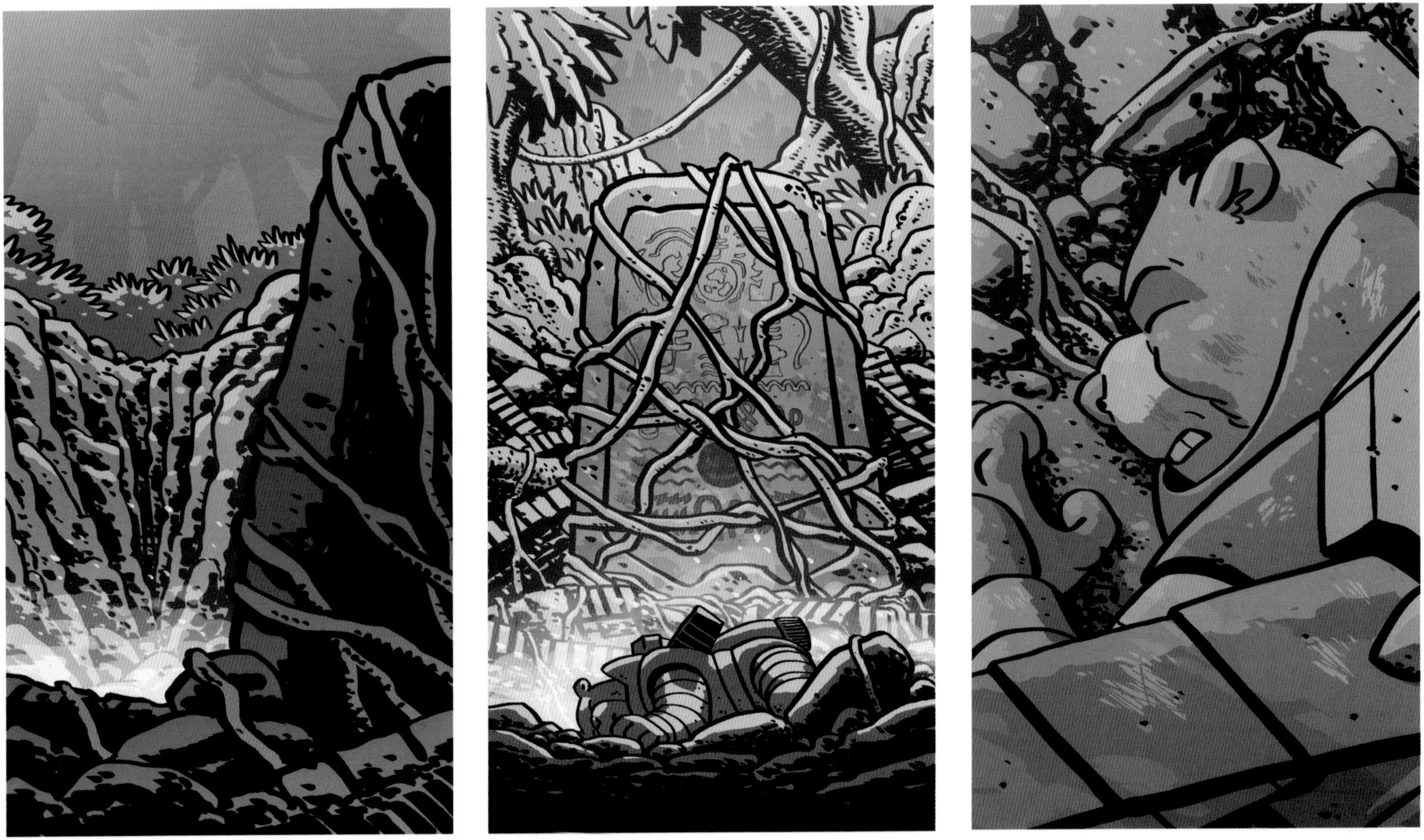

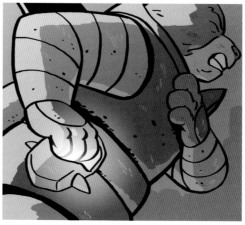

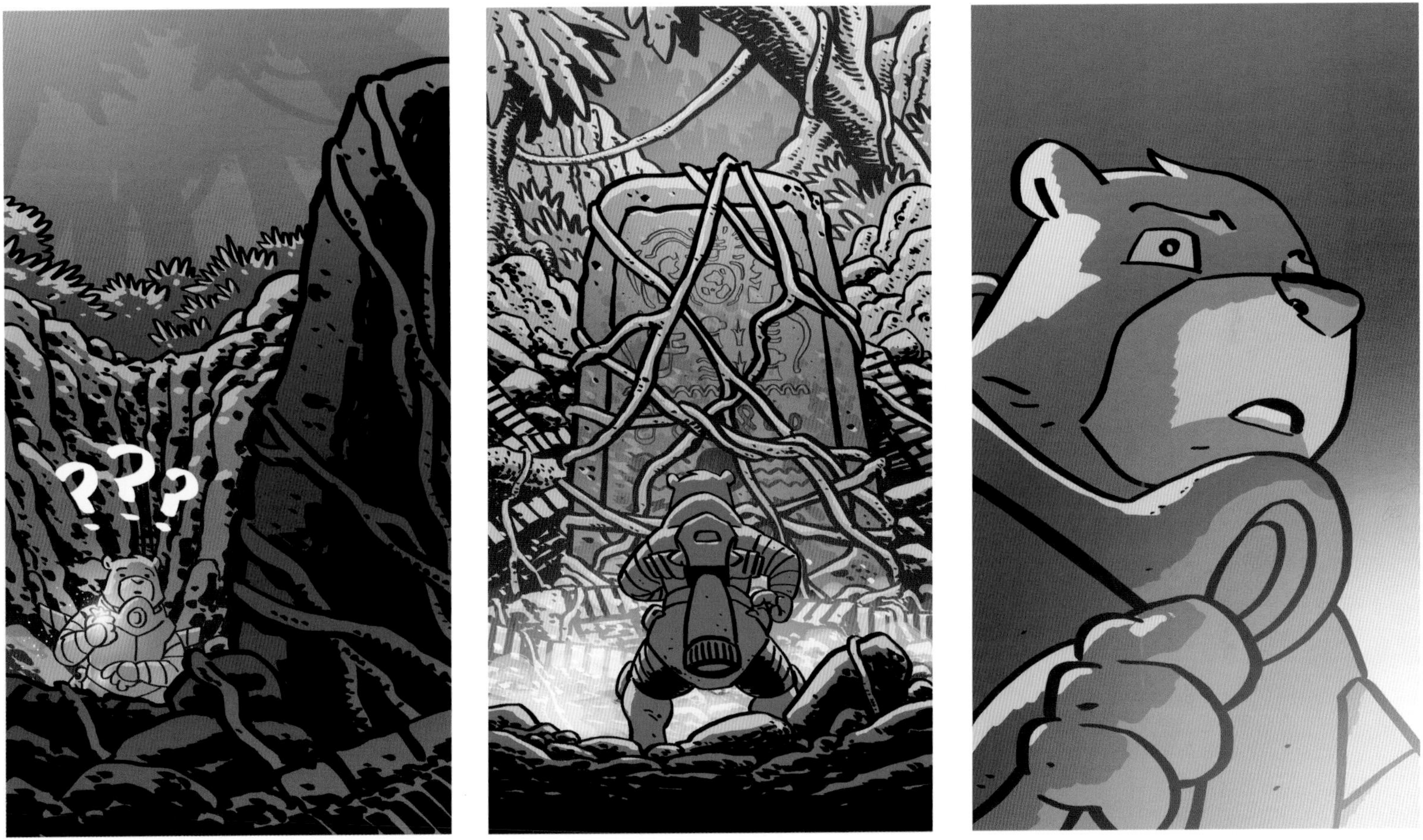
???

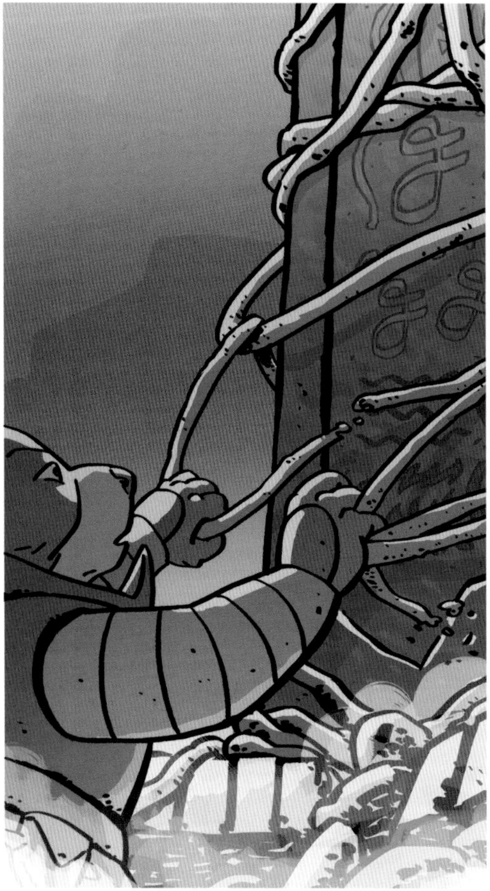
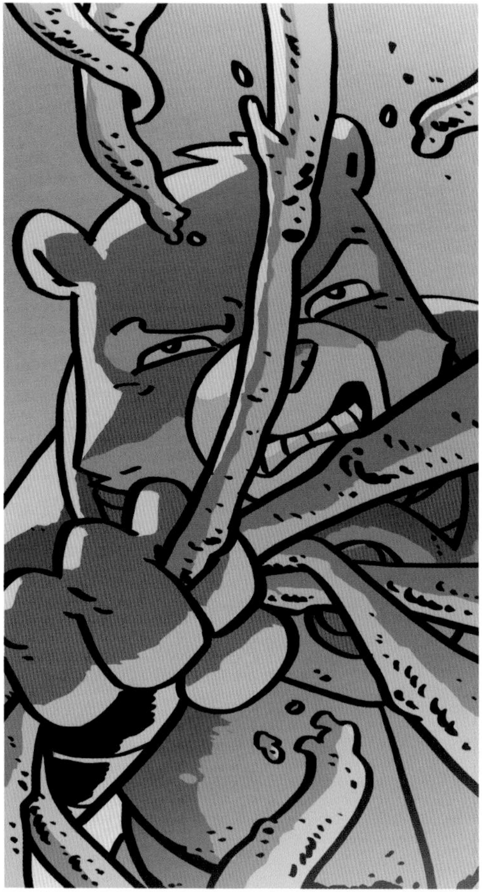
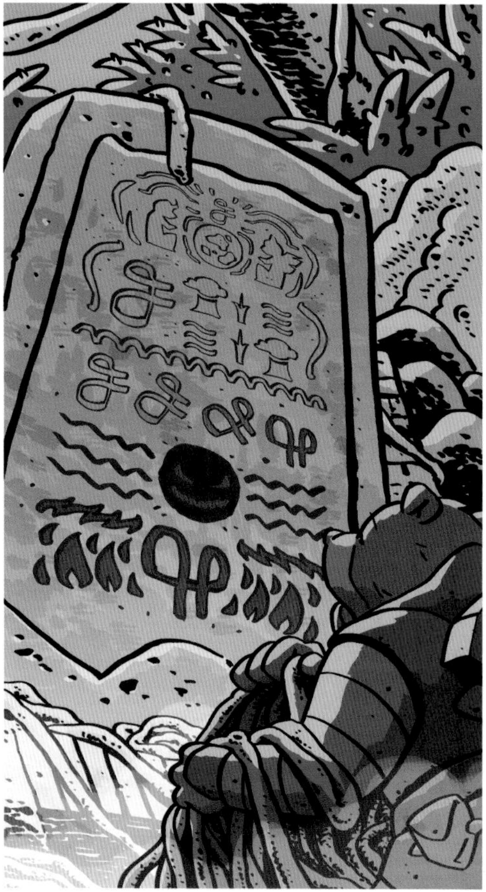

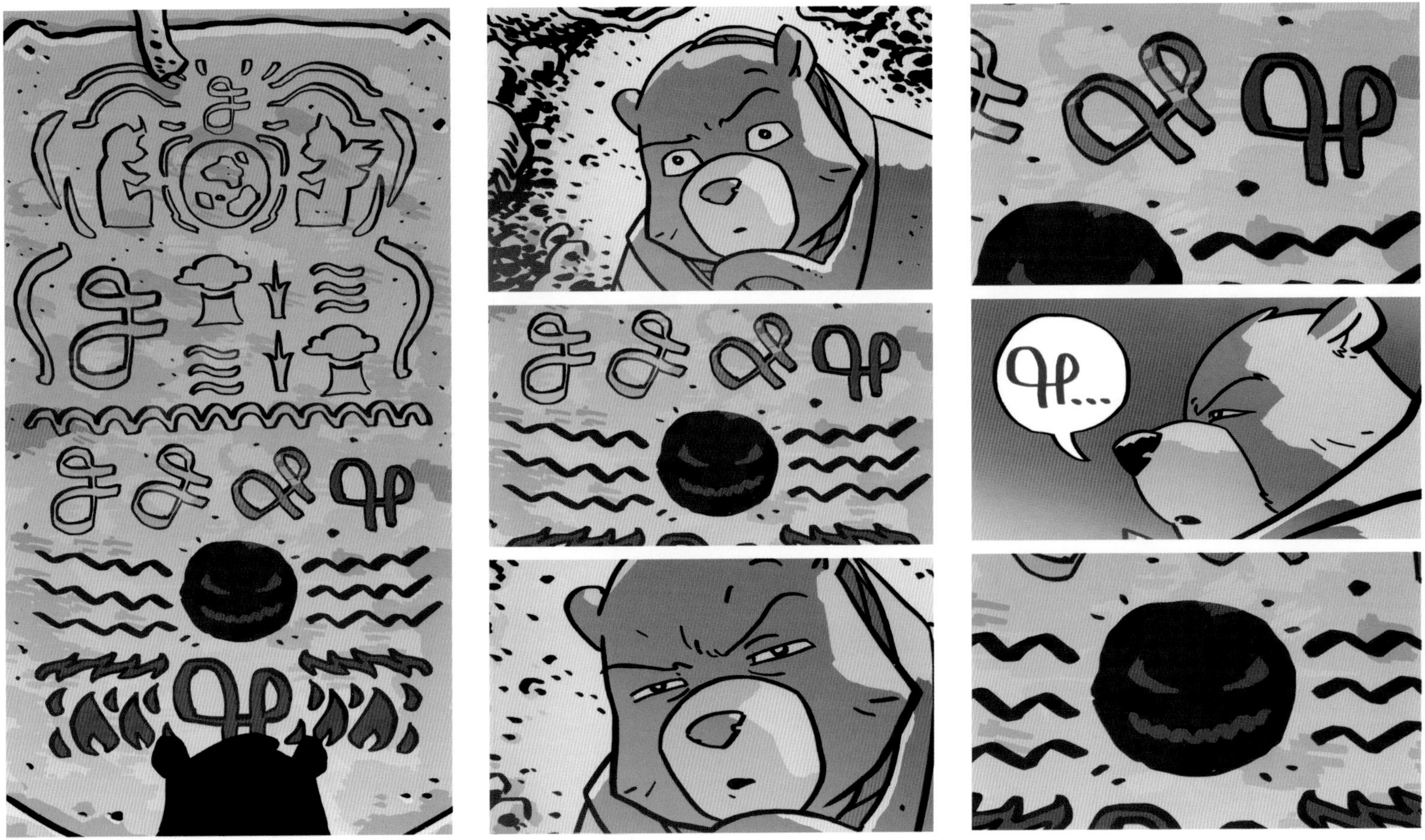

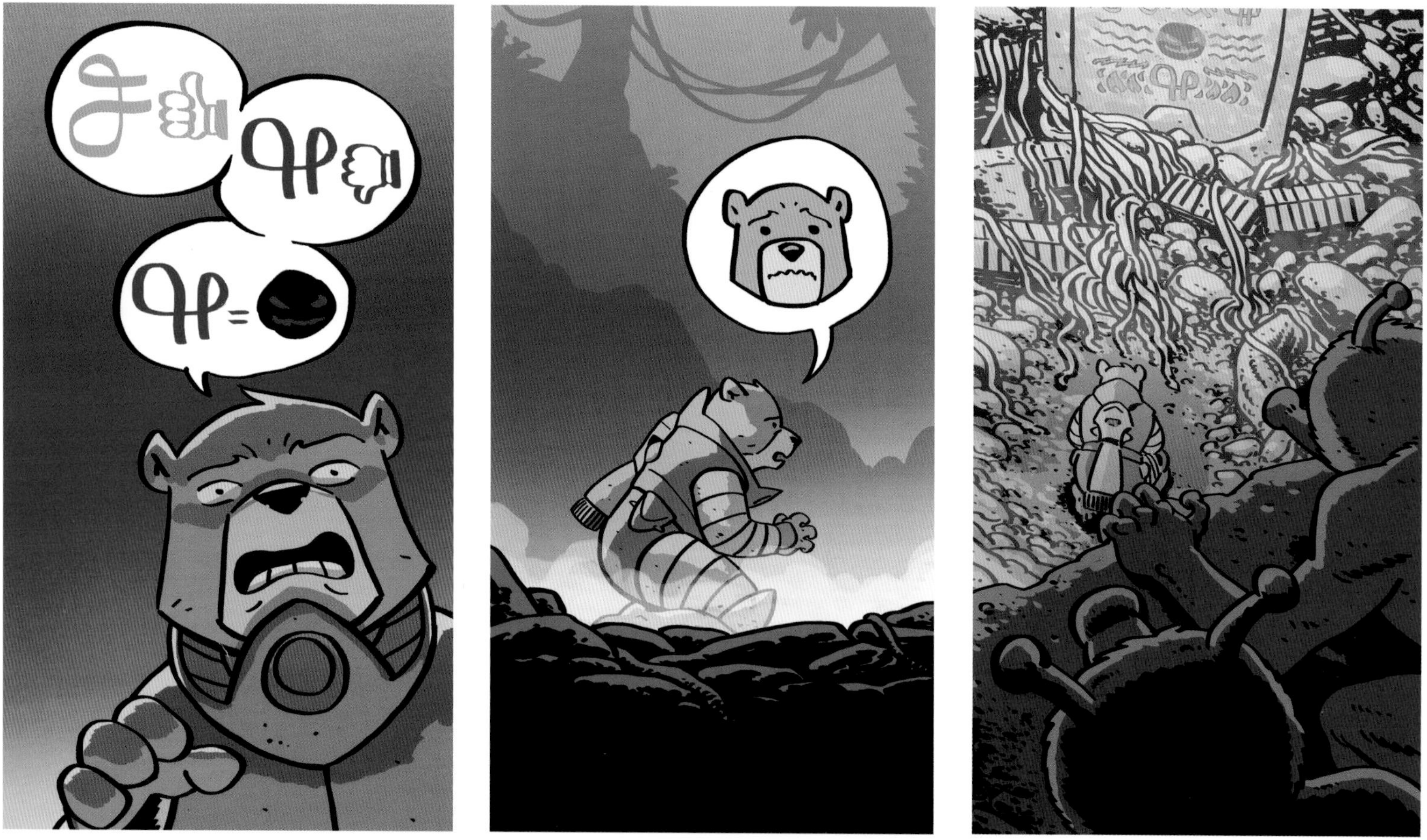

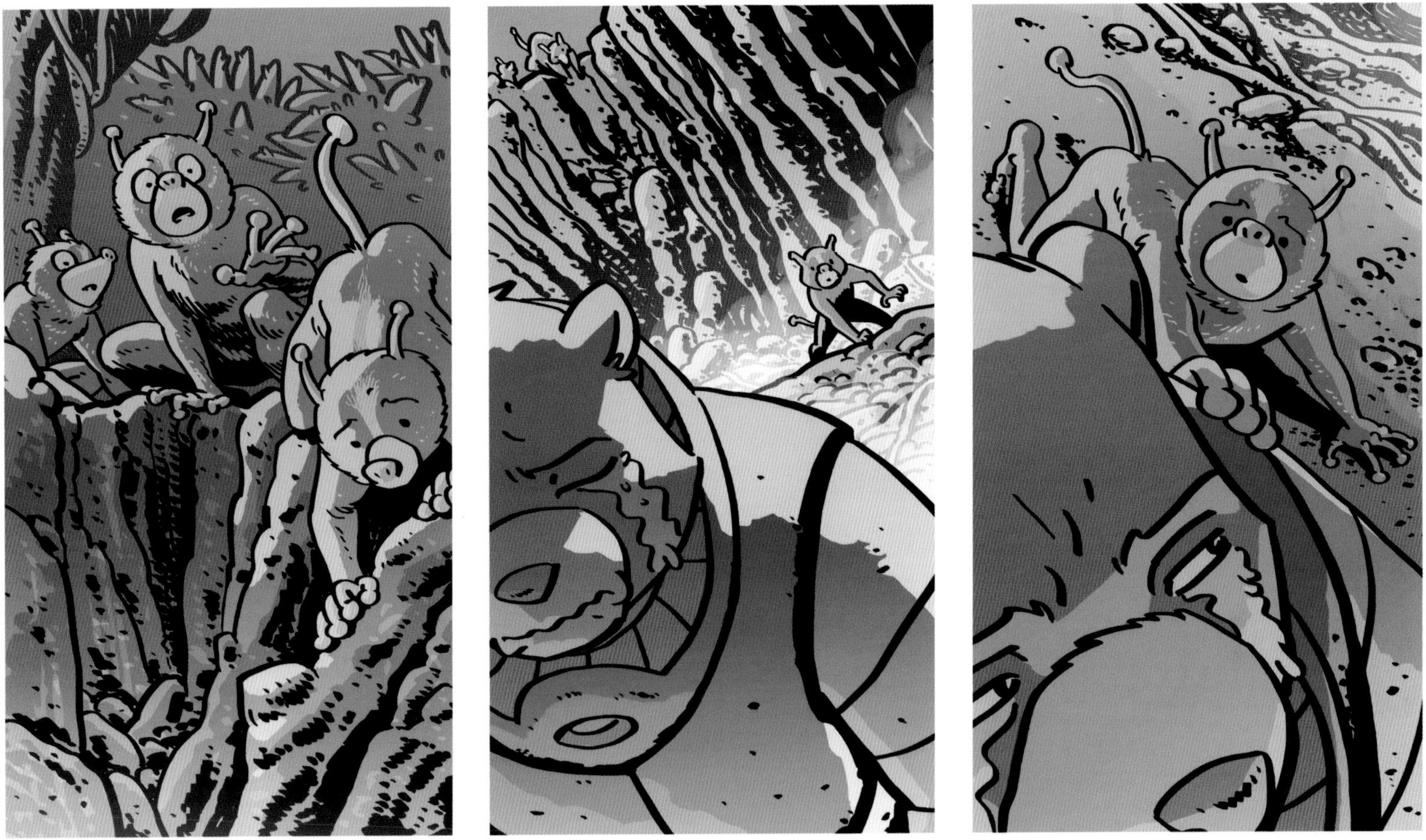

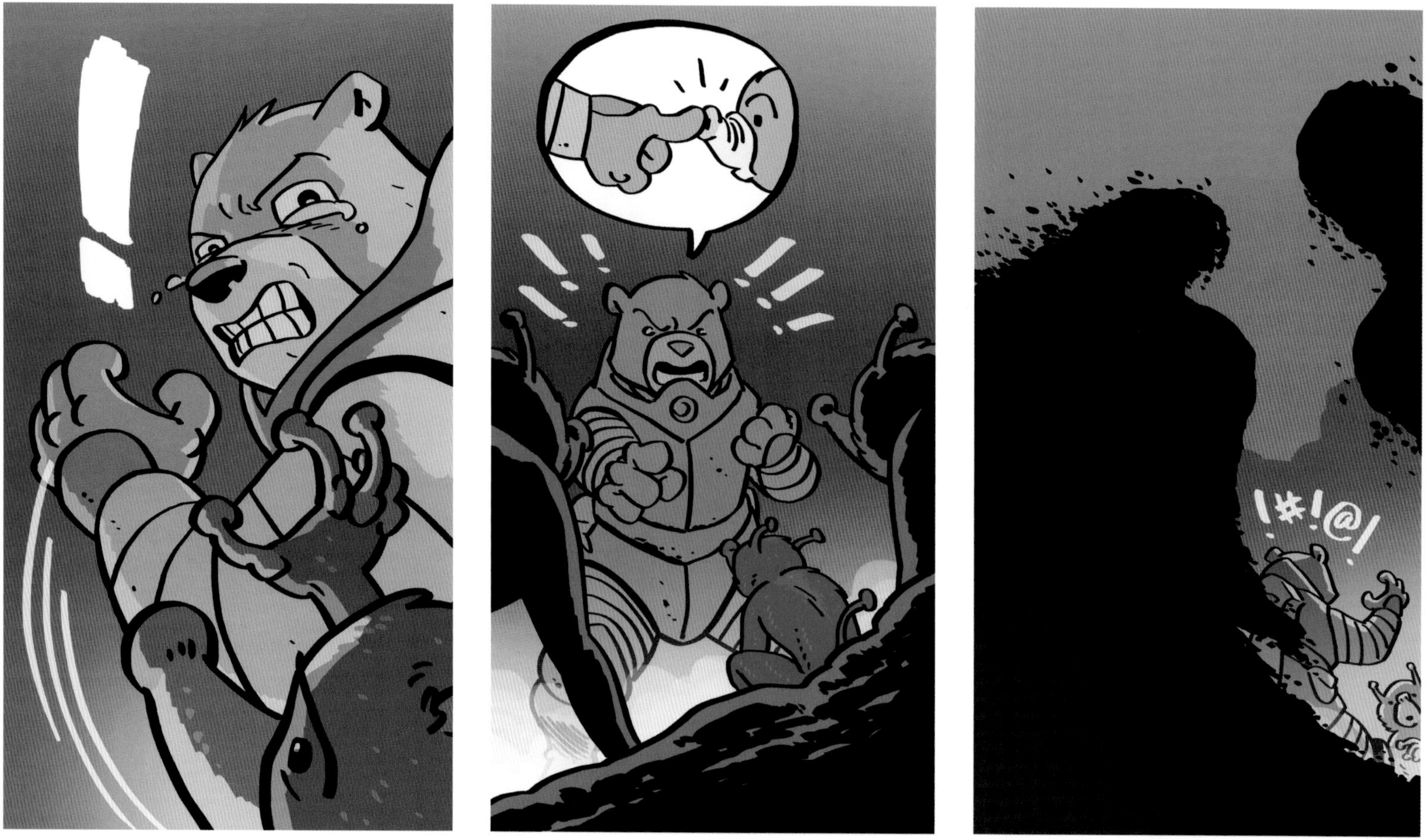
!
!#!@!

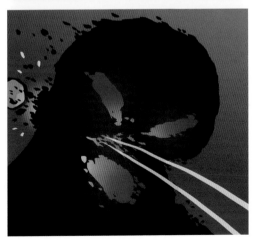

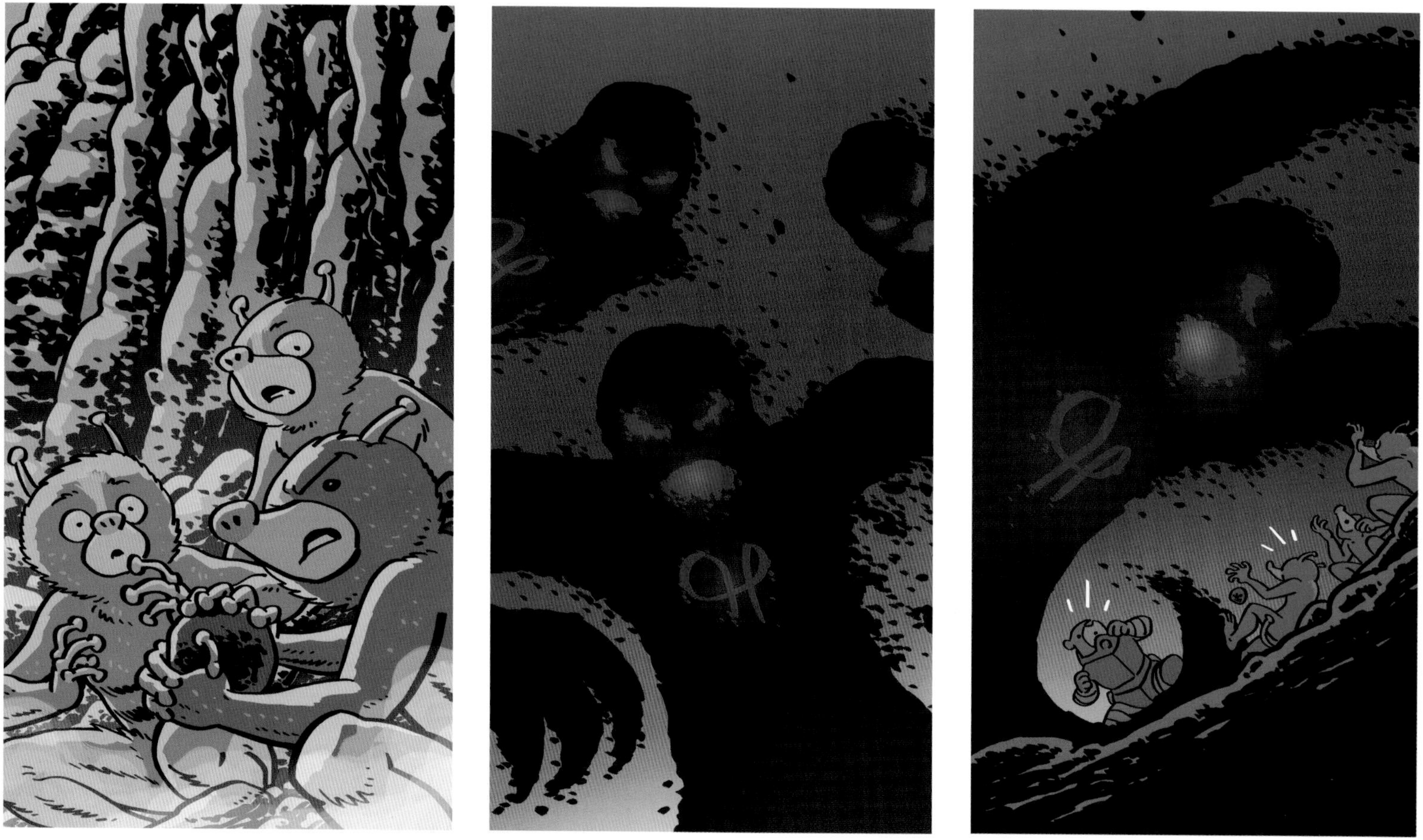

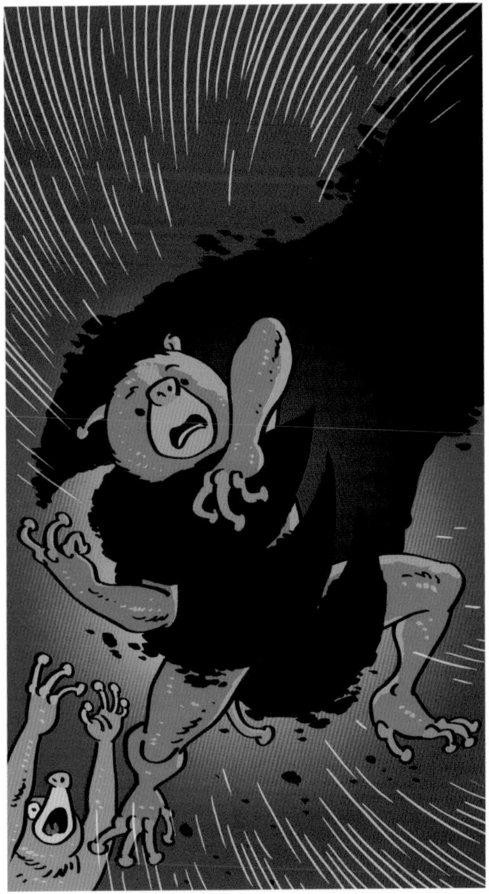
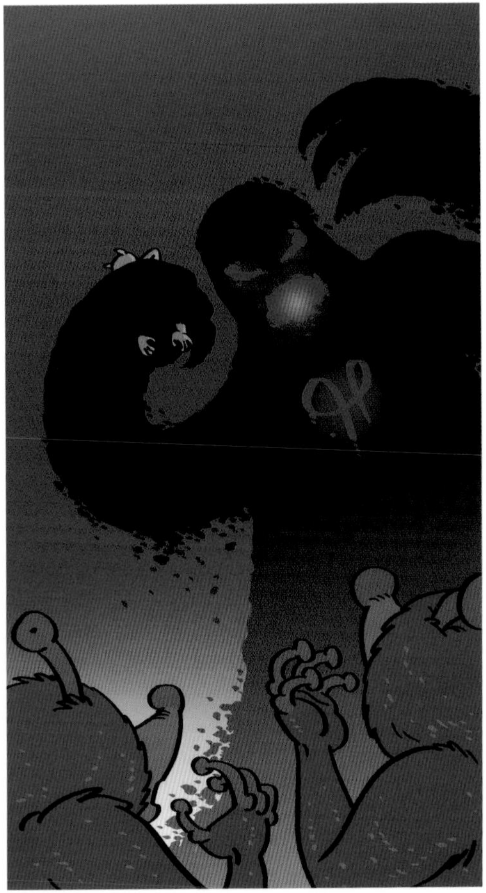
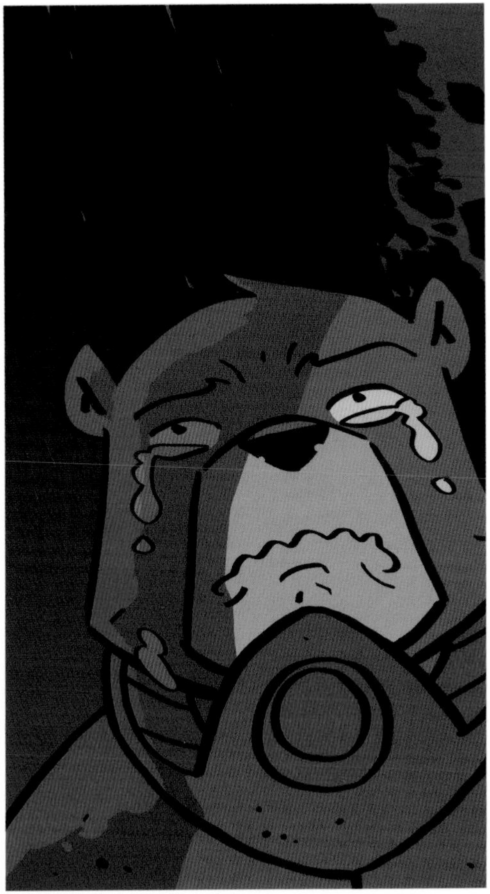

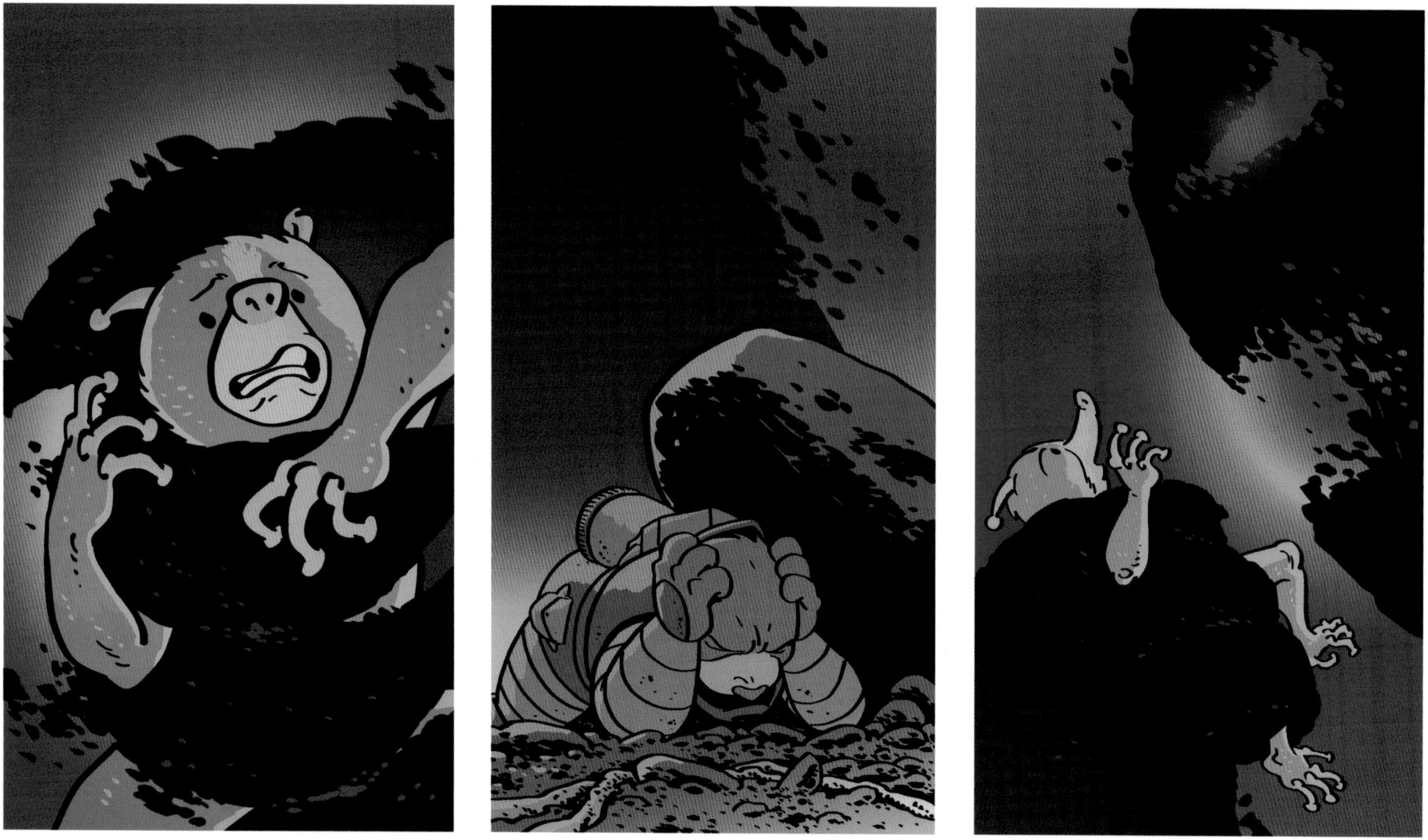

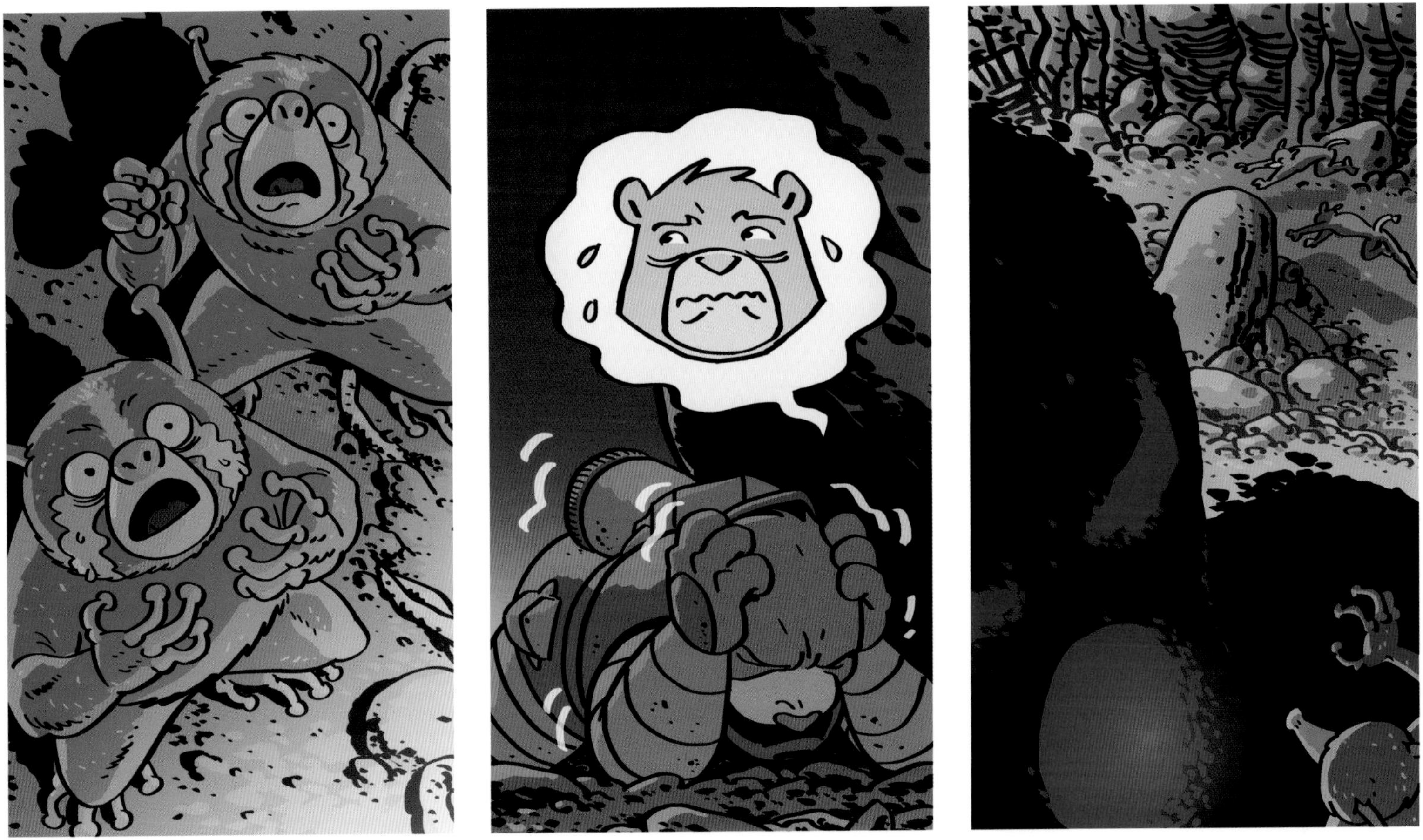

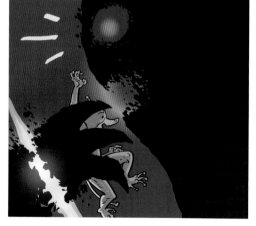

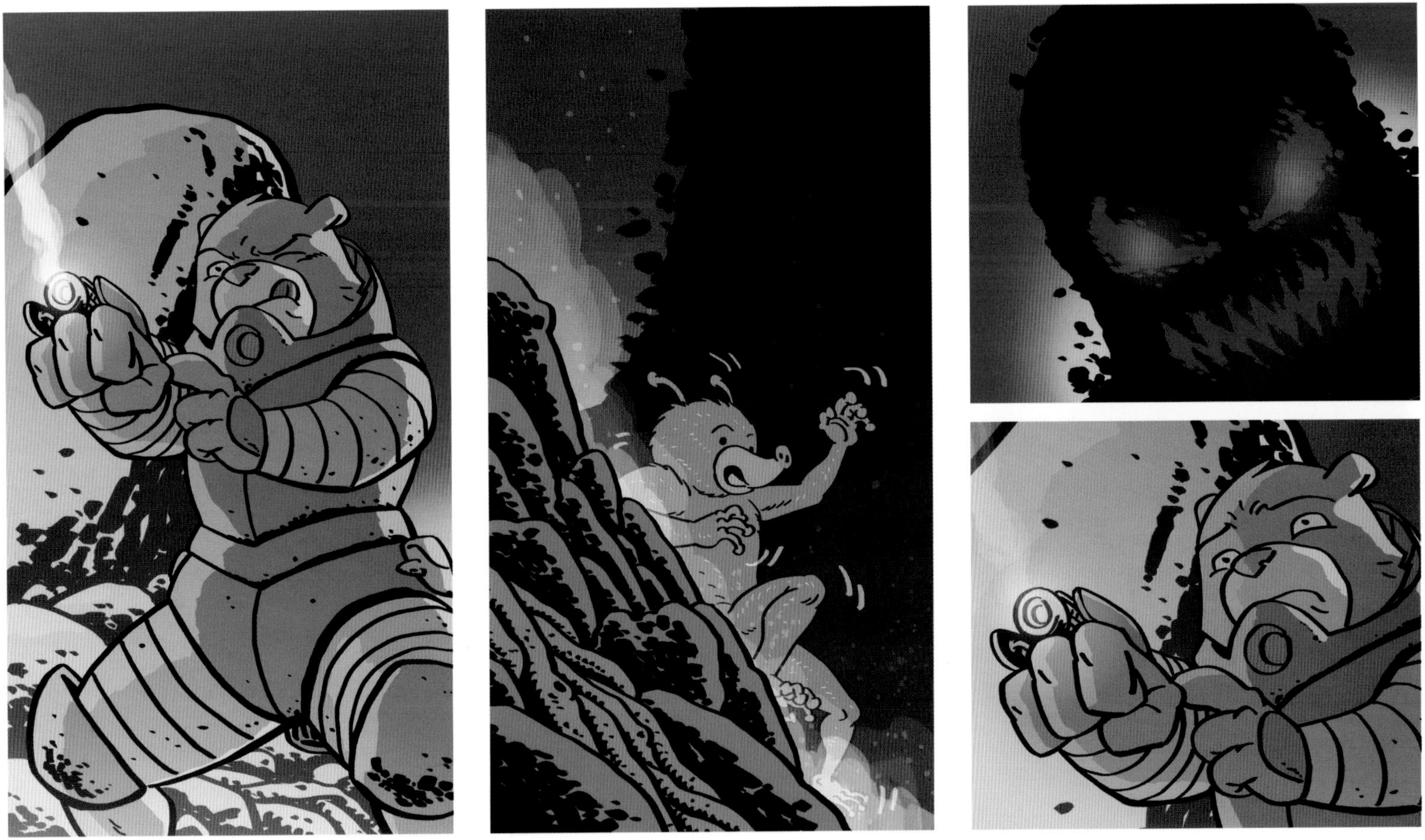

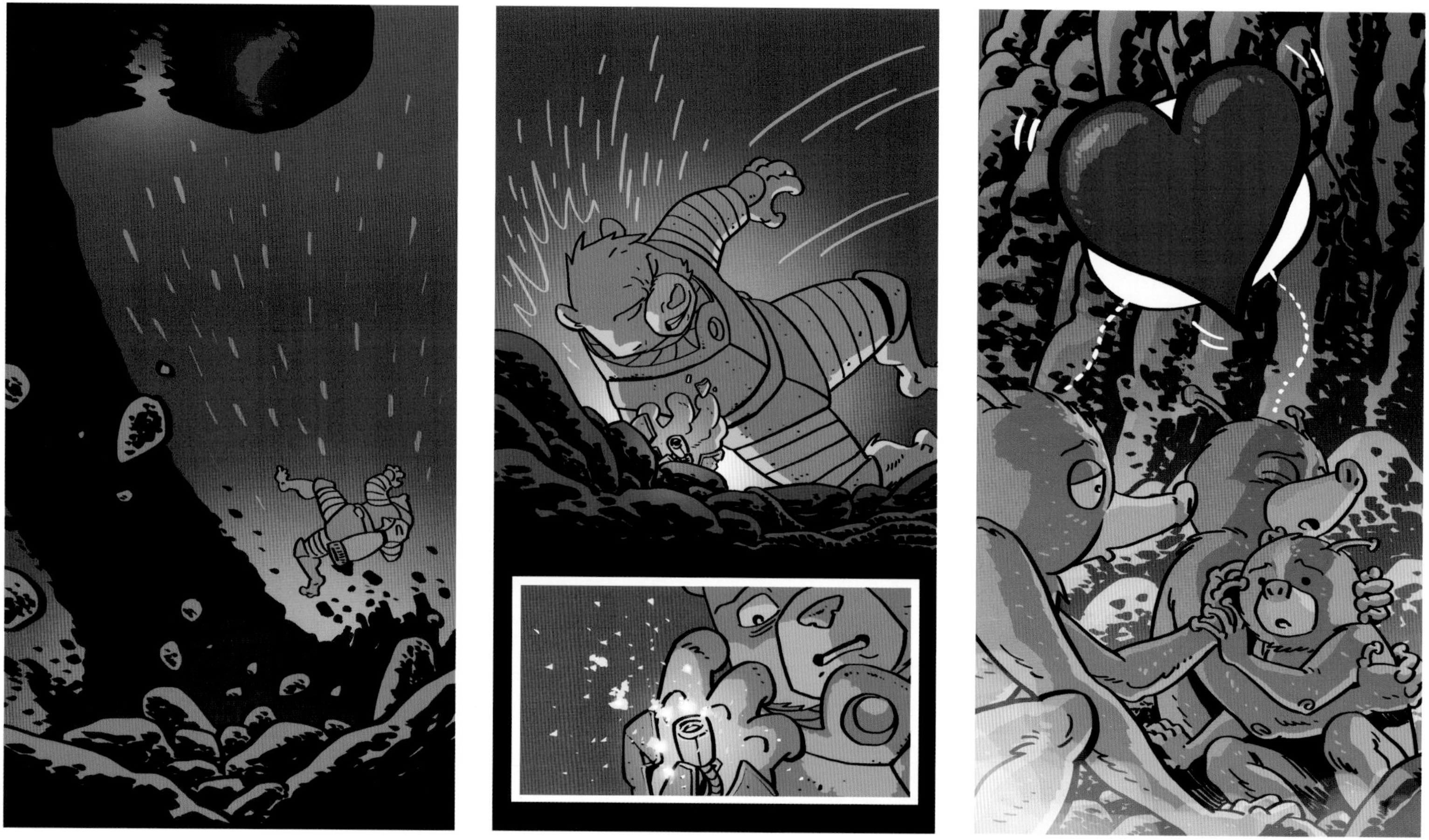

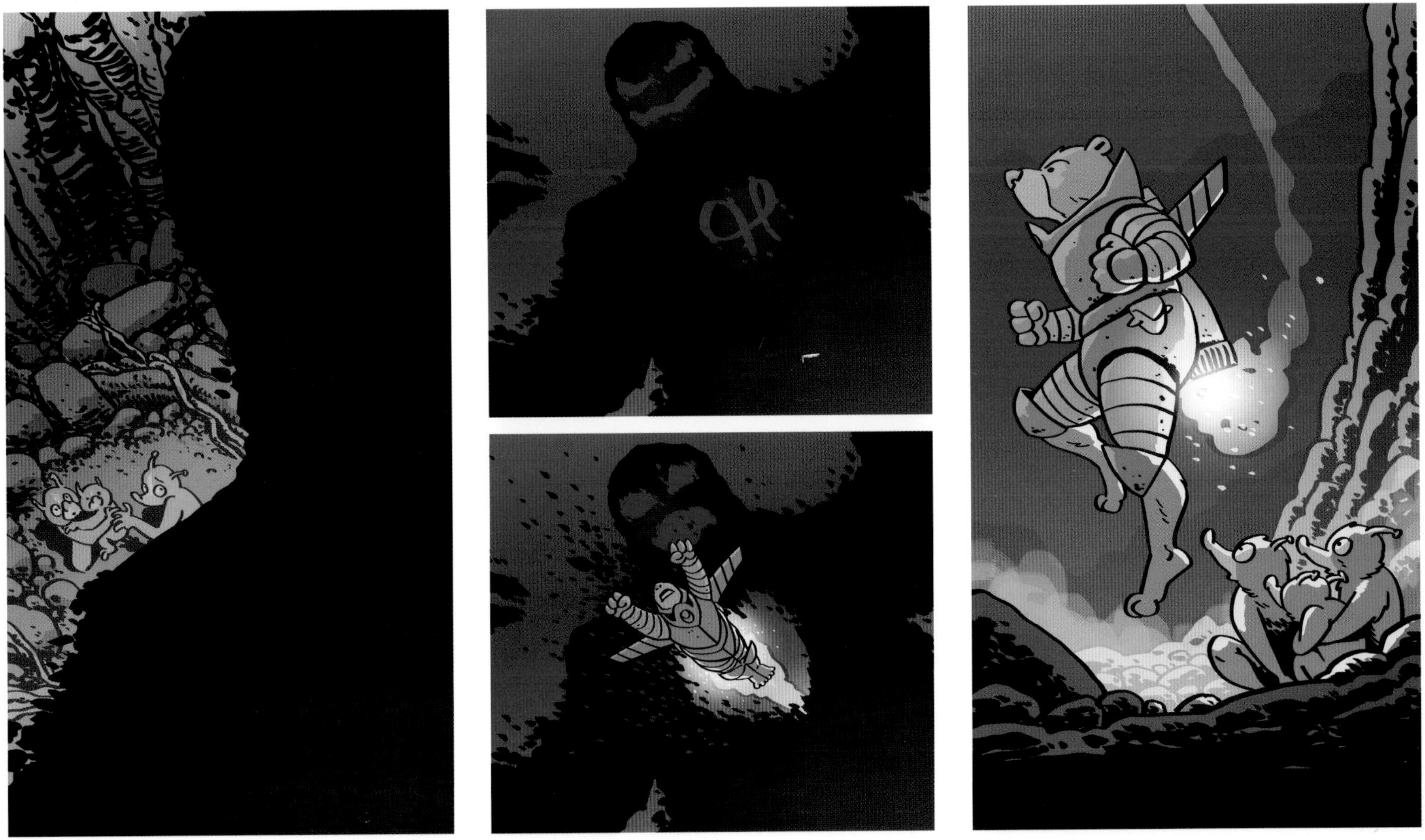

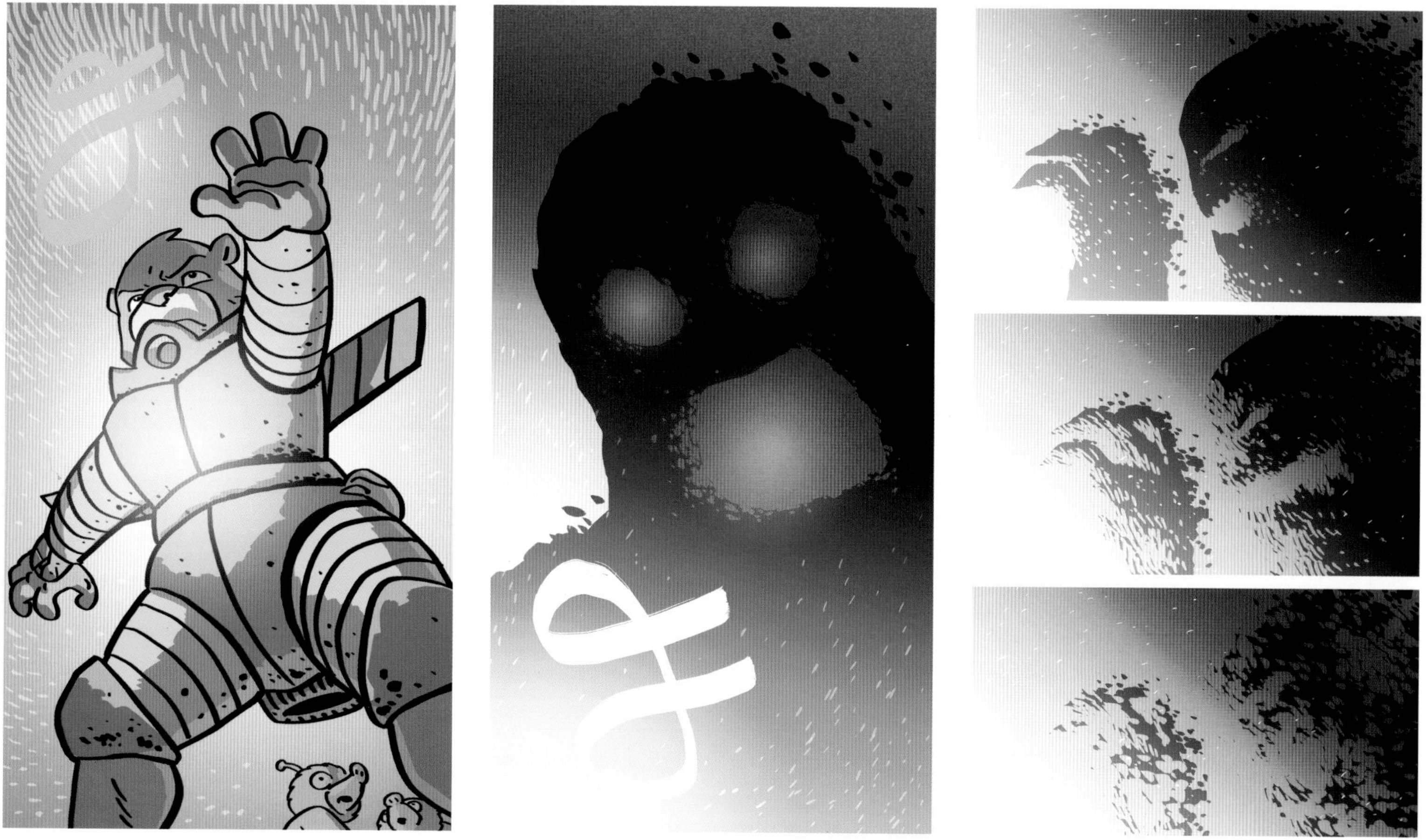

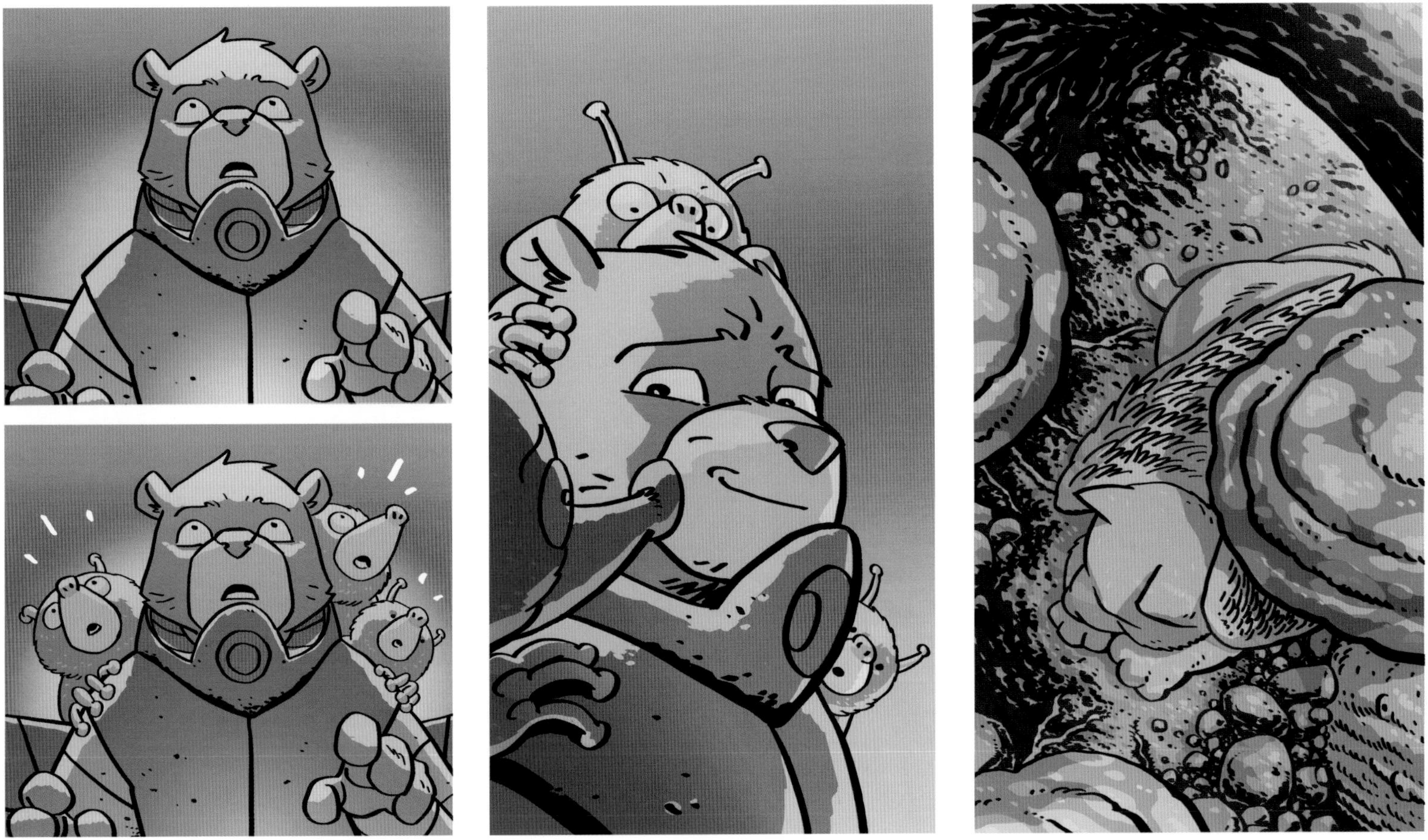

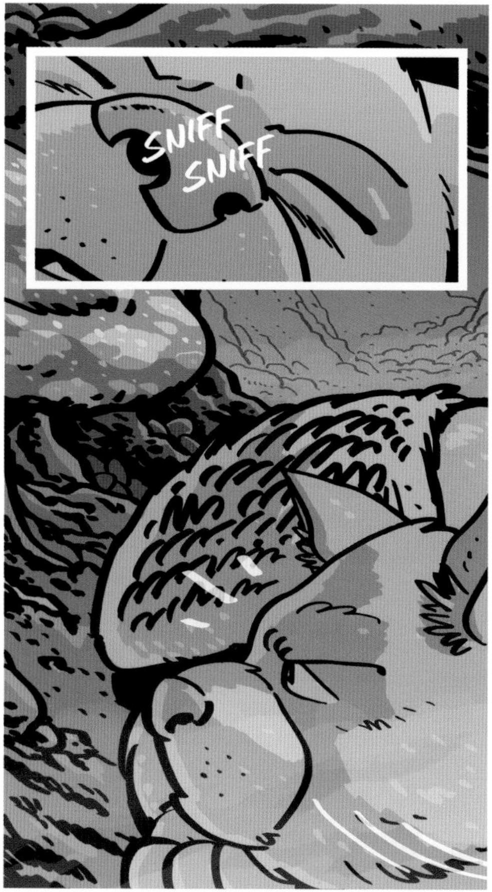
SNIFF
SNIFF
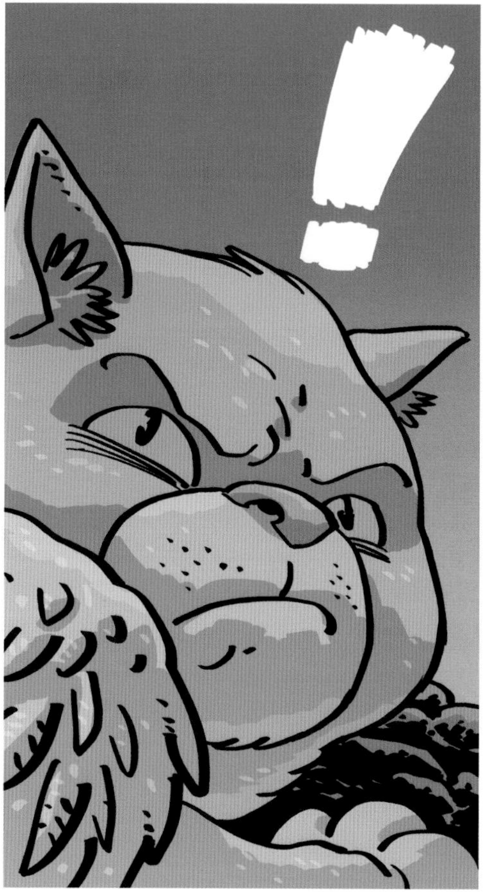
!
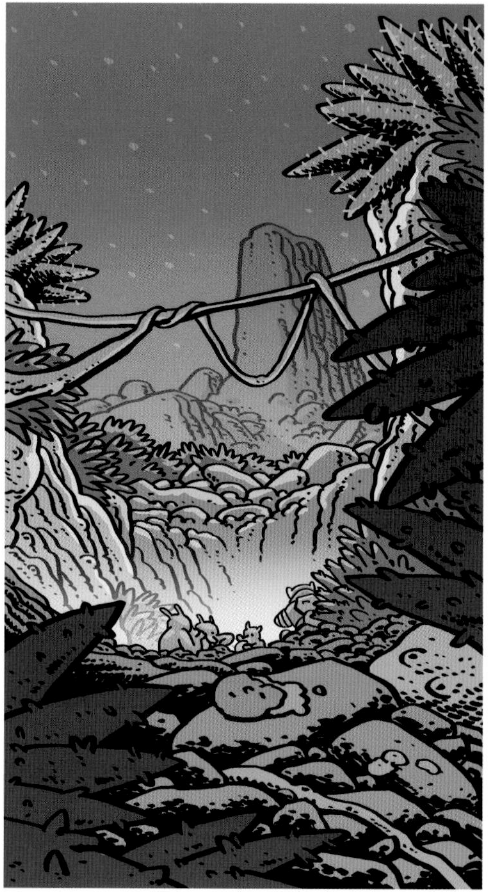

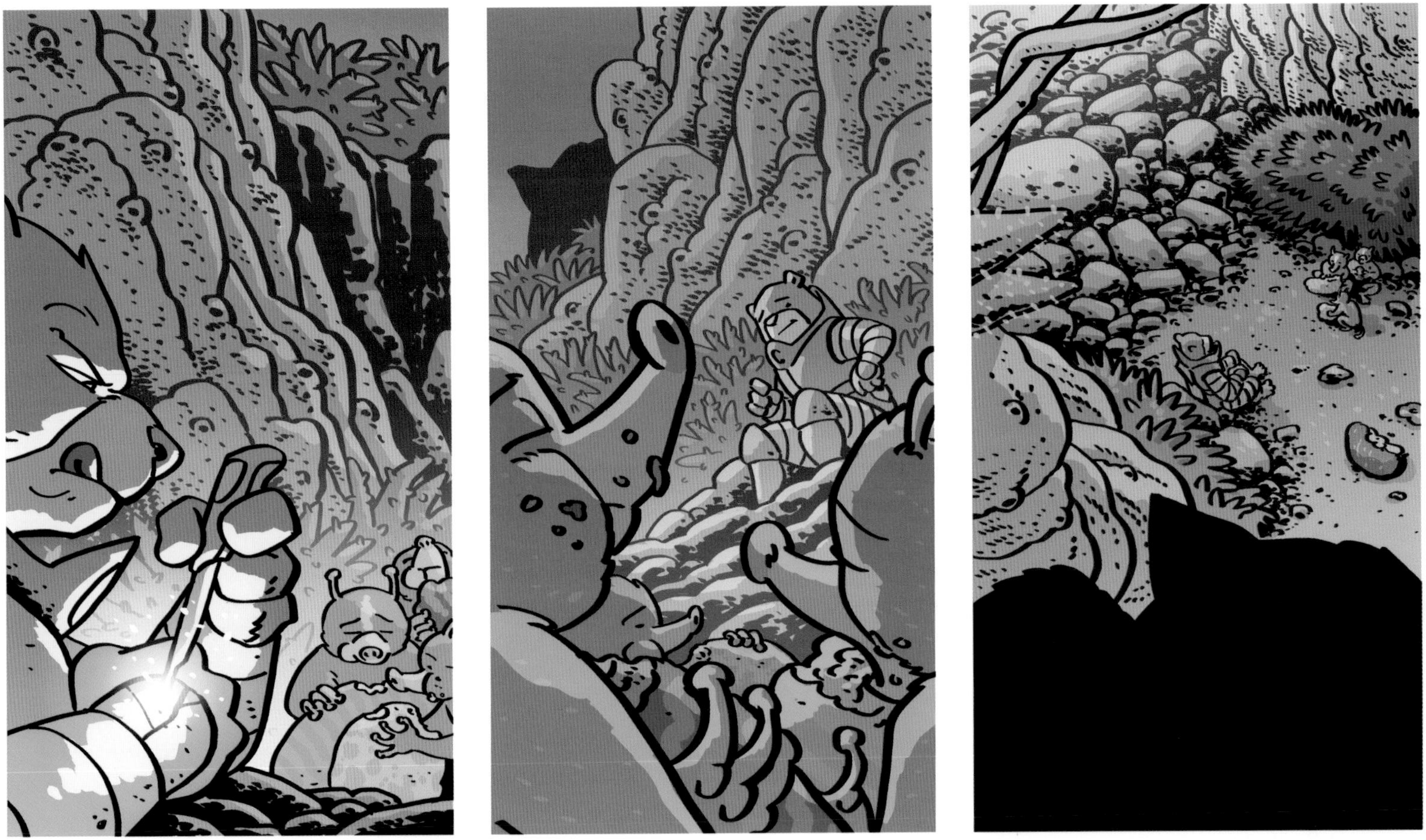

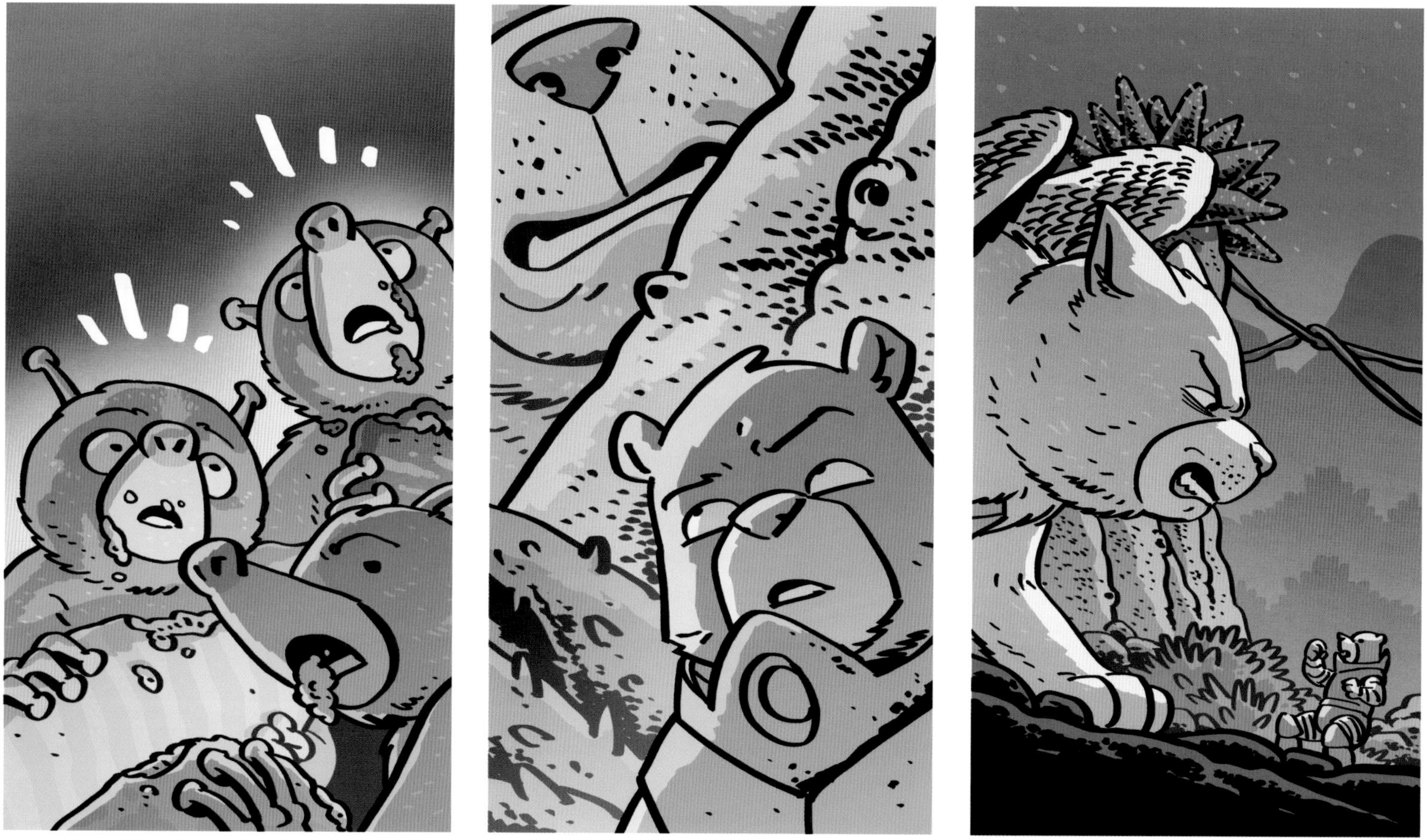

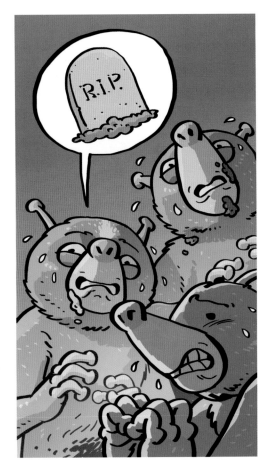

R.I.P.

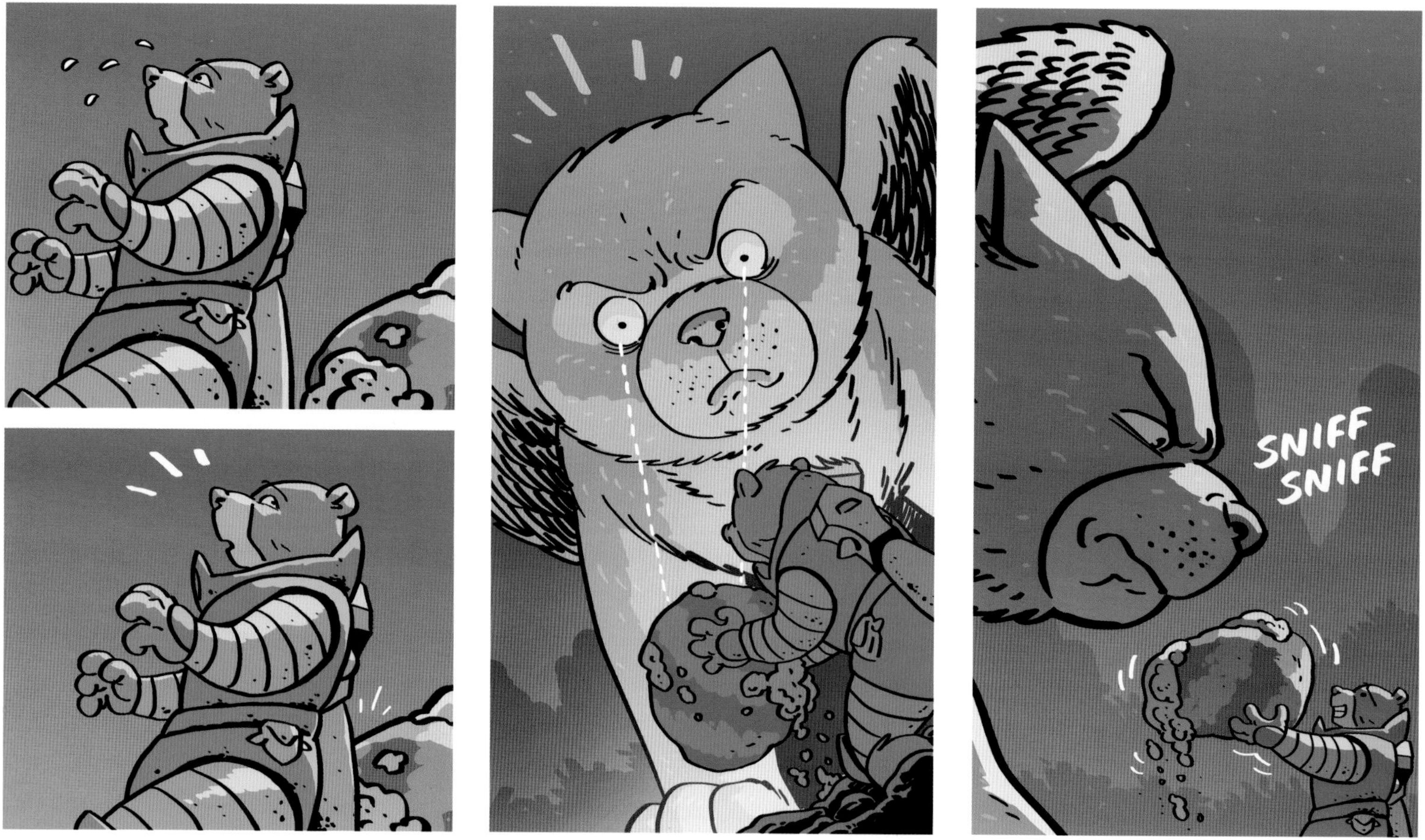
SNIFF
SNIFF

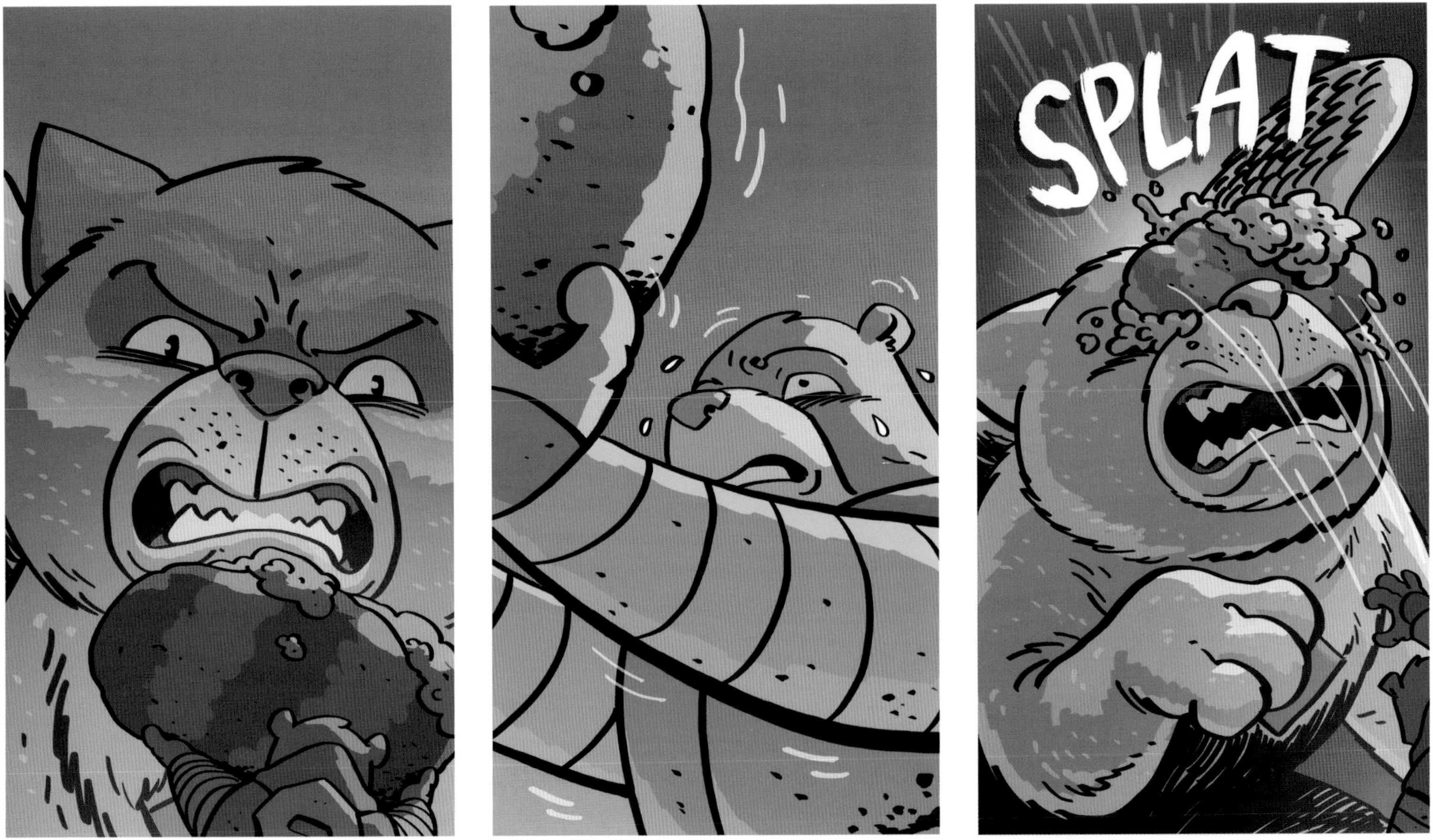
SPLAT

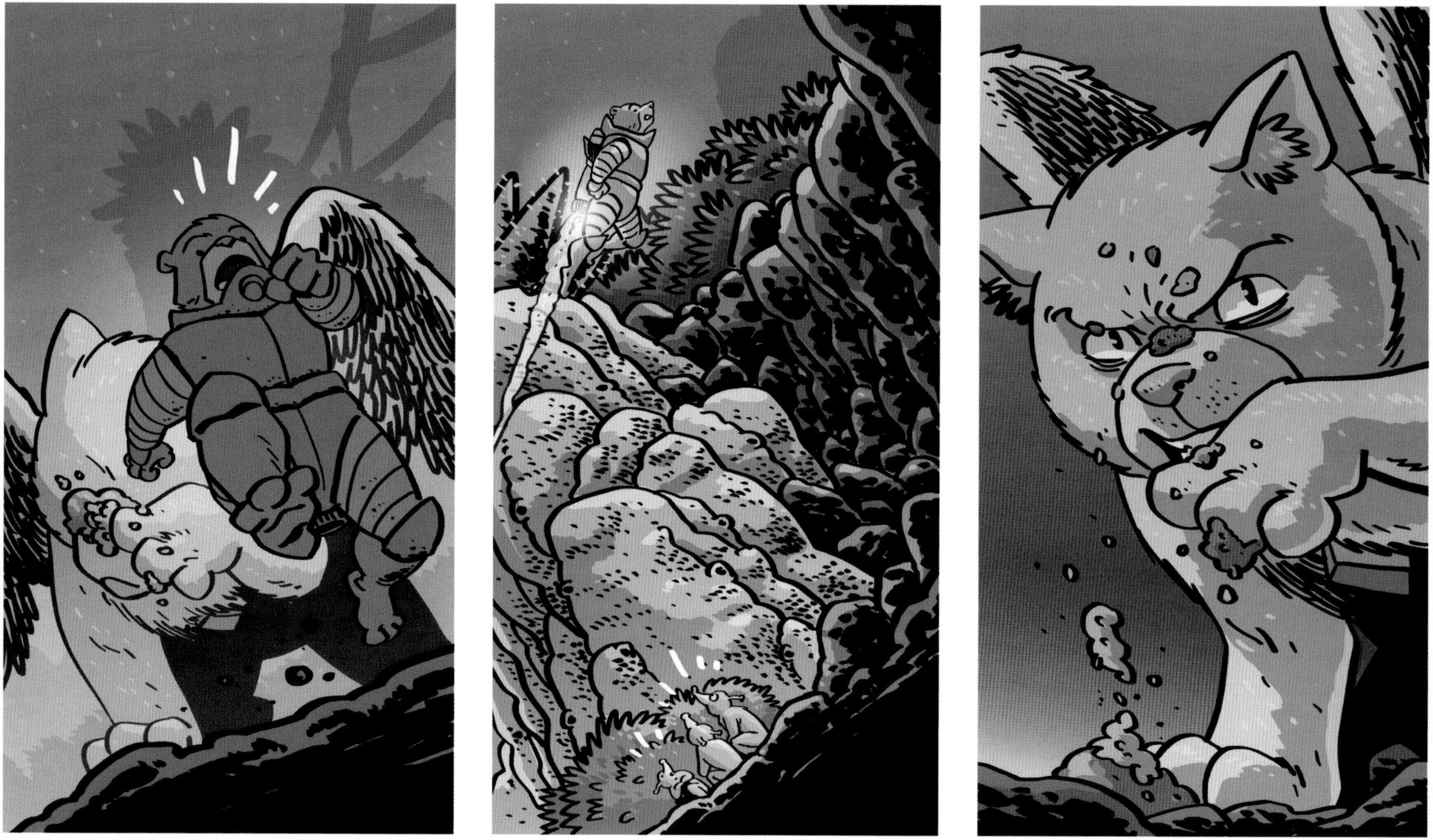

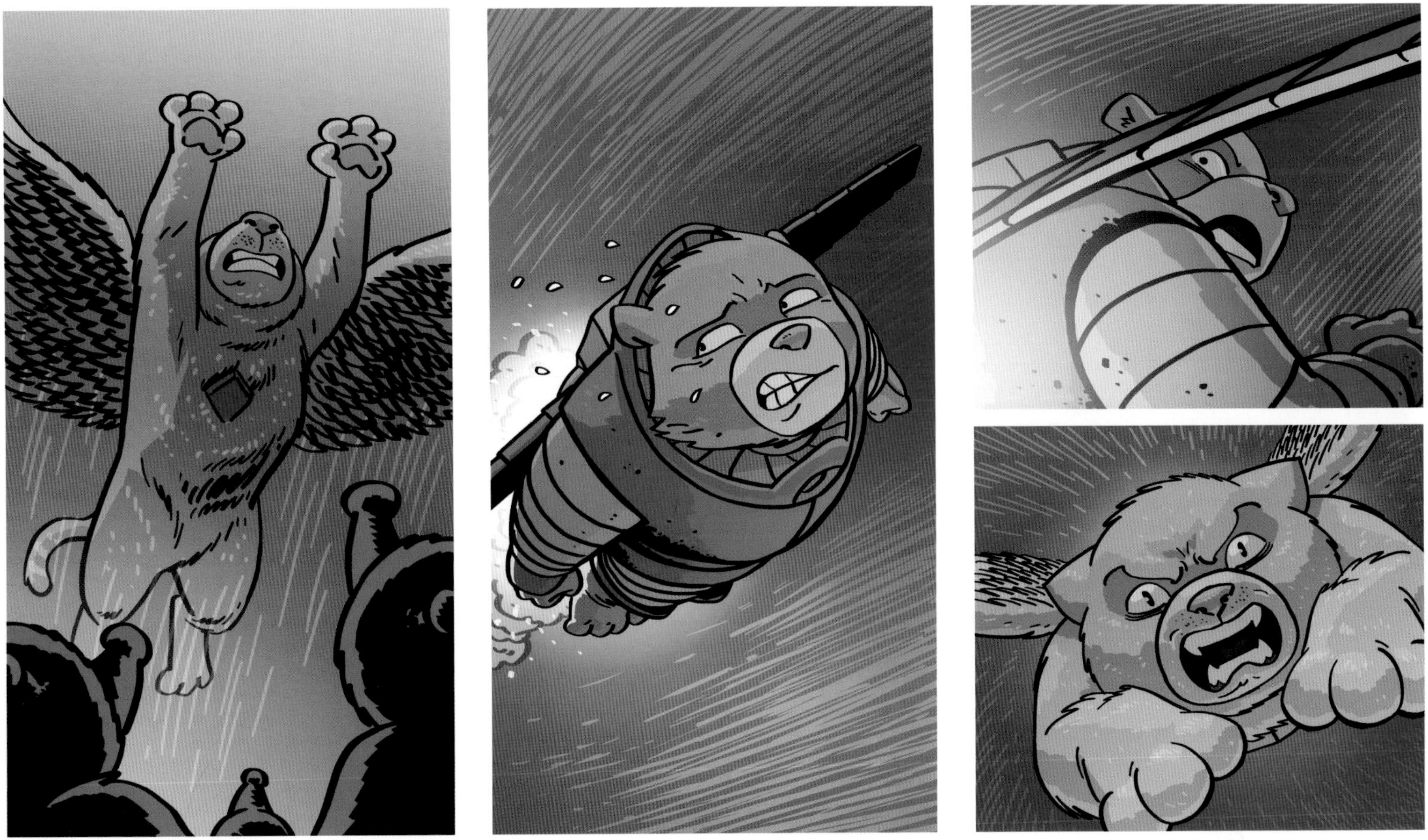

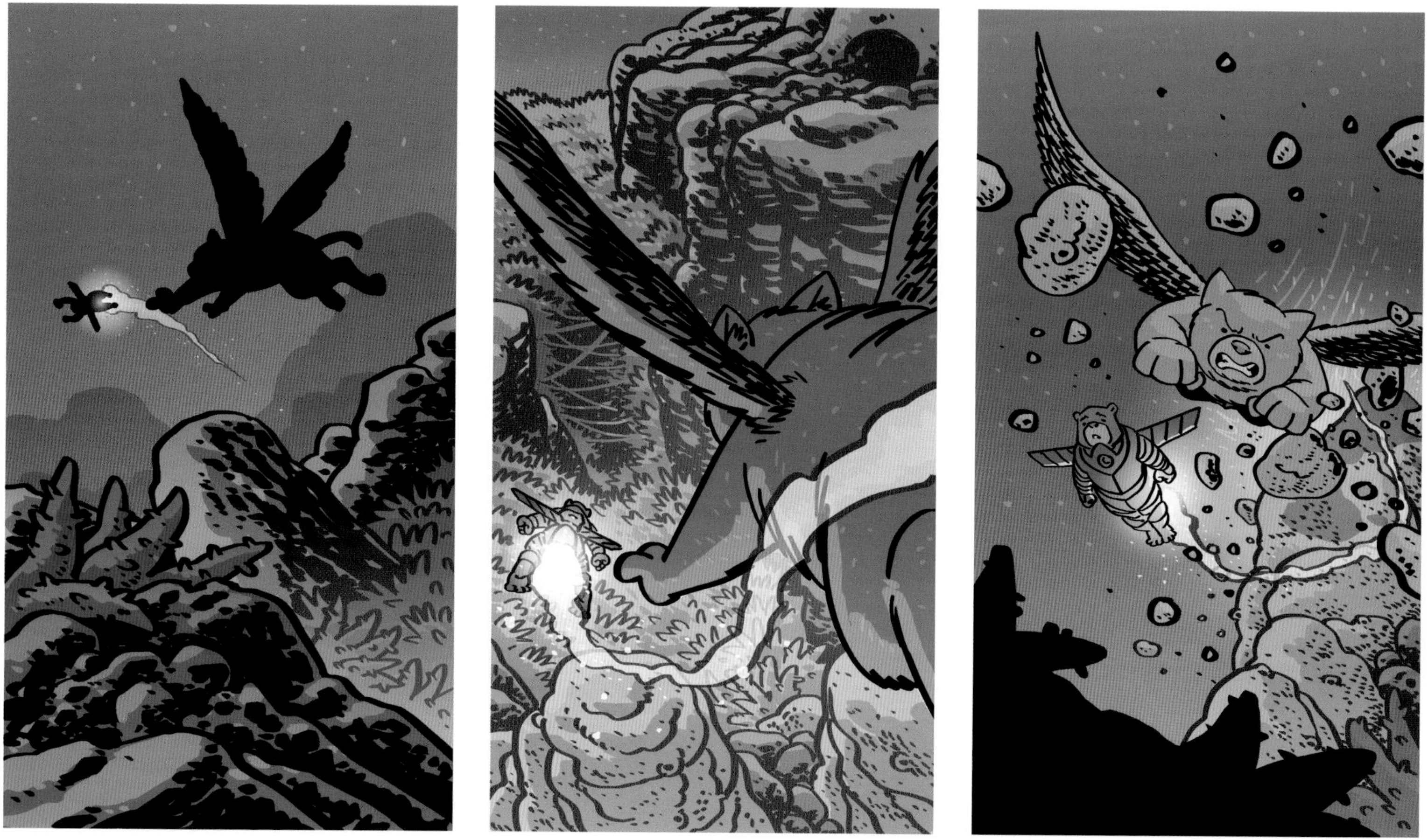

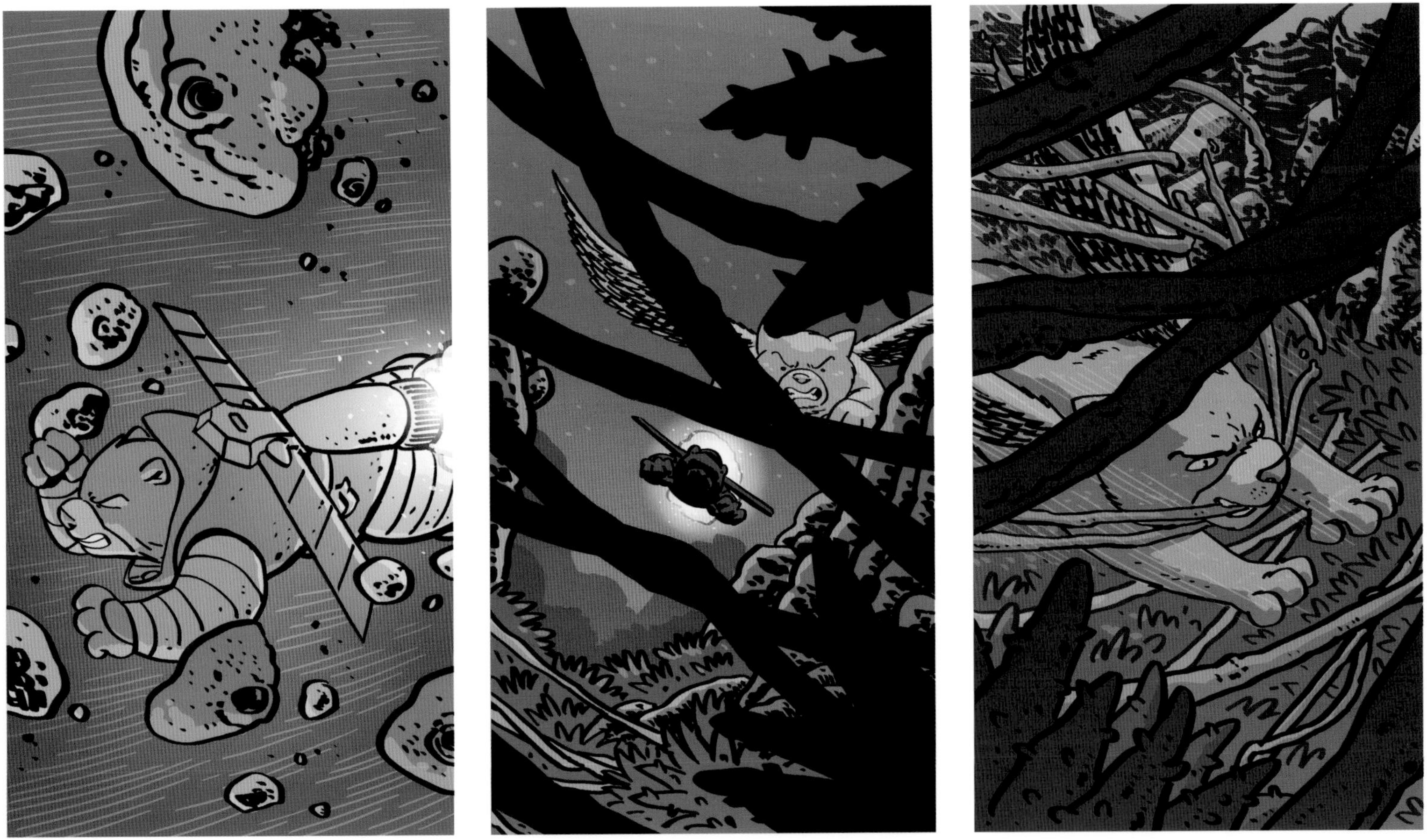

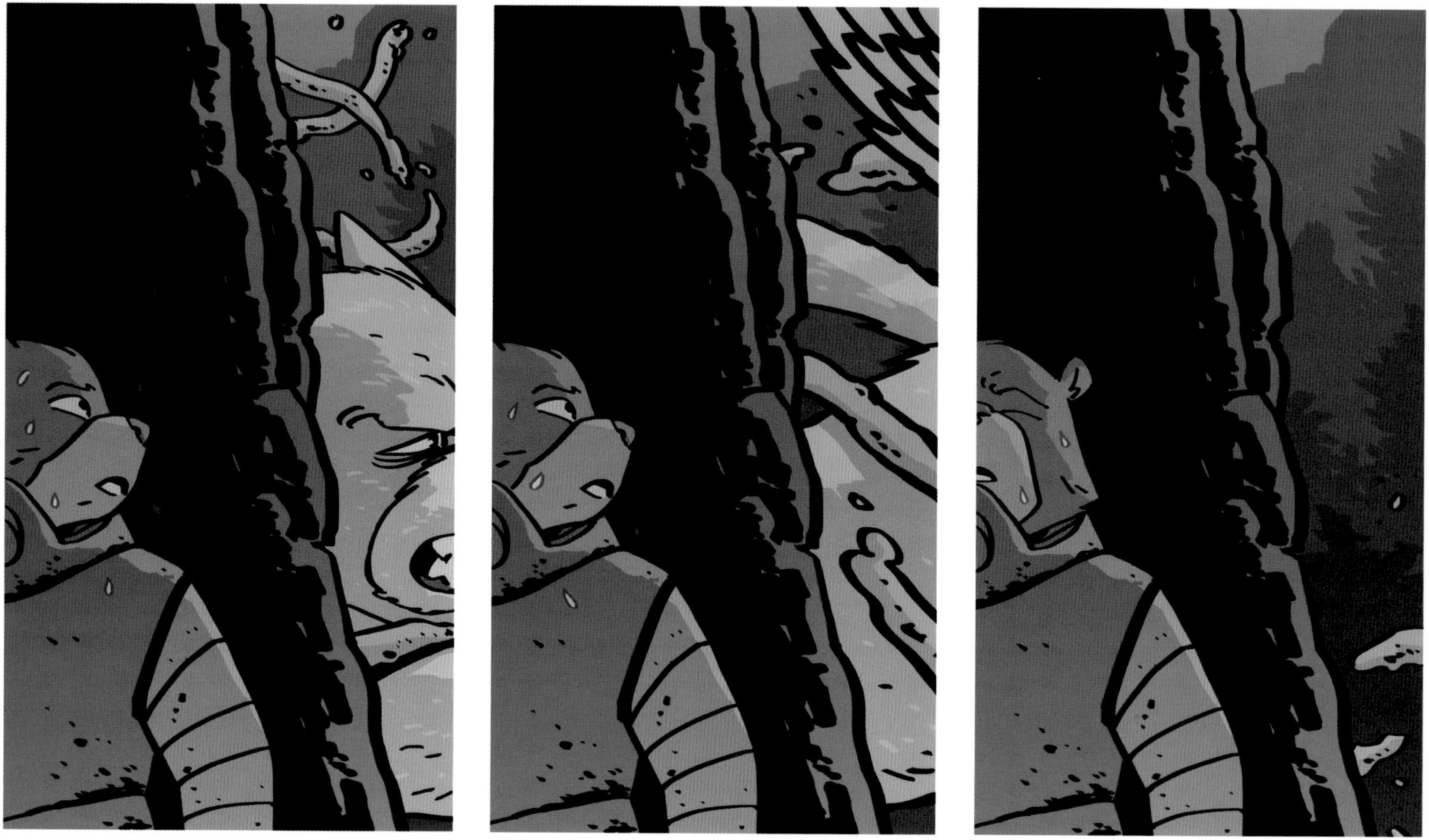

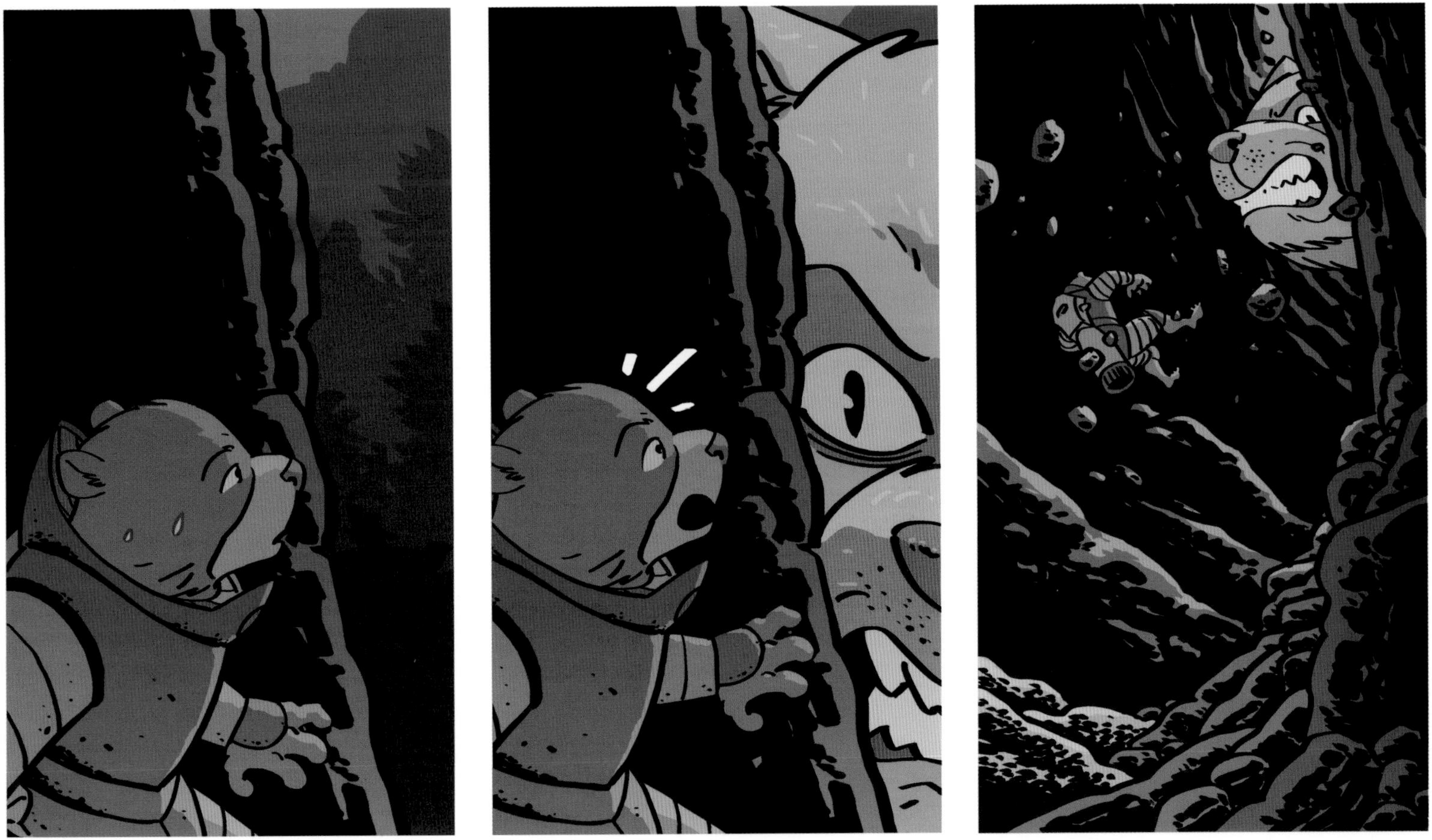

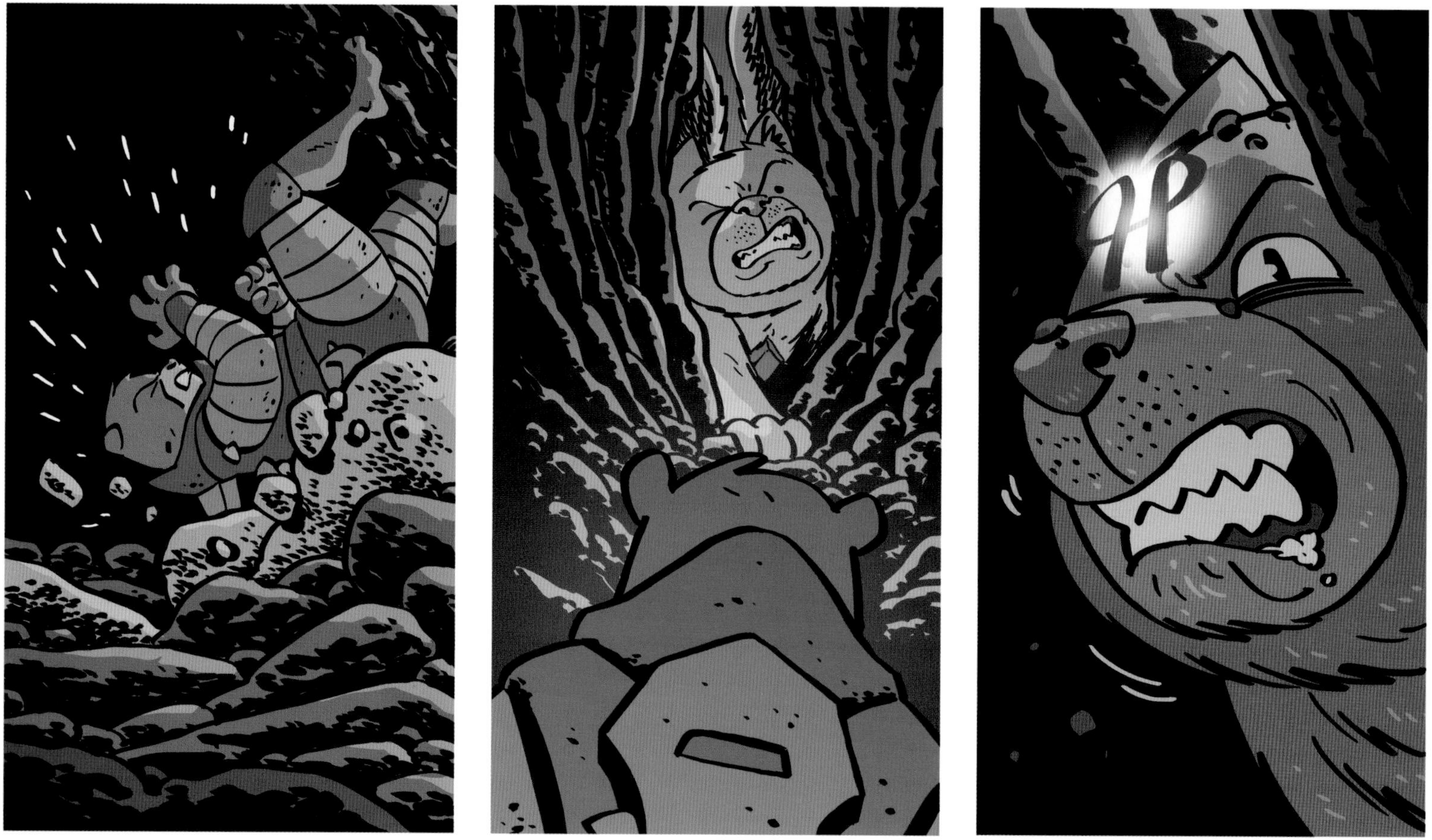

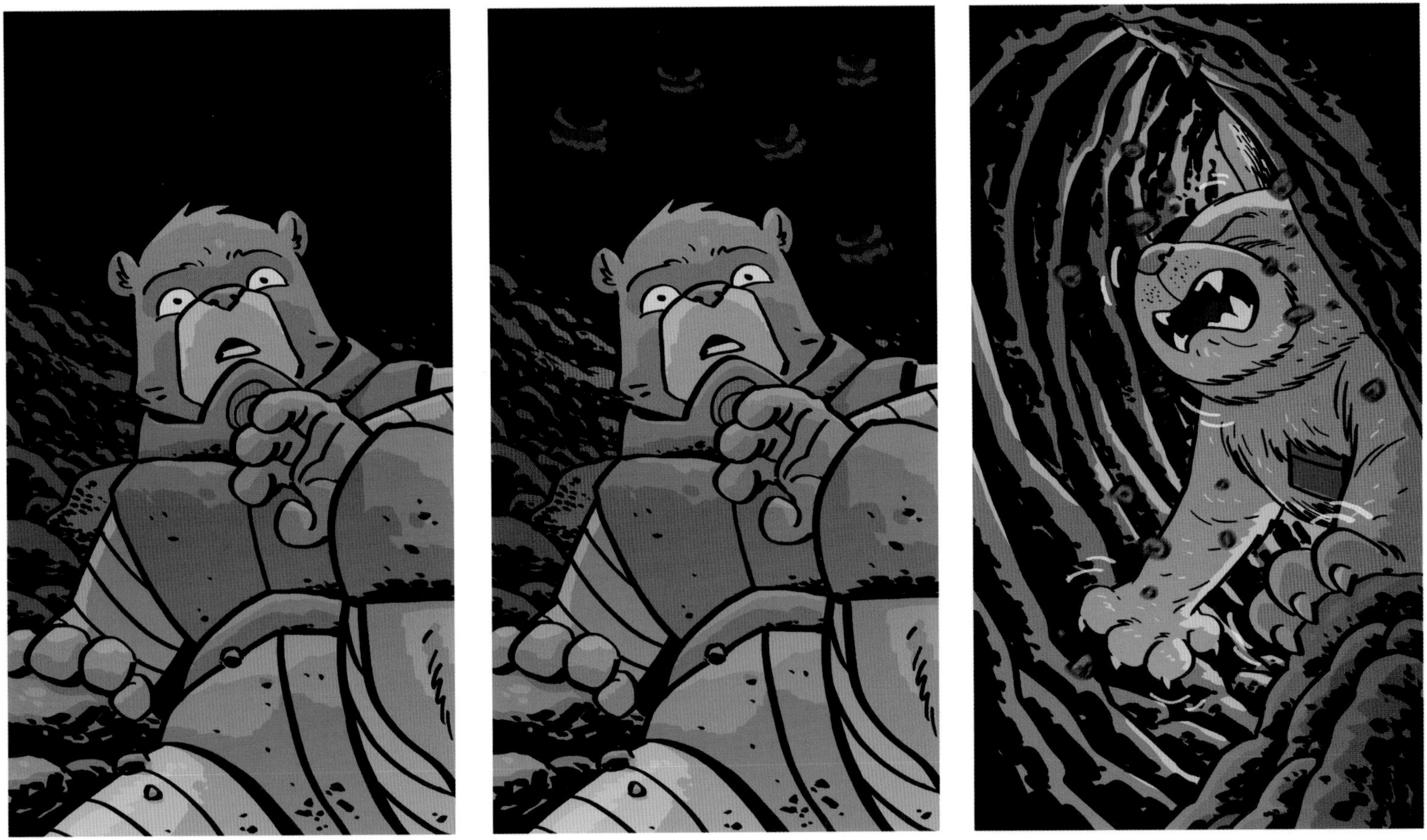

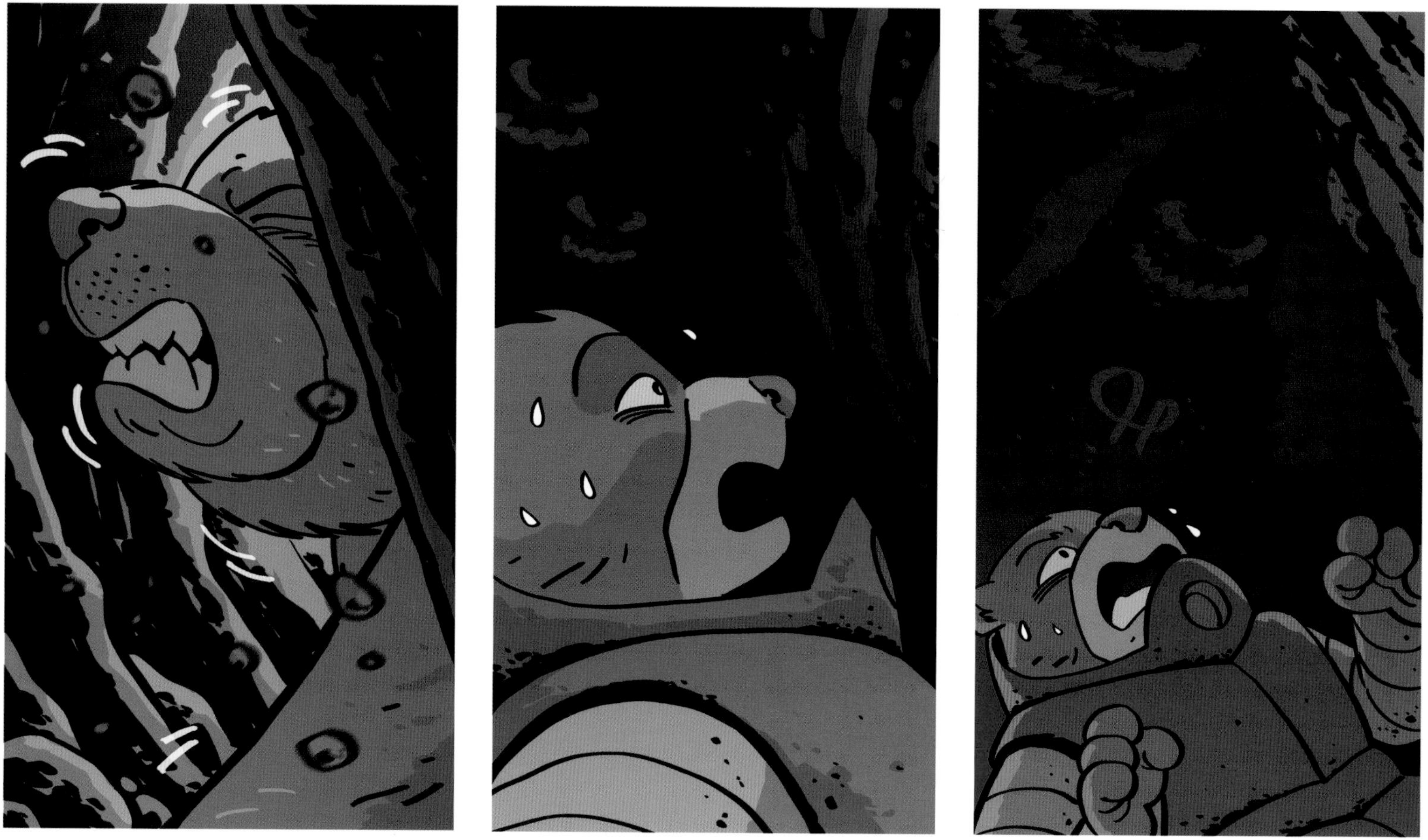

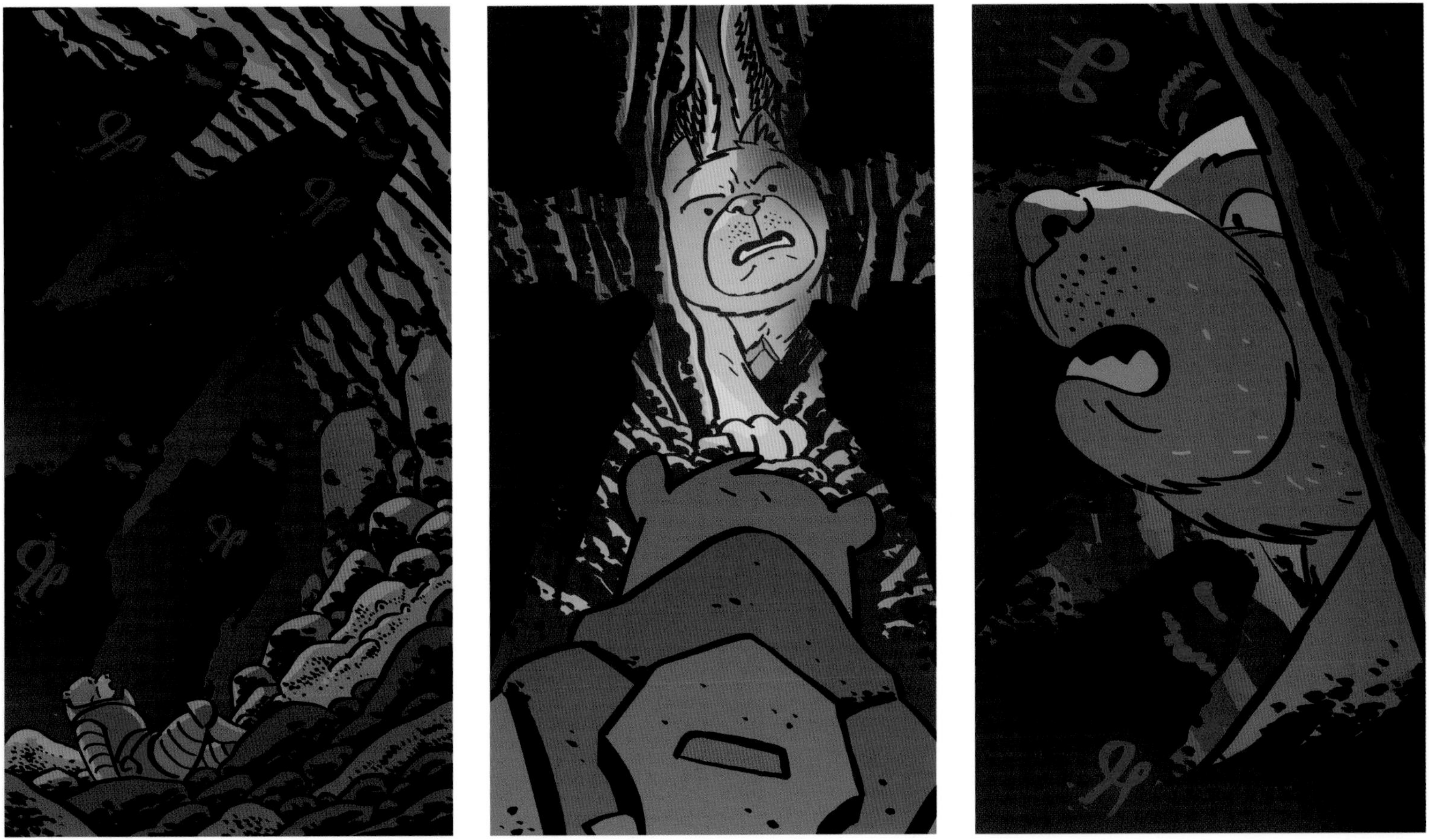

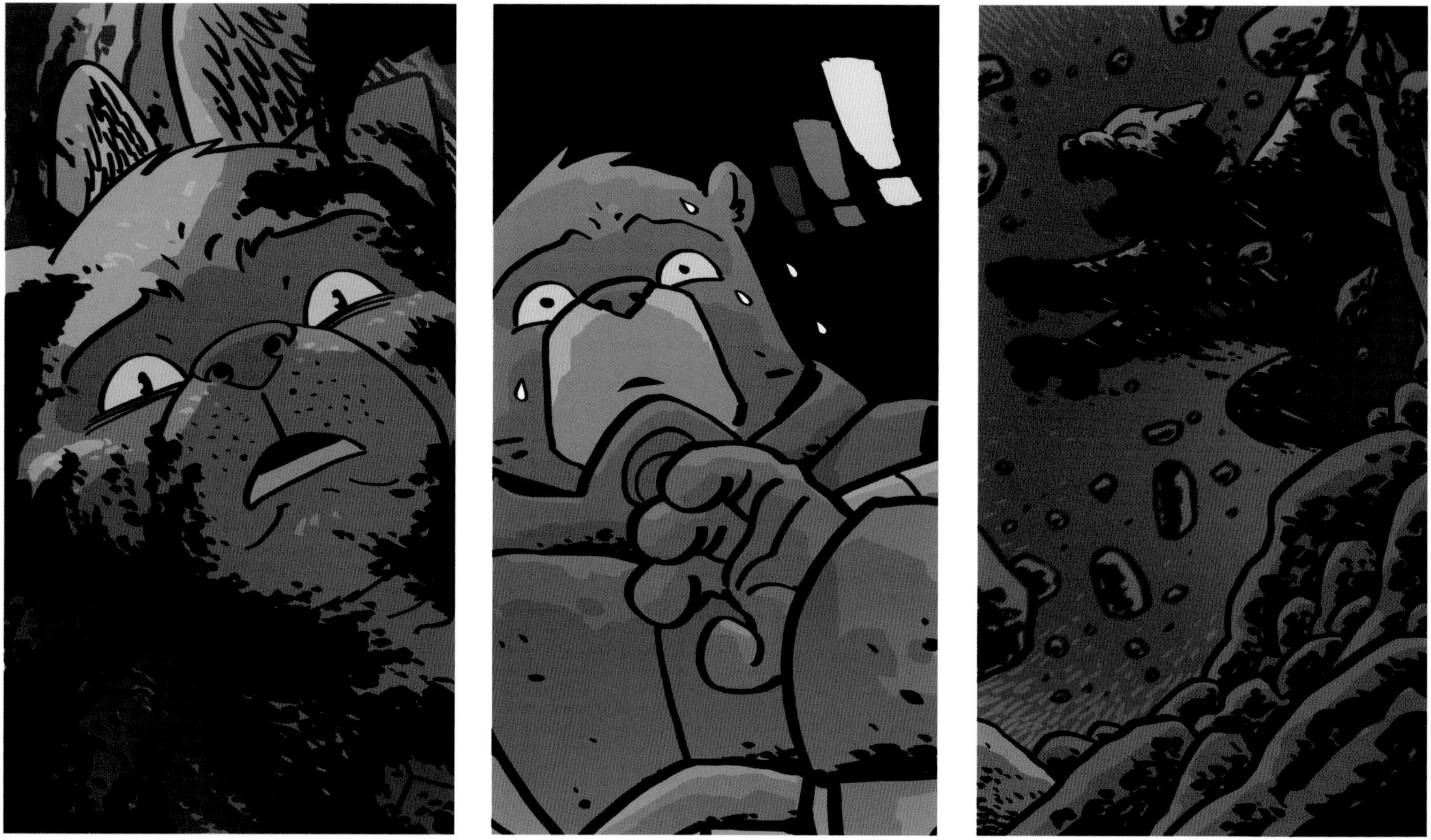
!!!

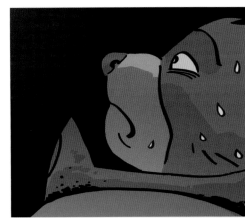

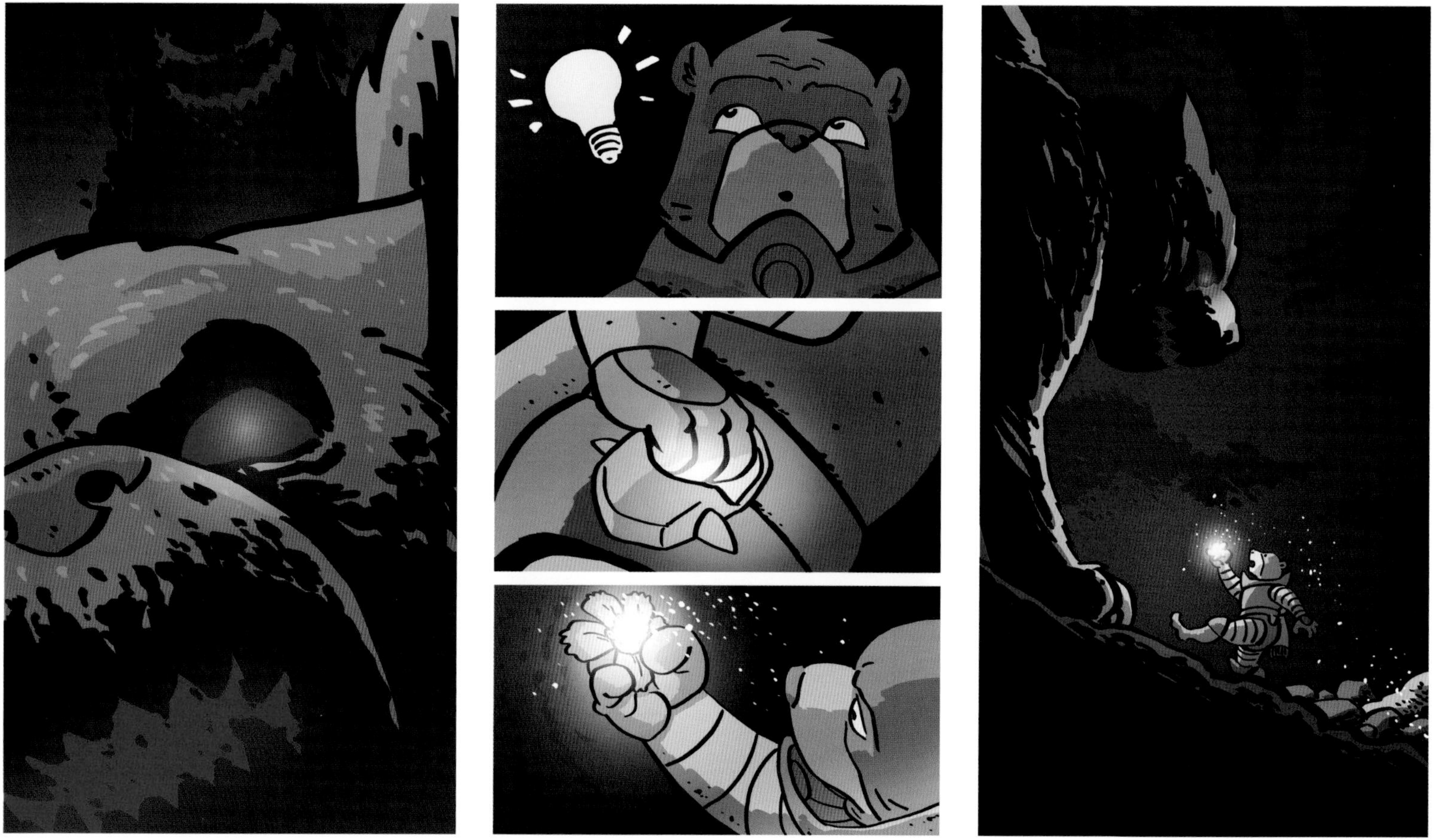

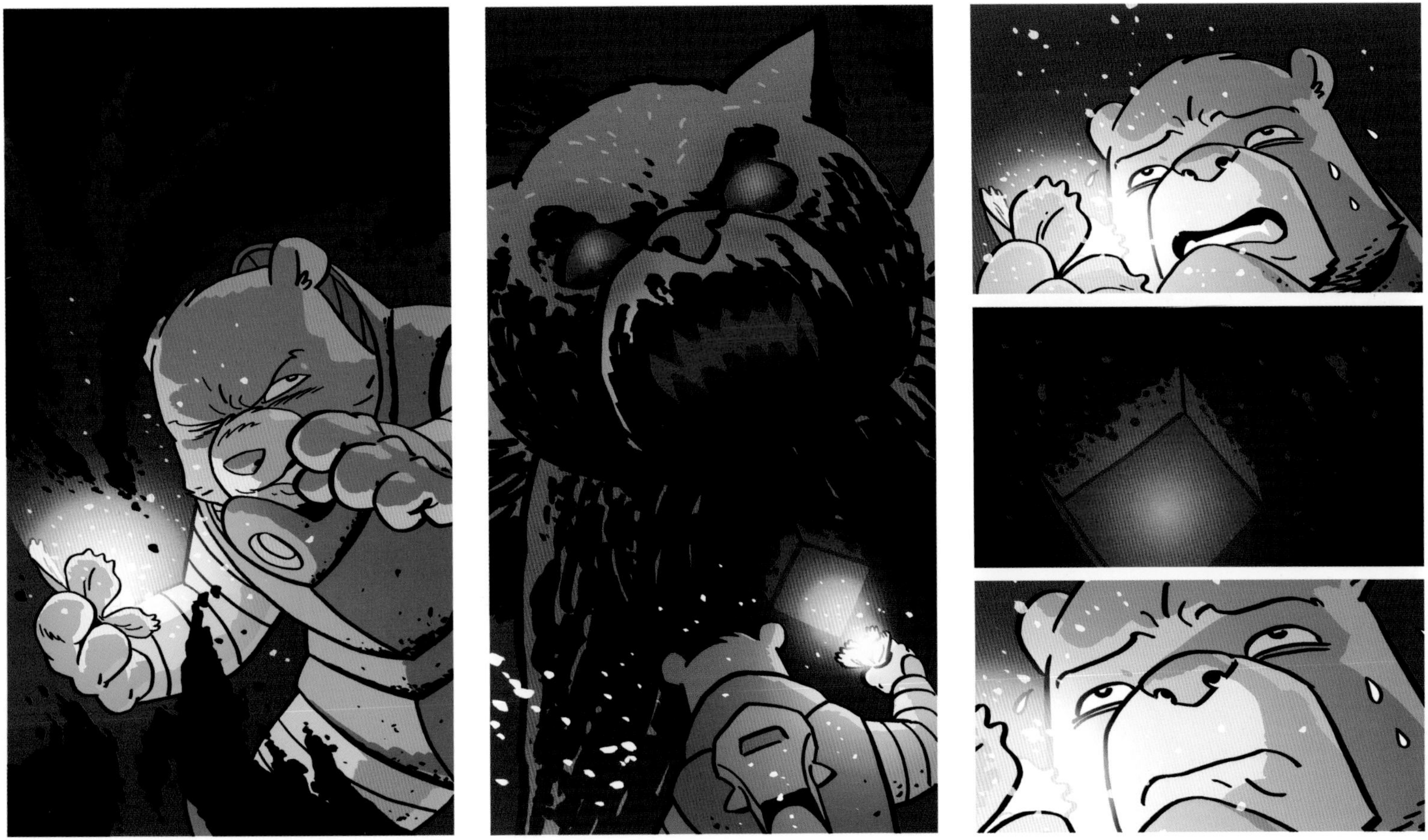

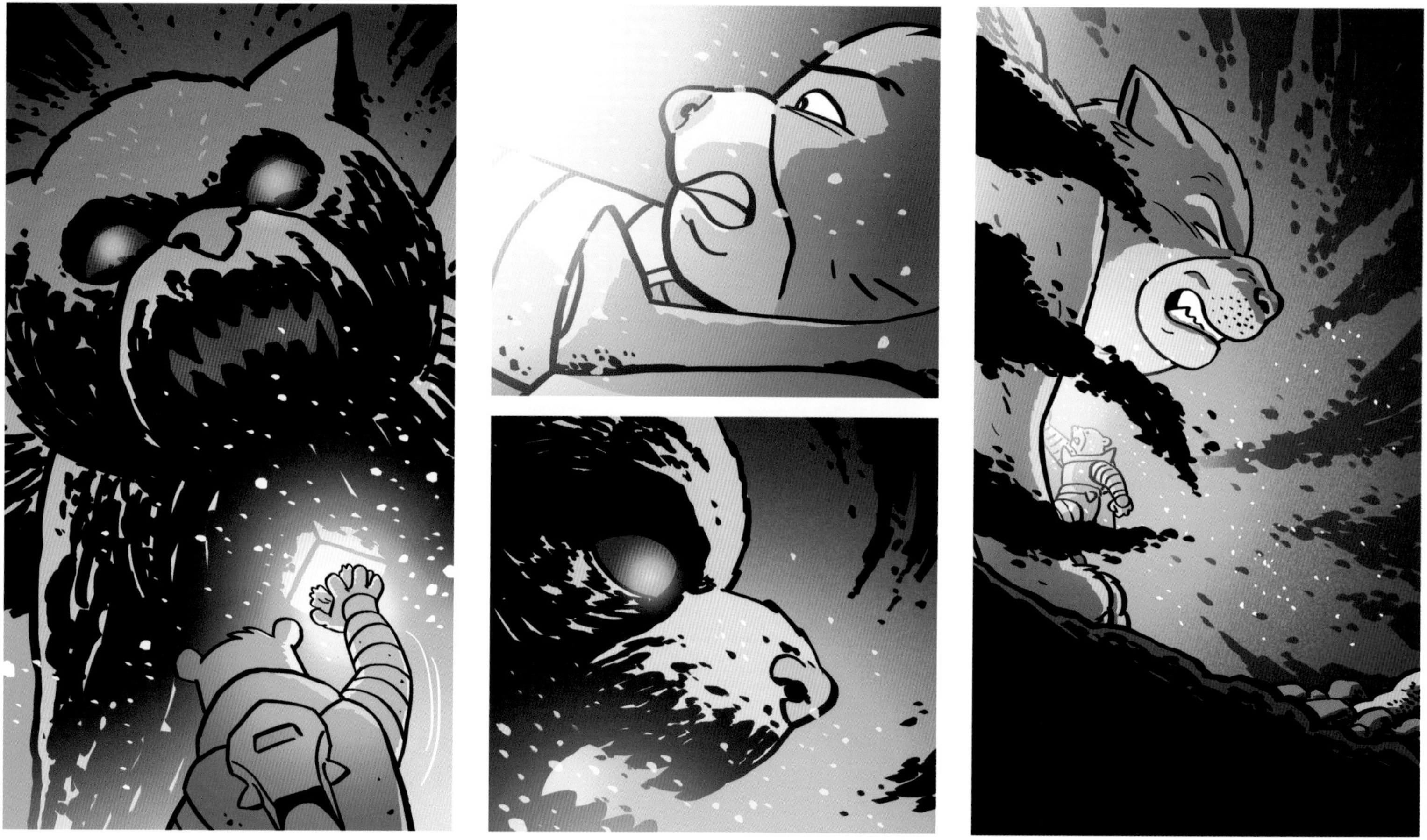

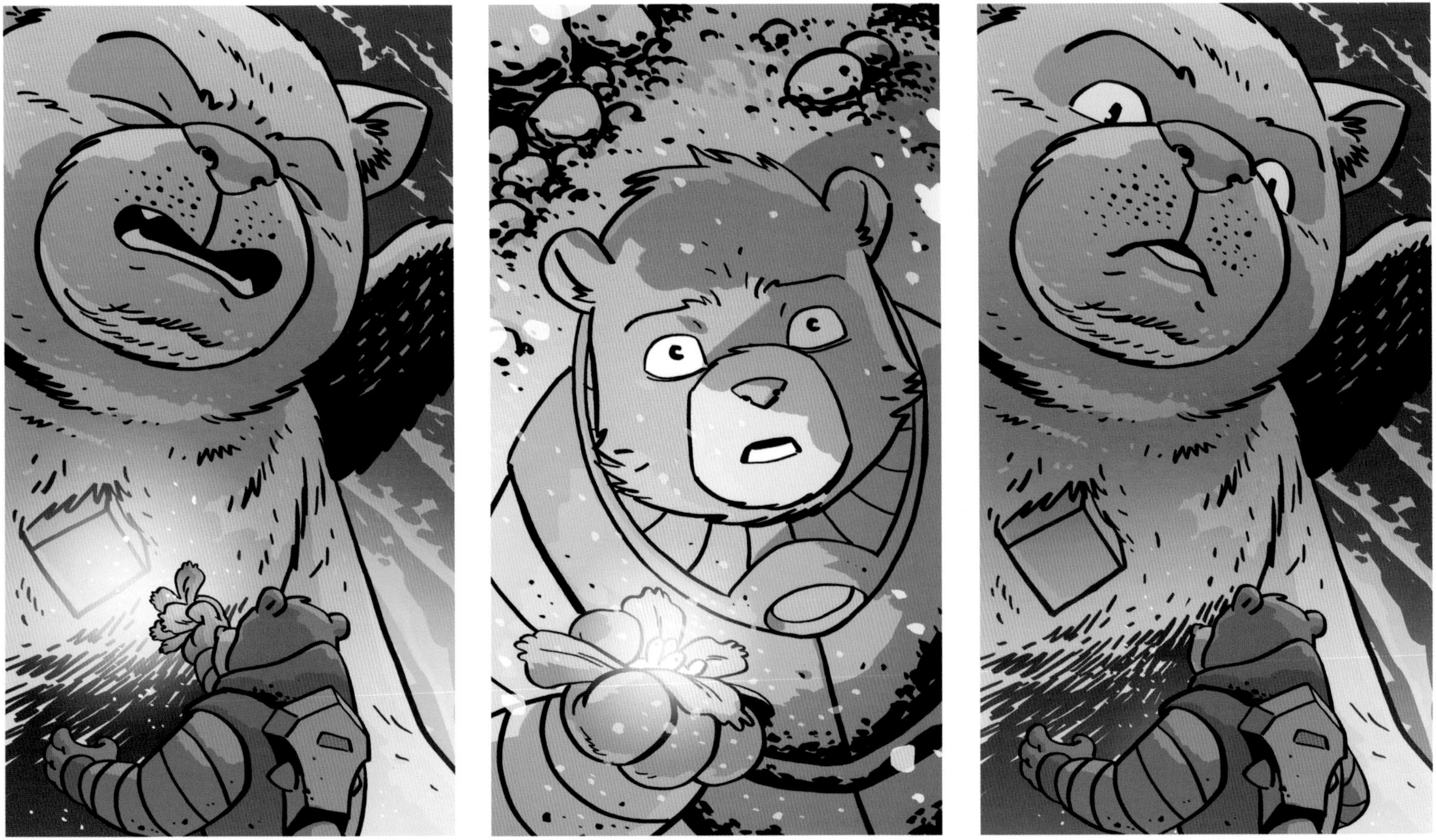

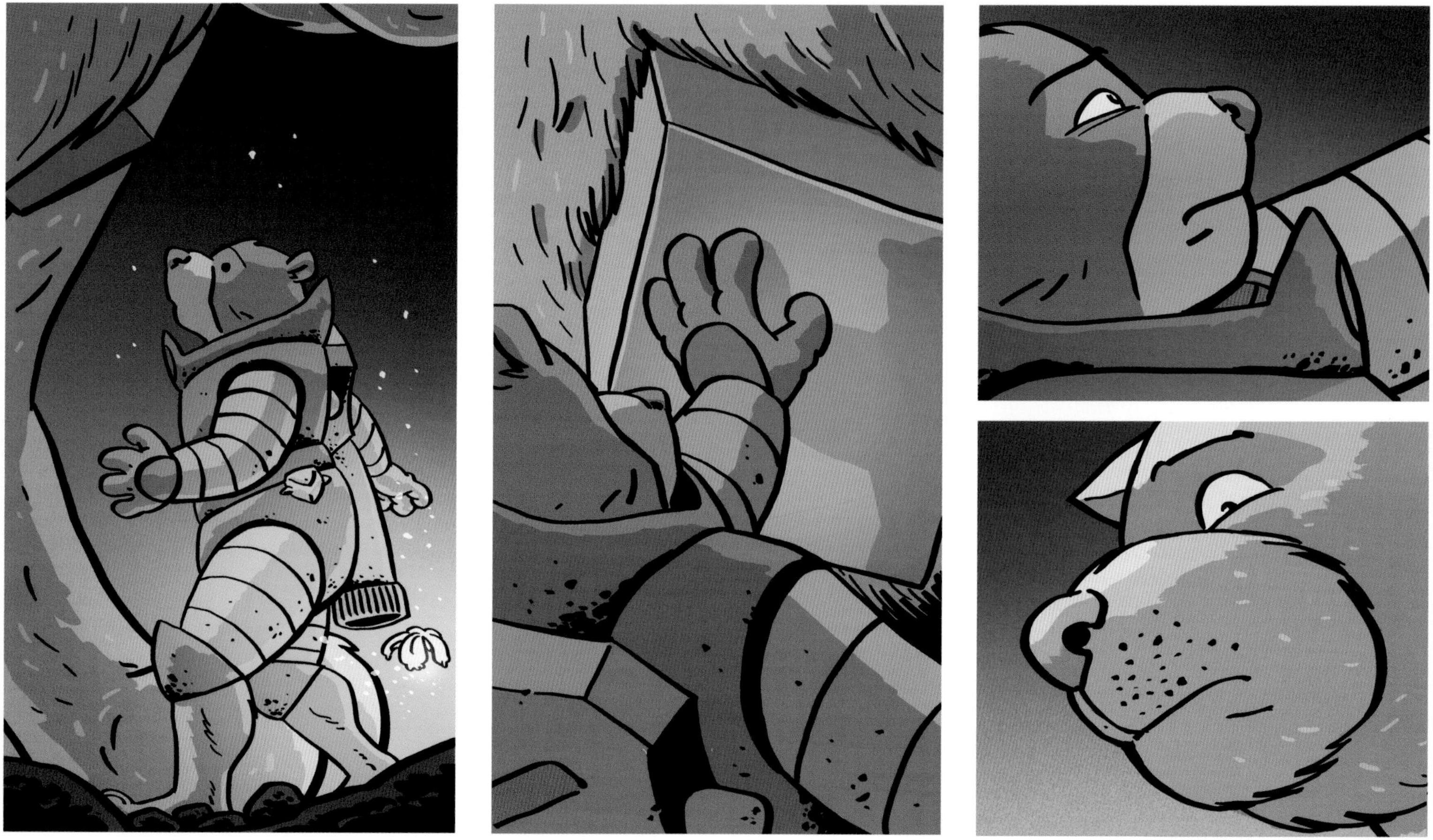

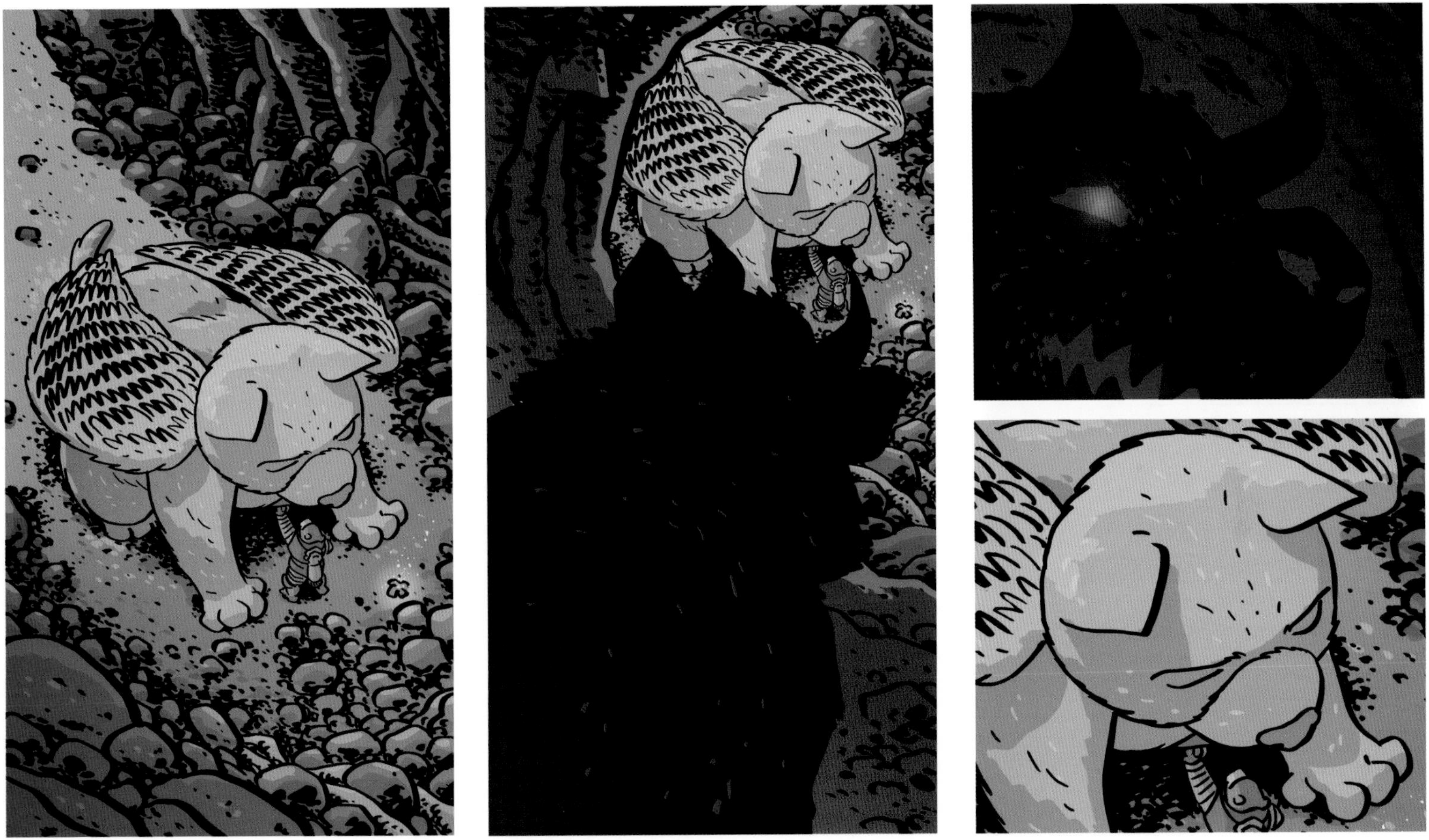

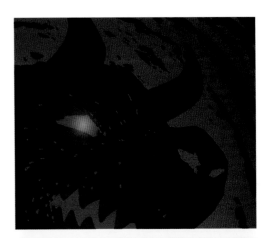

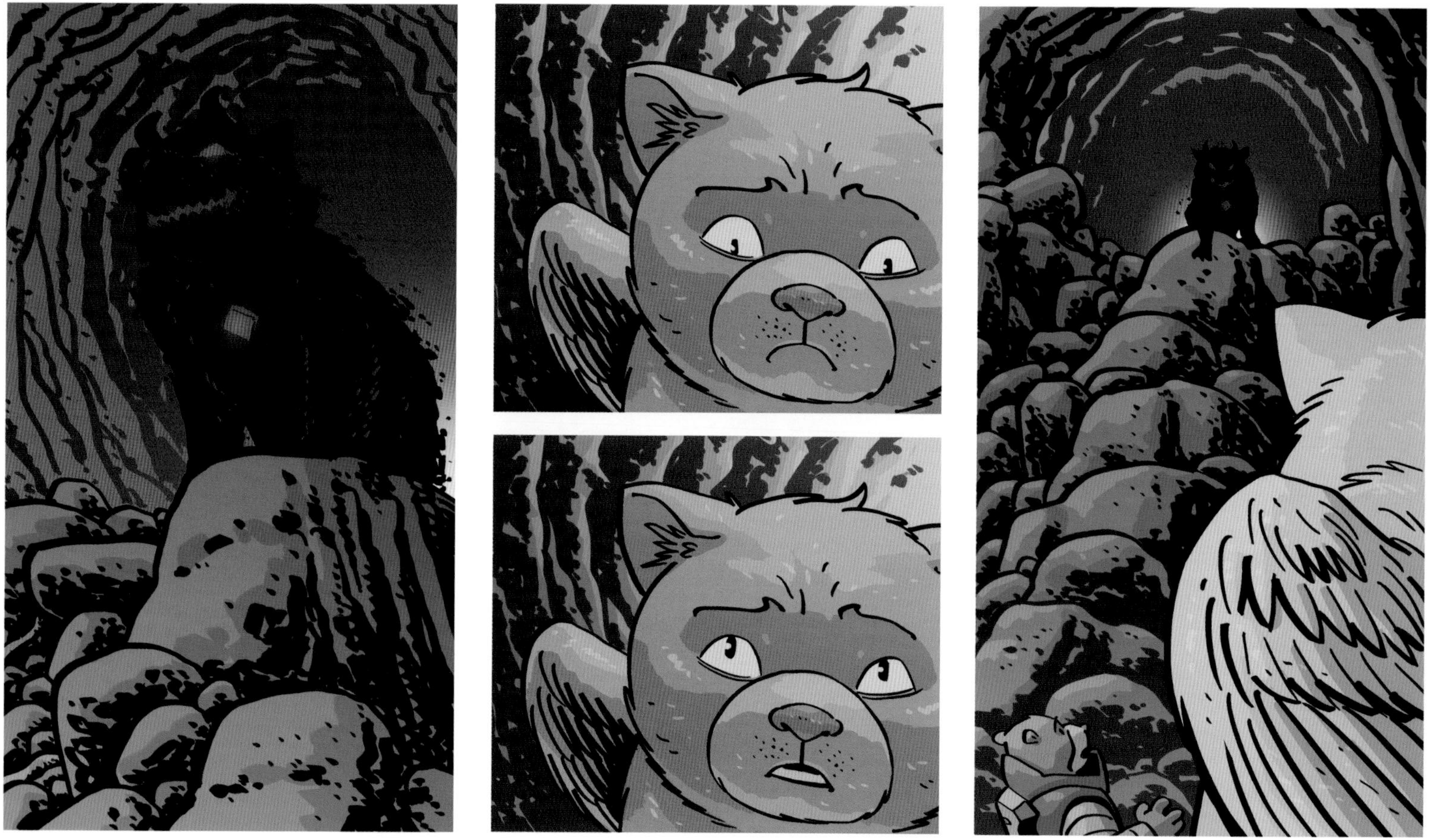

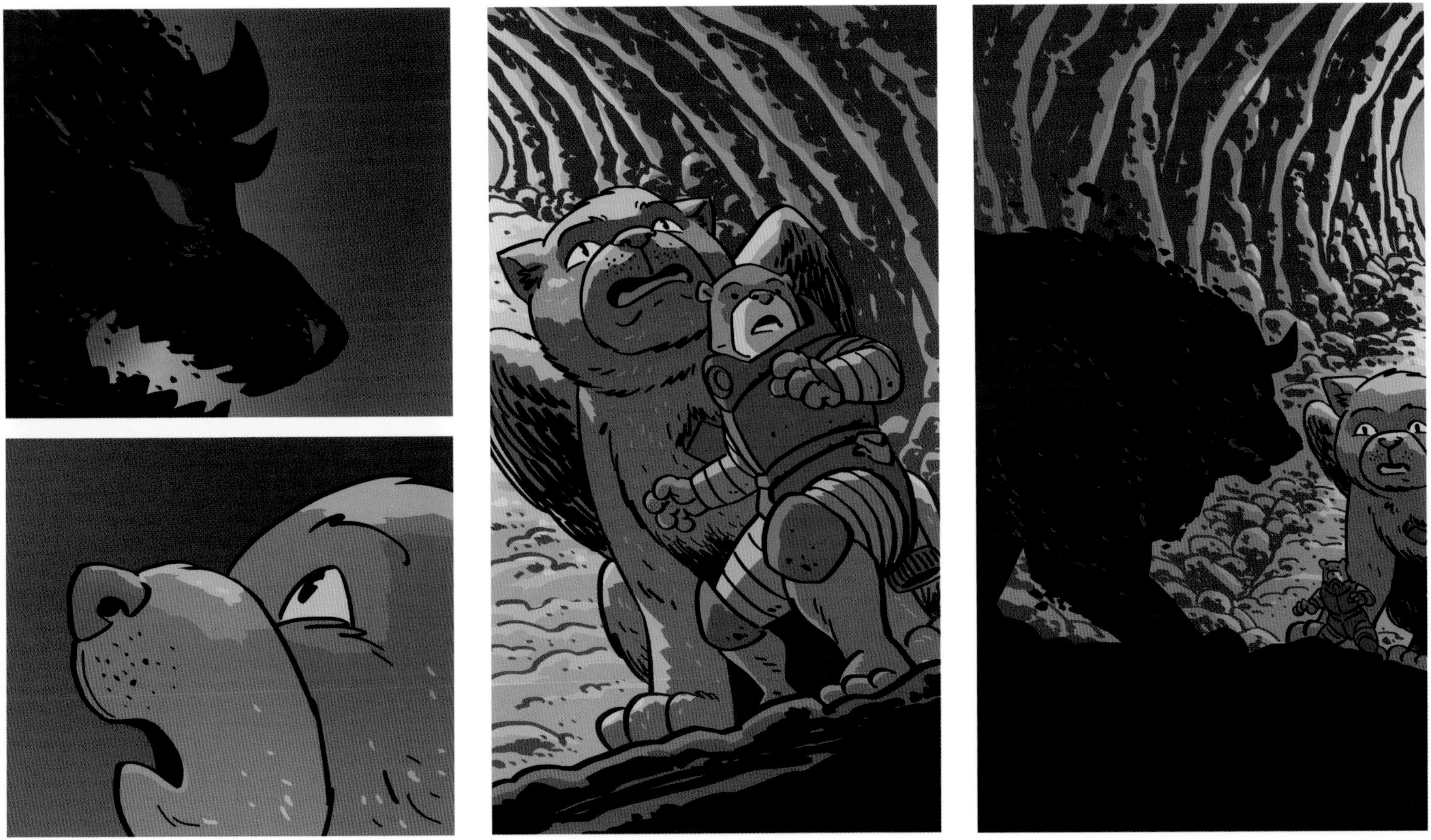

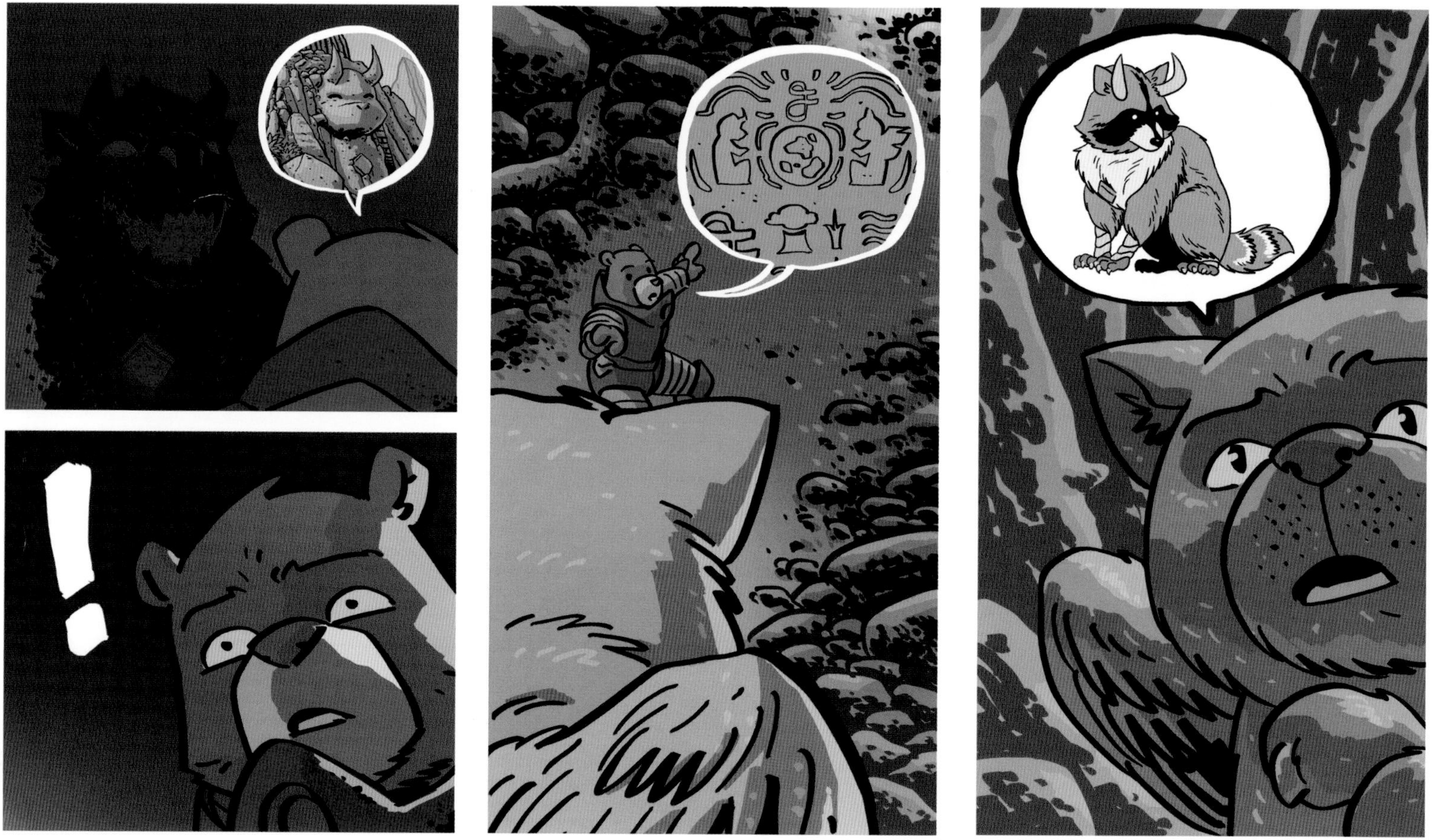
!

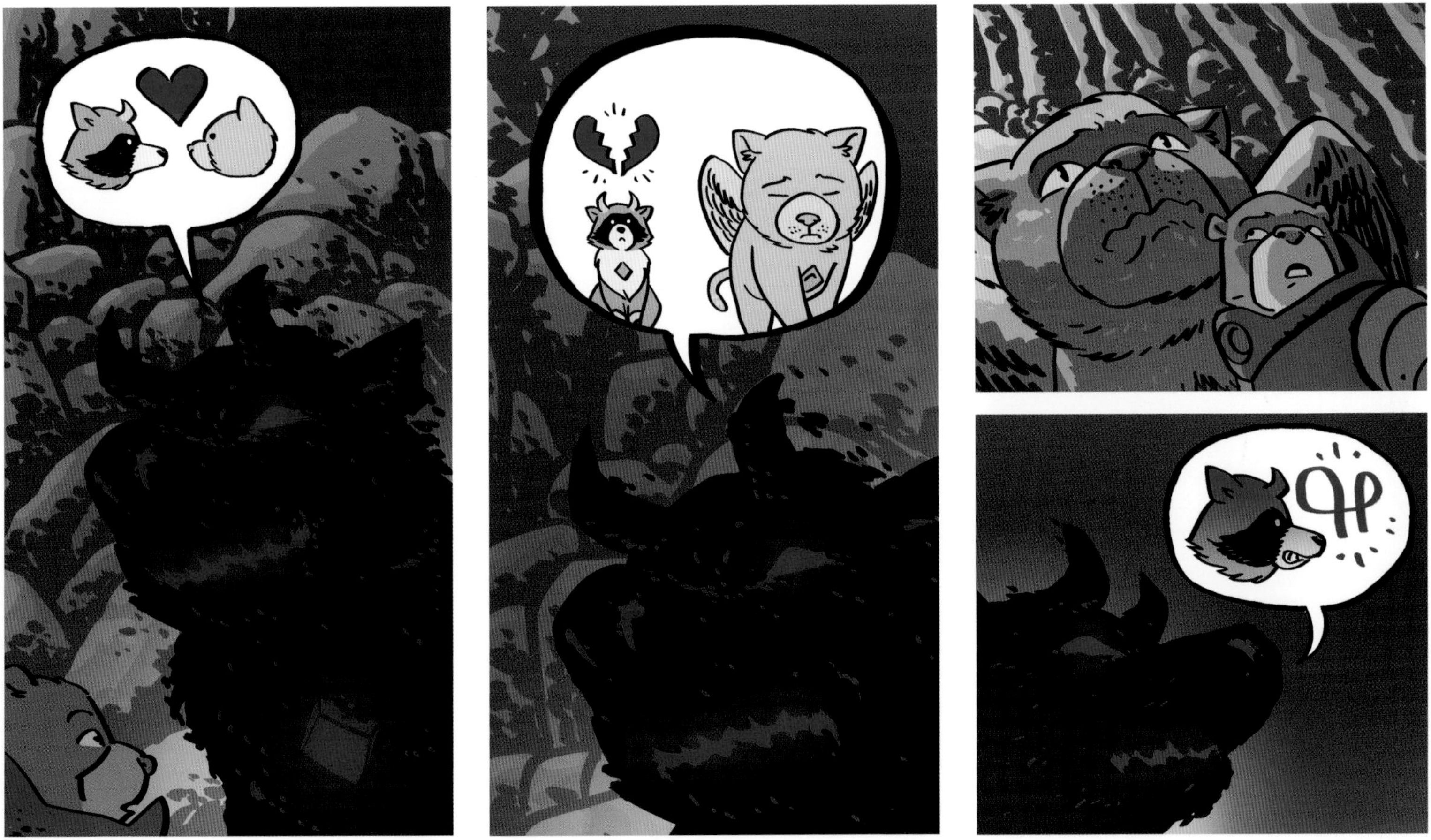

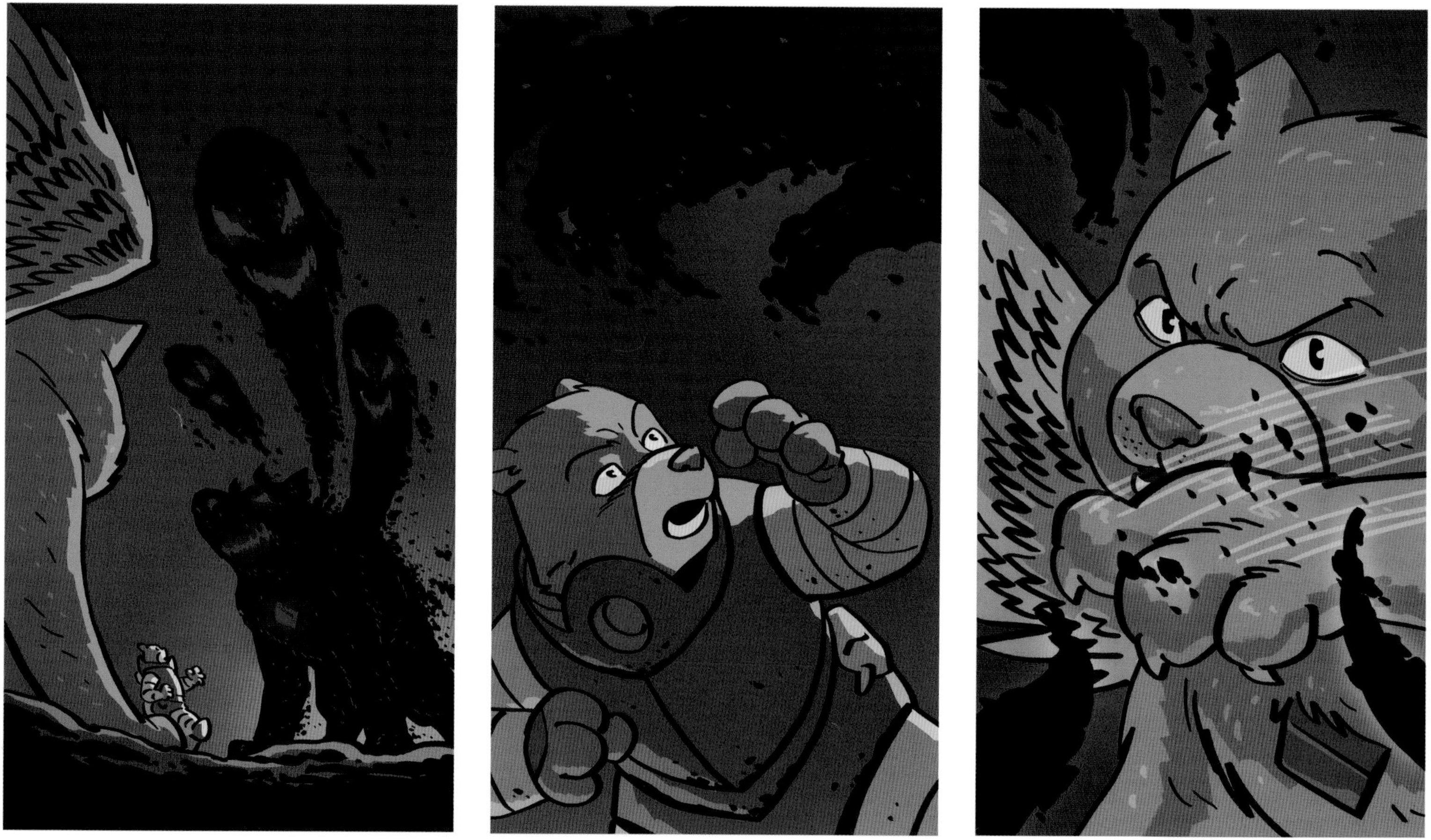

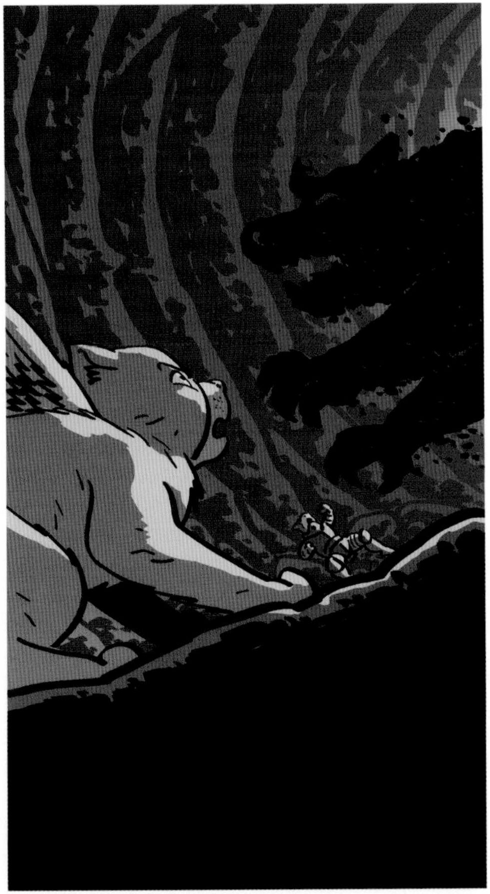
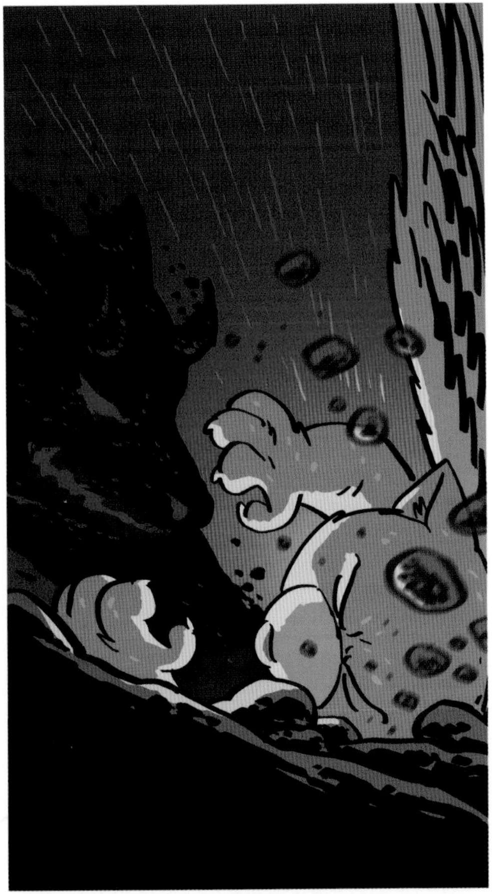
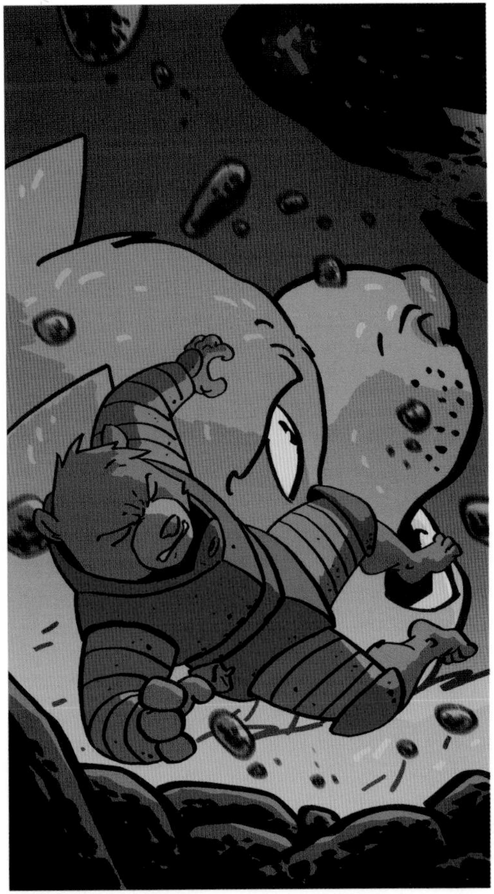

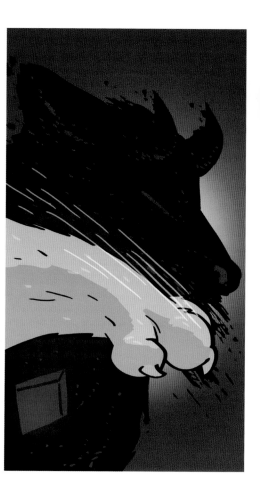

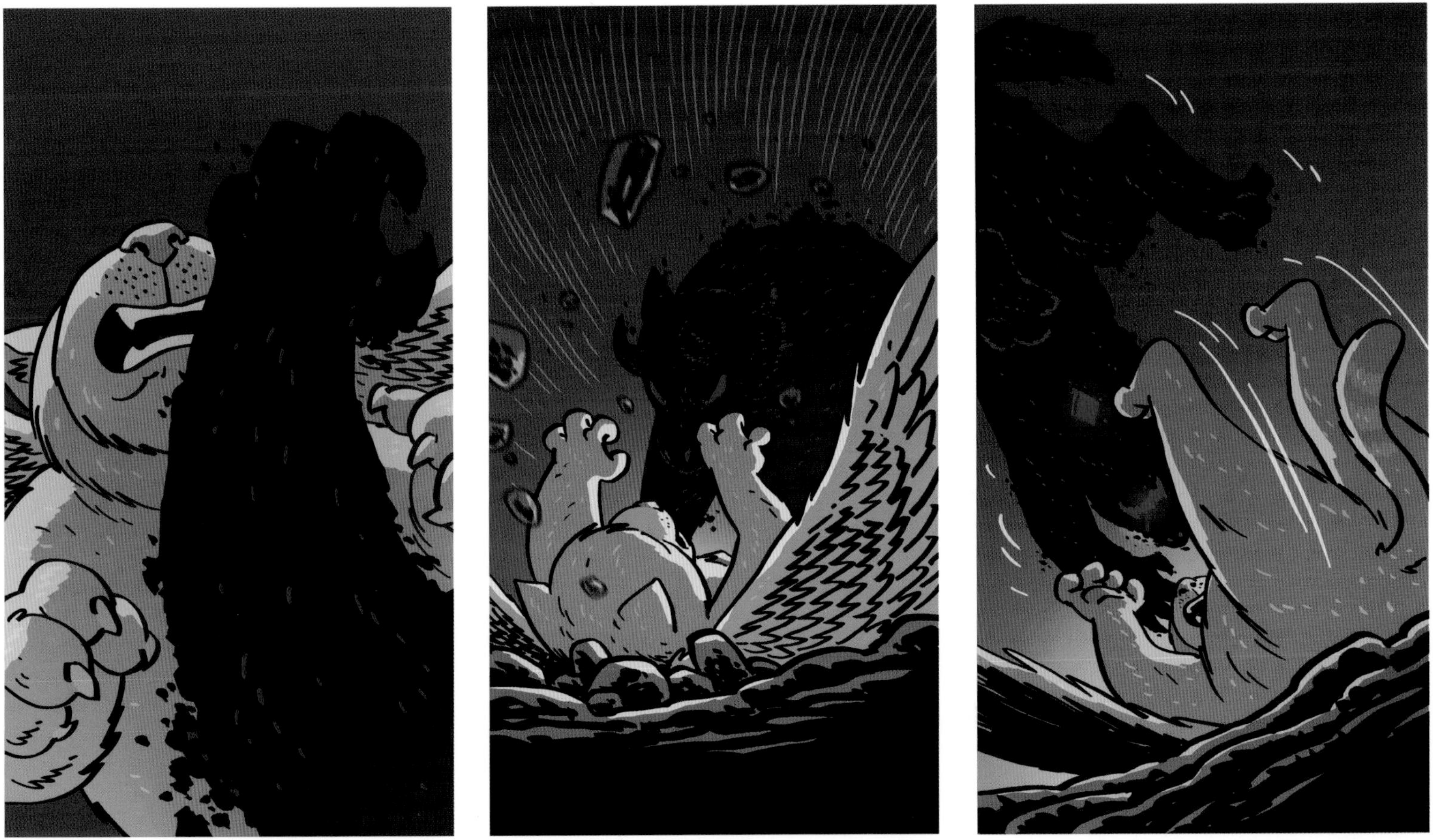

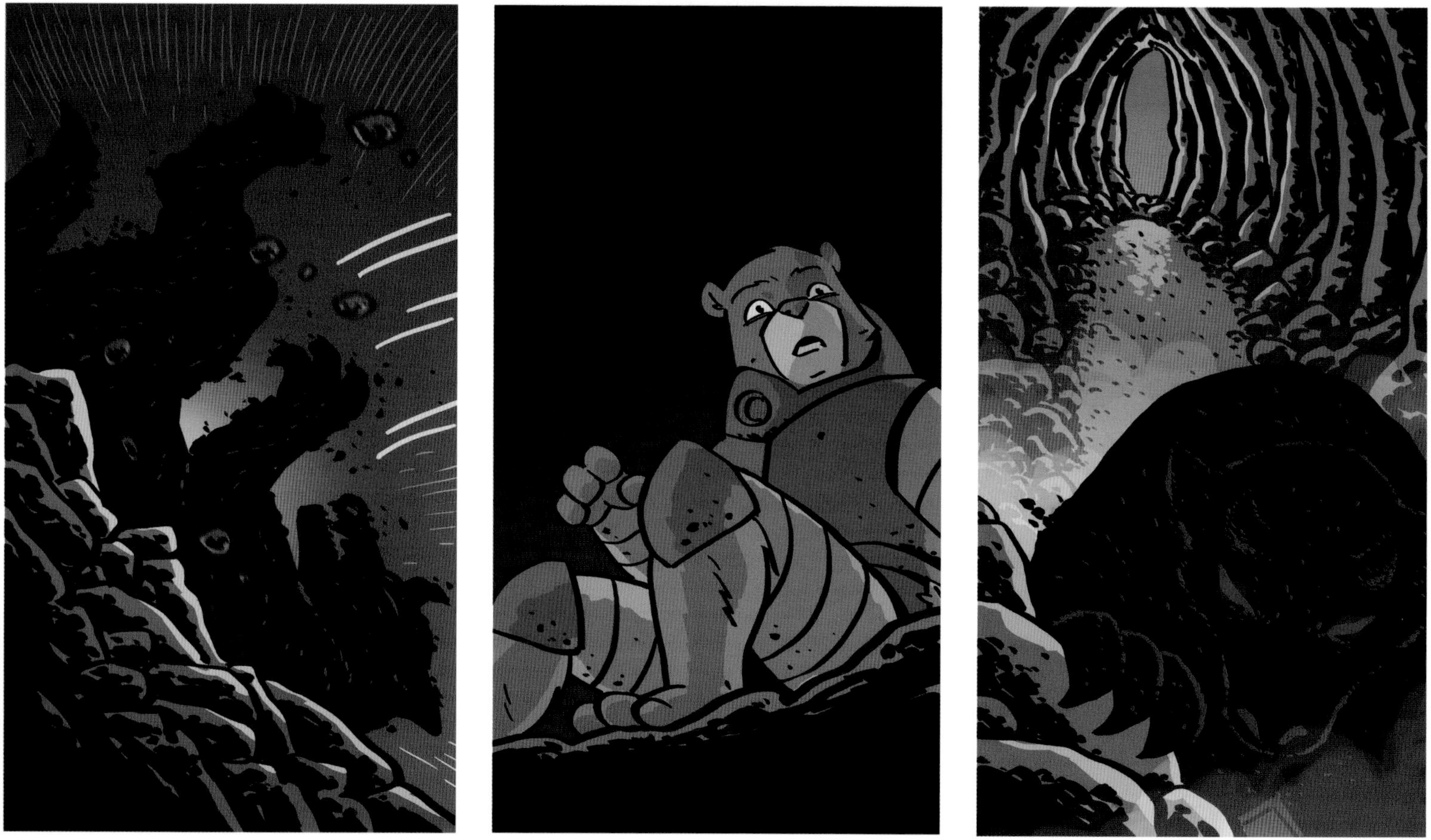

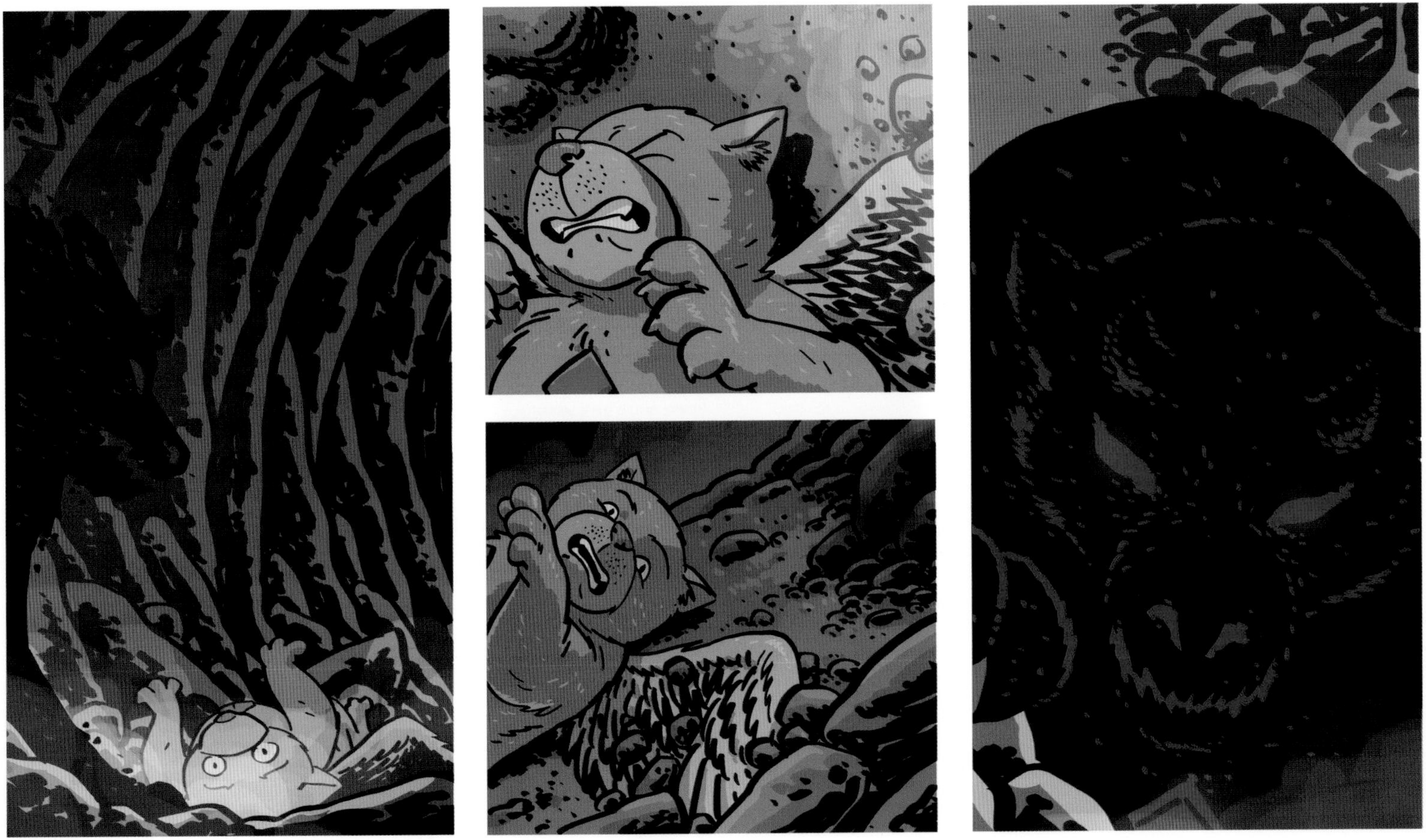

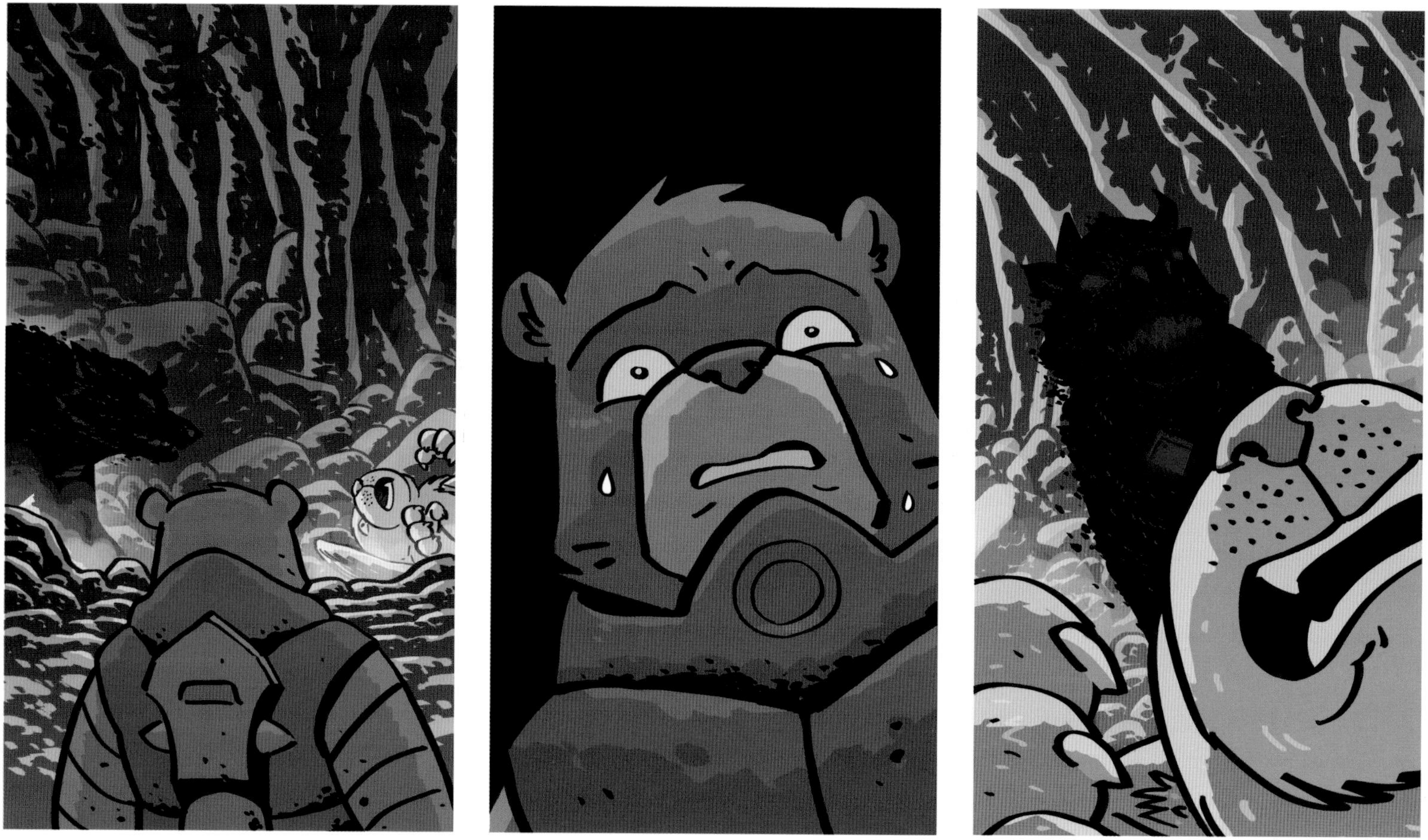

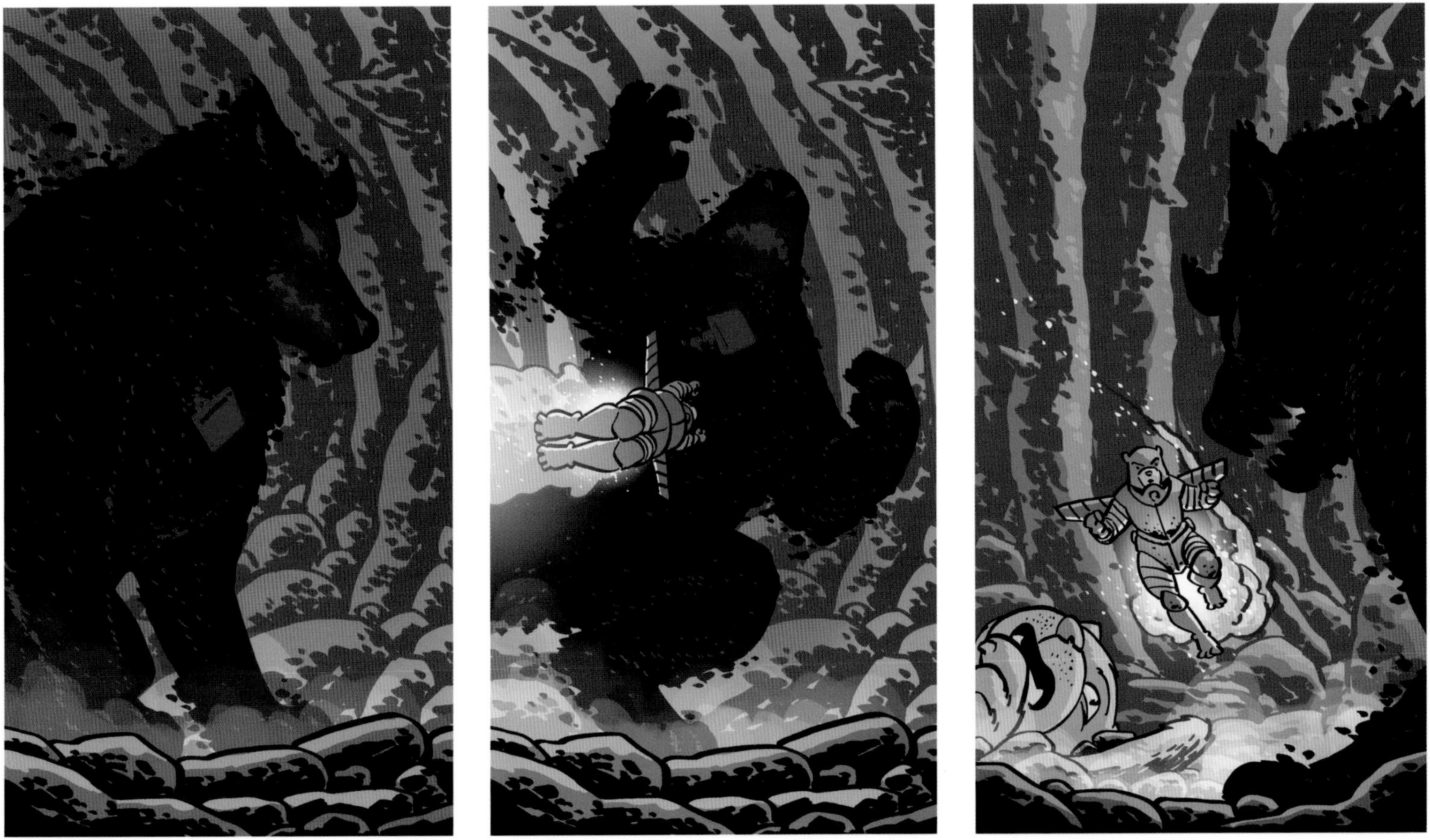

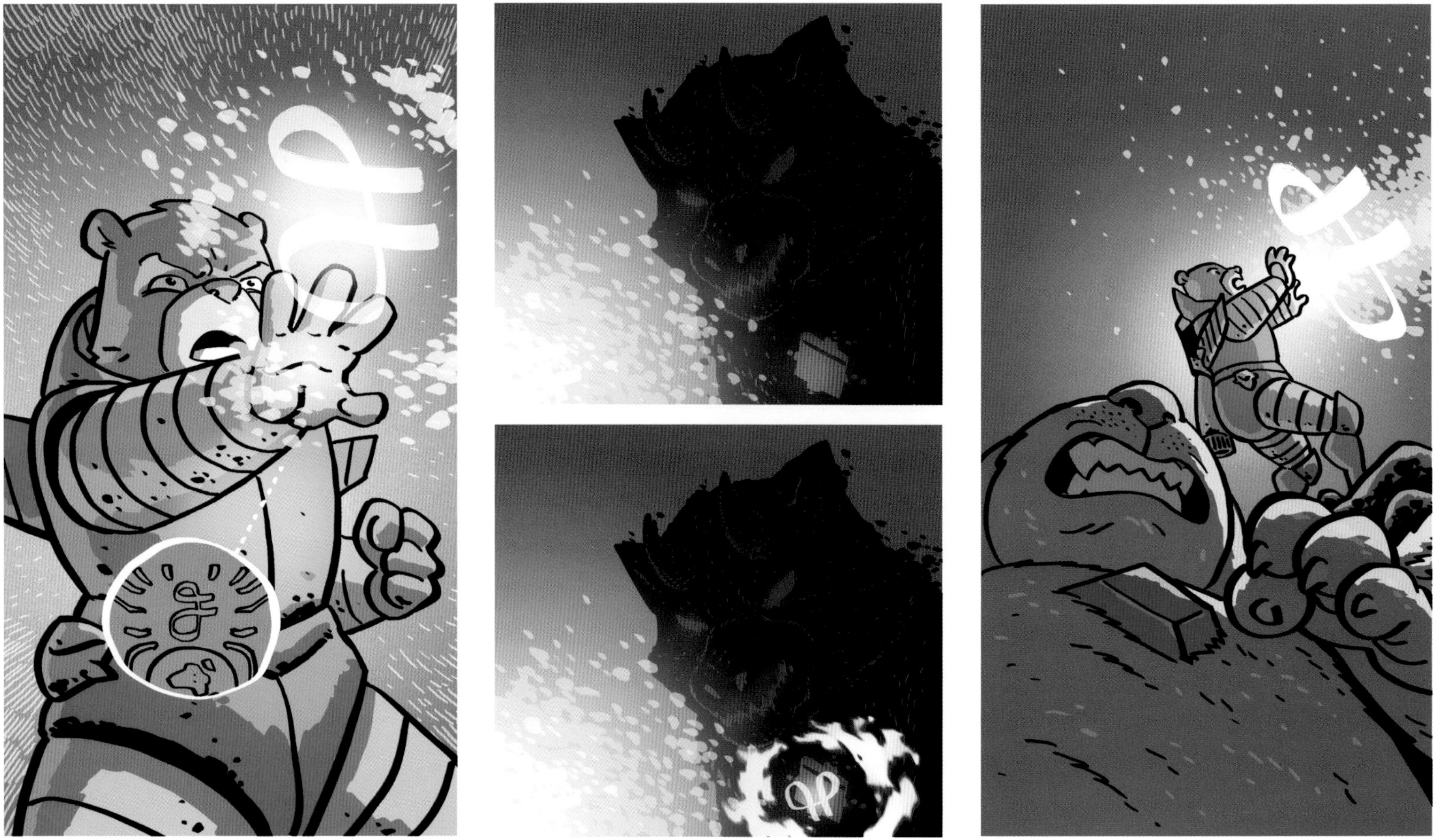

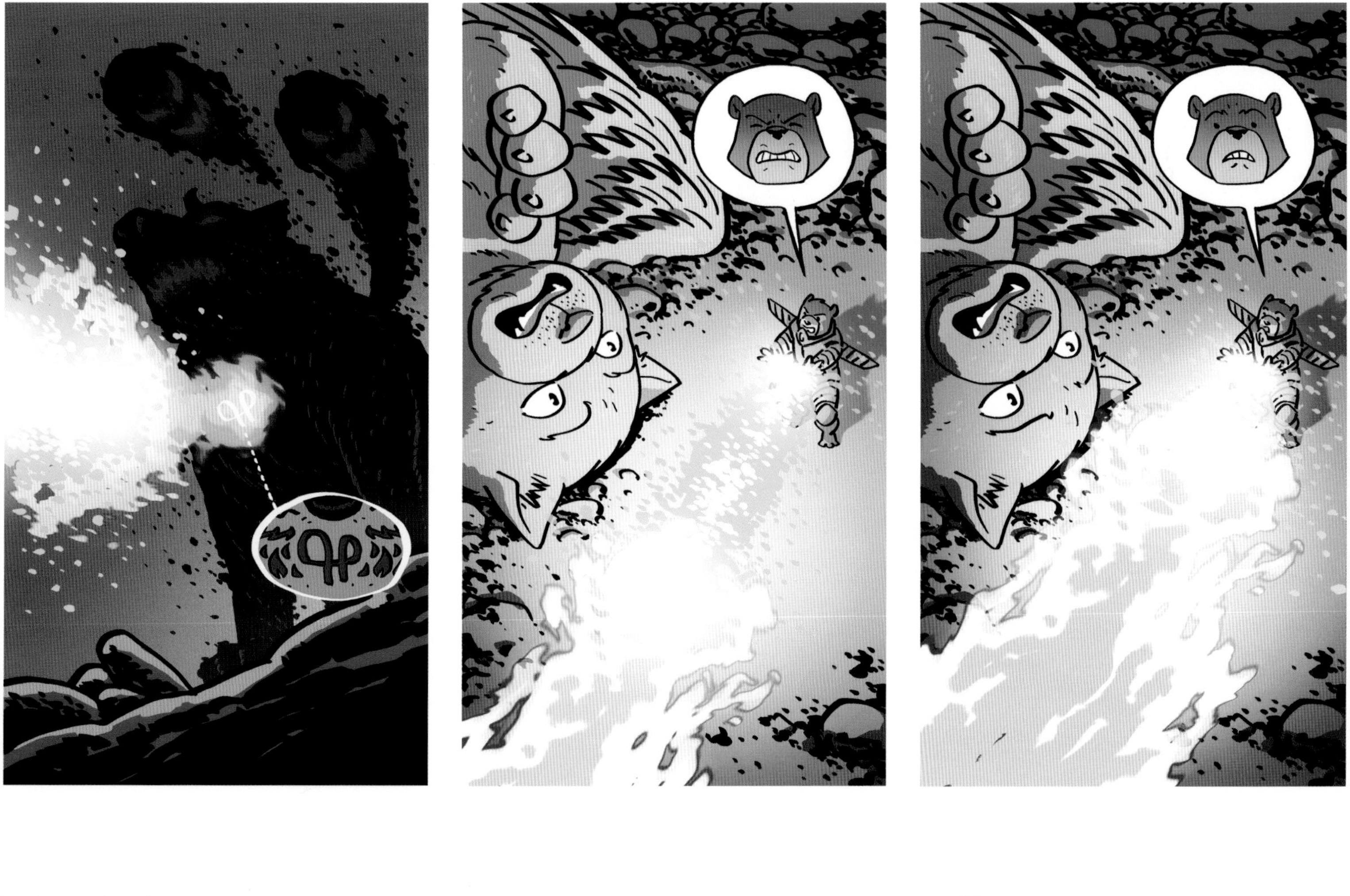

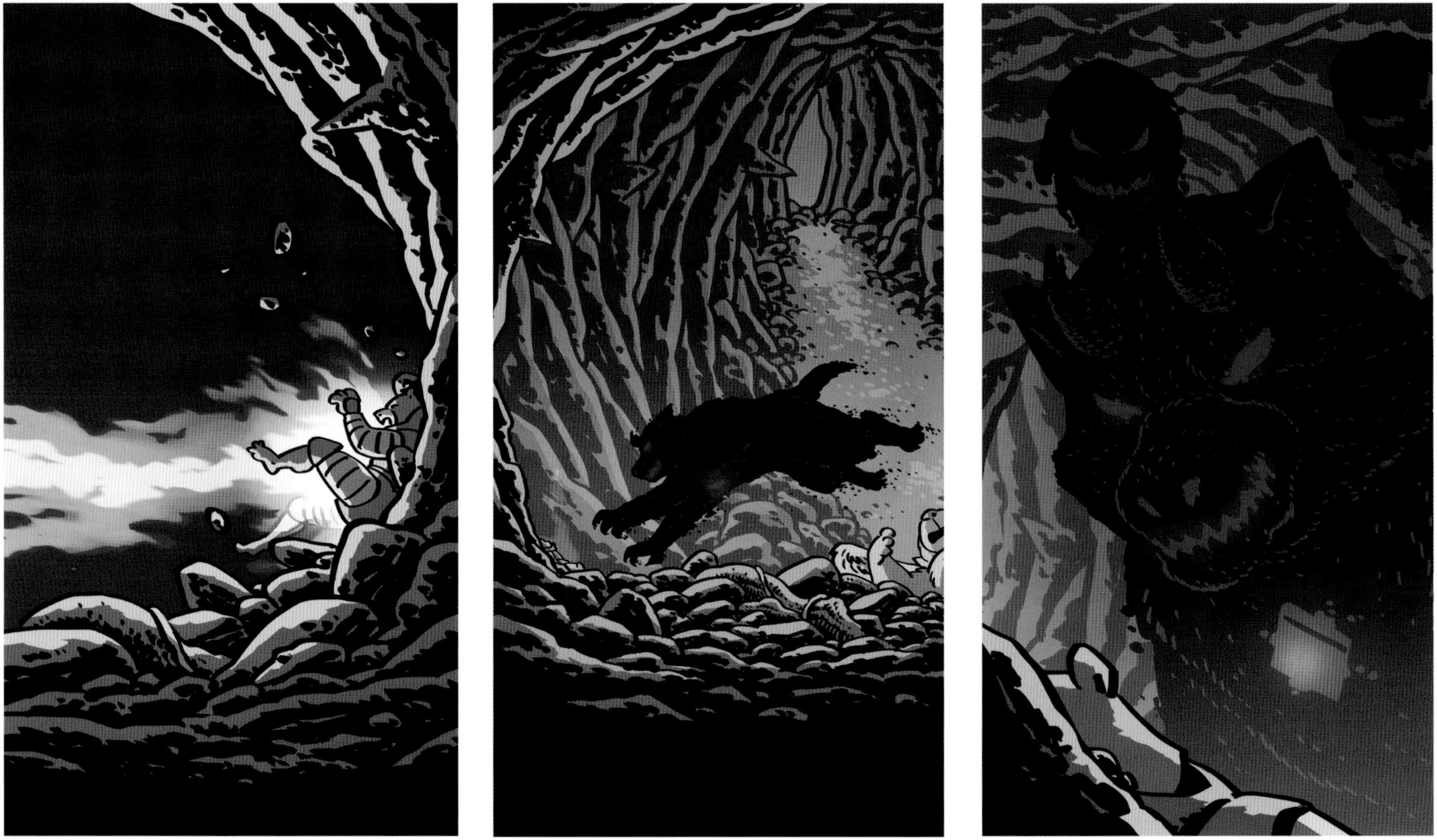

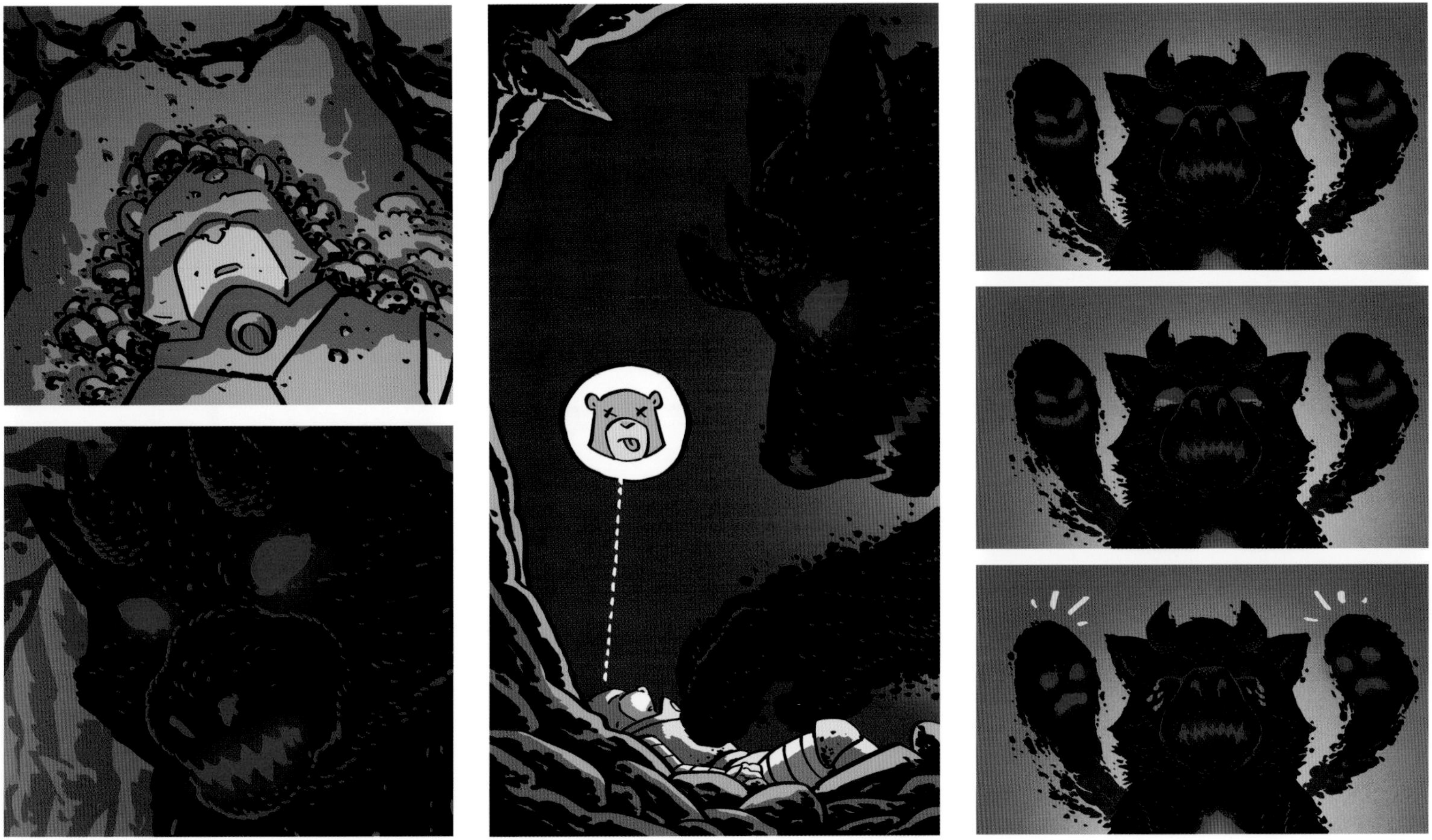

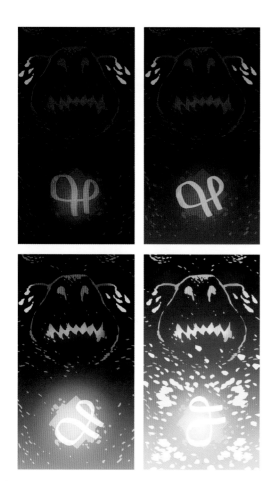

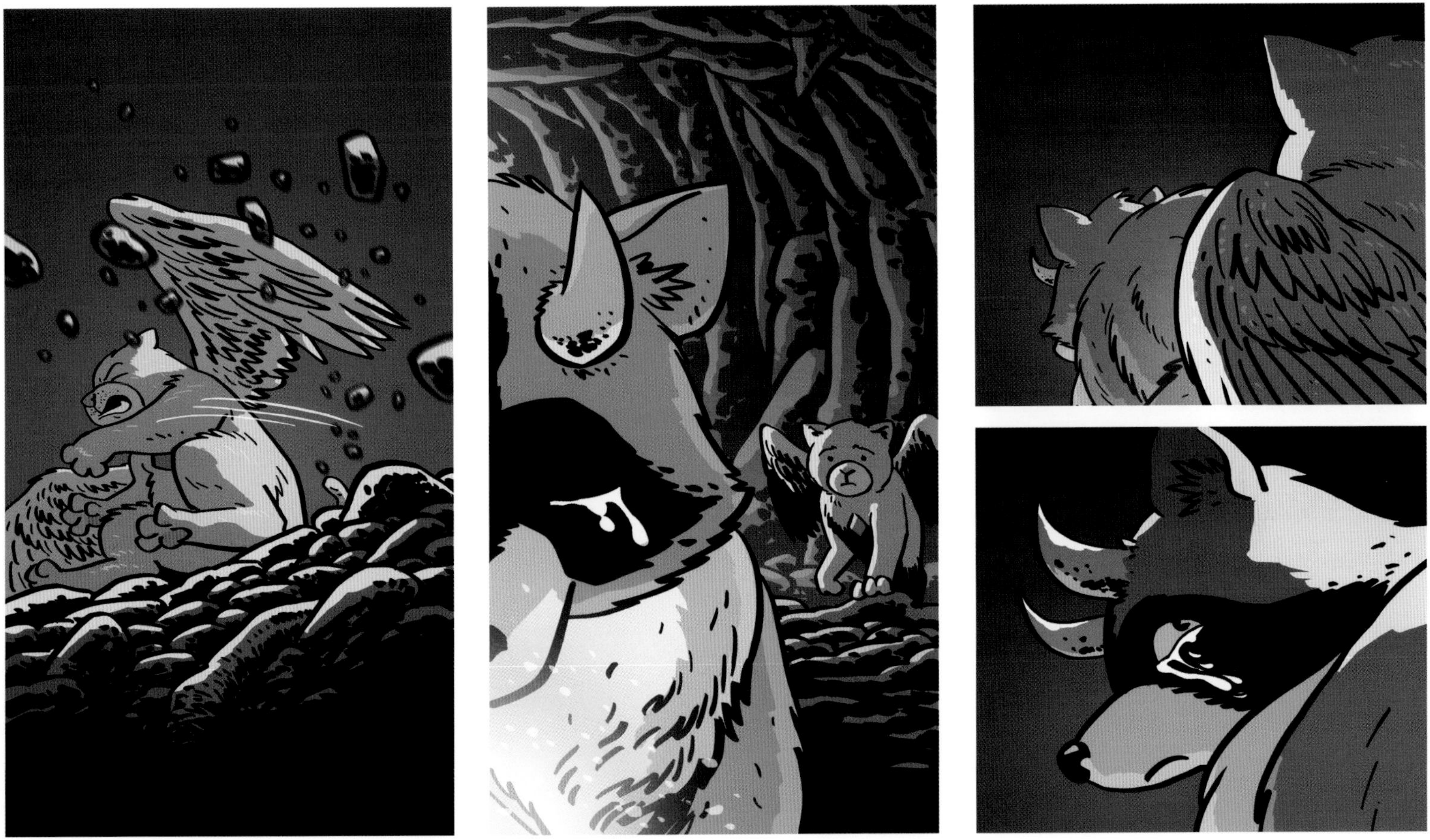

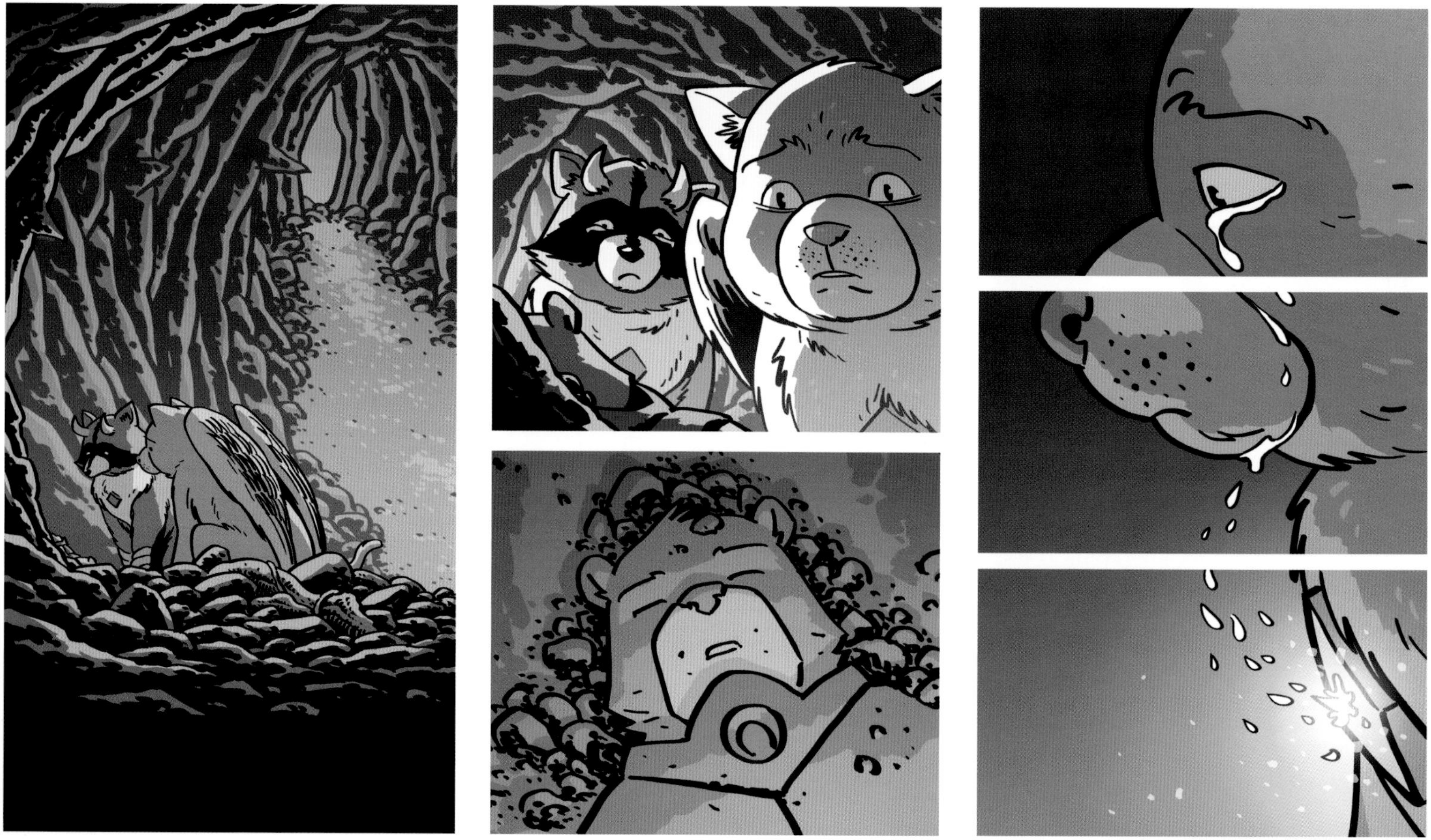

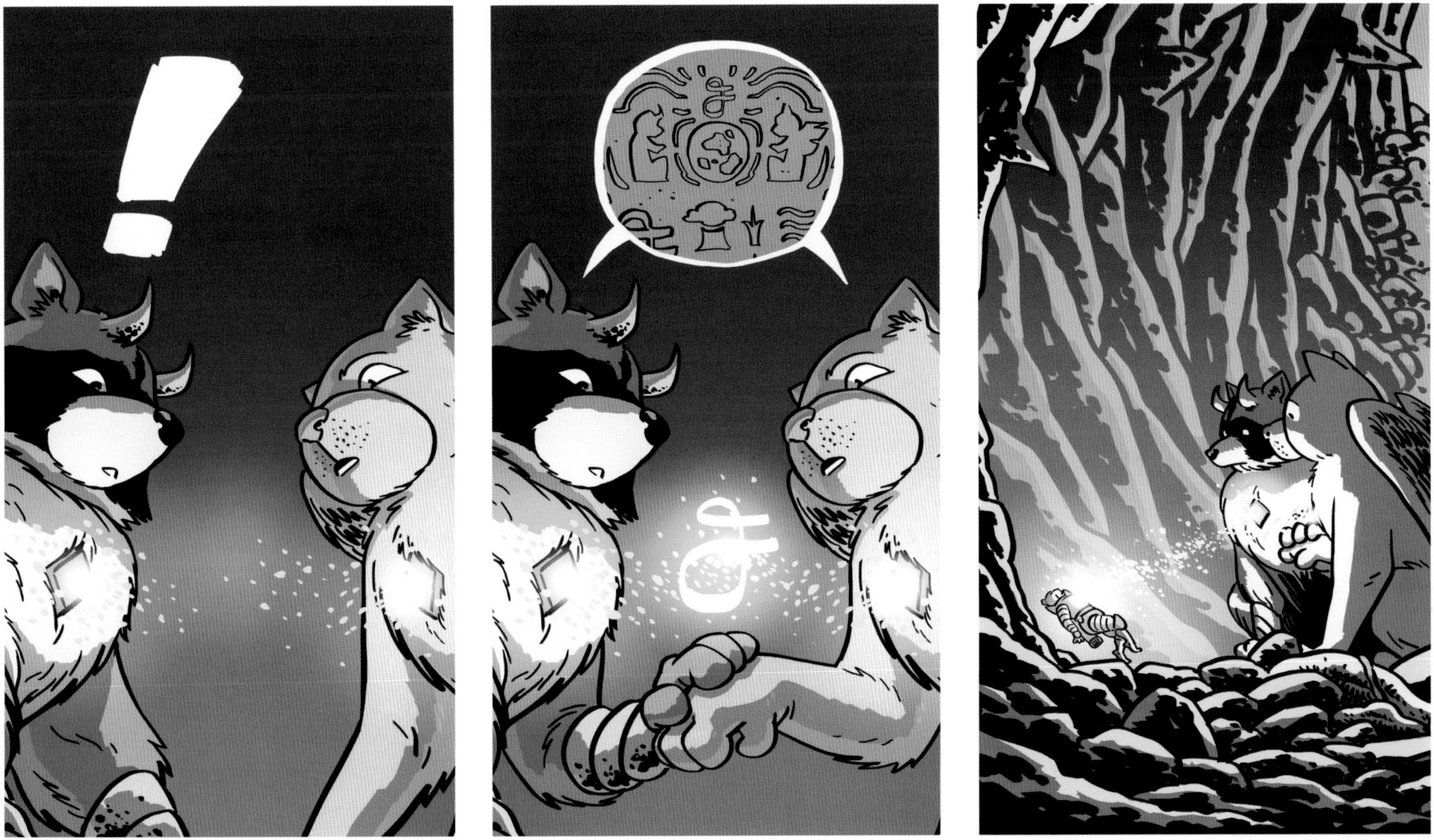
!

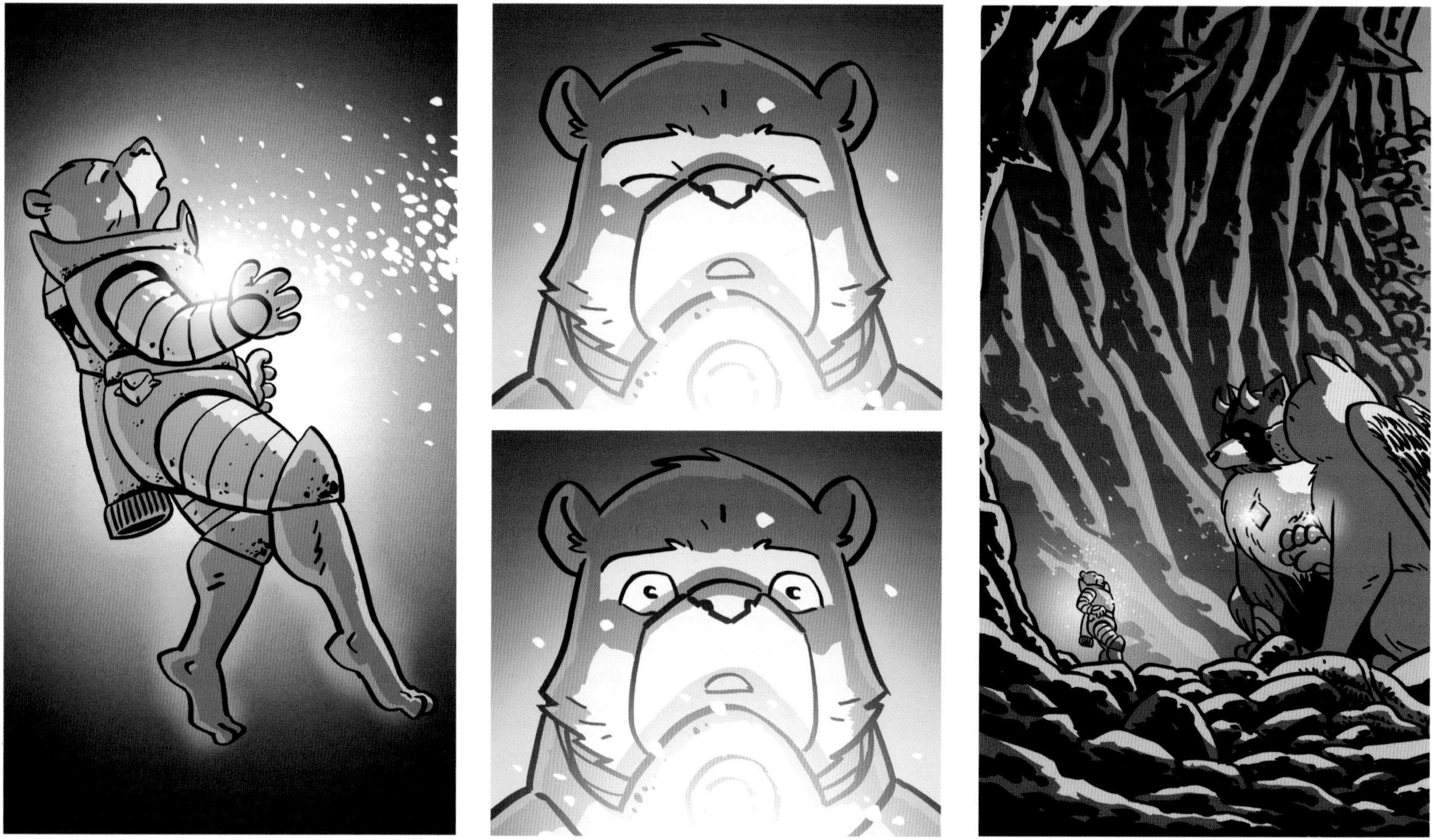

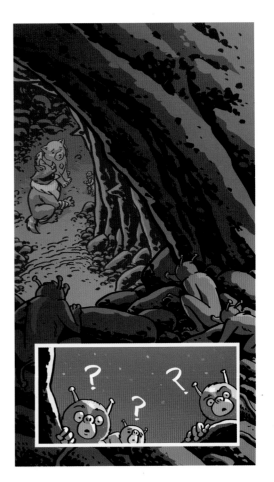

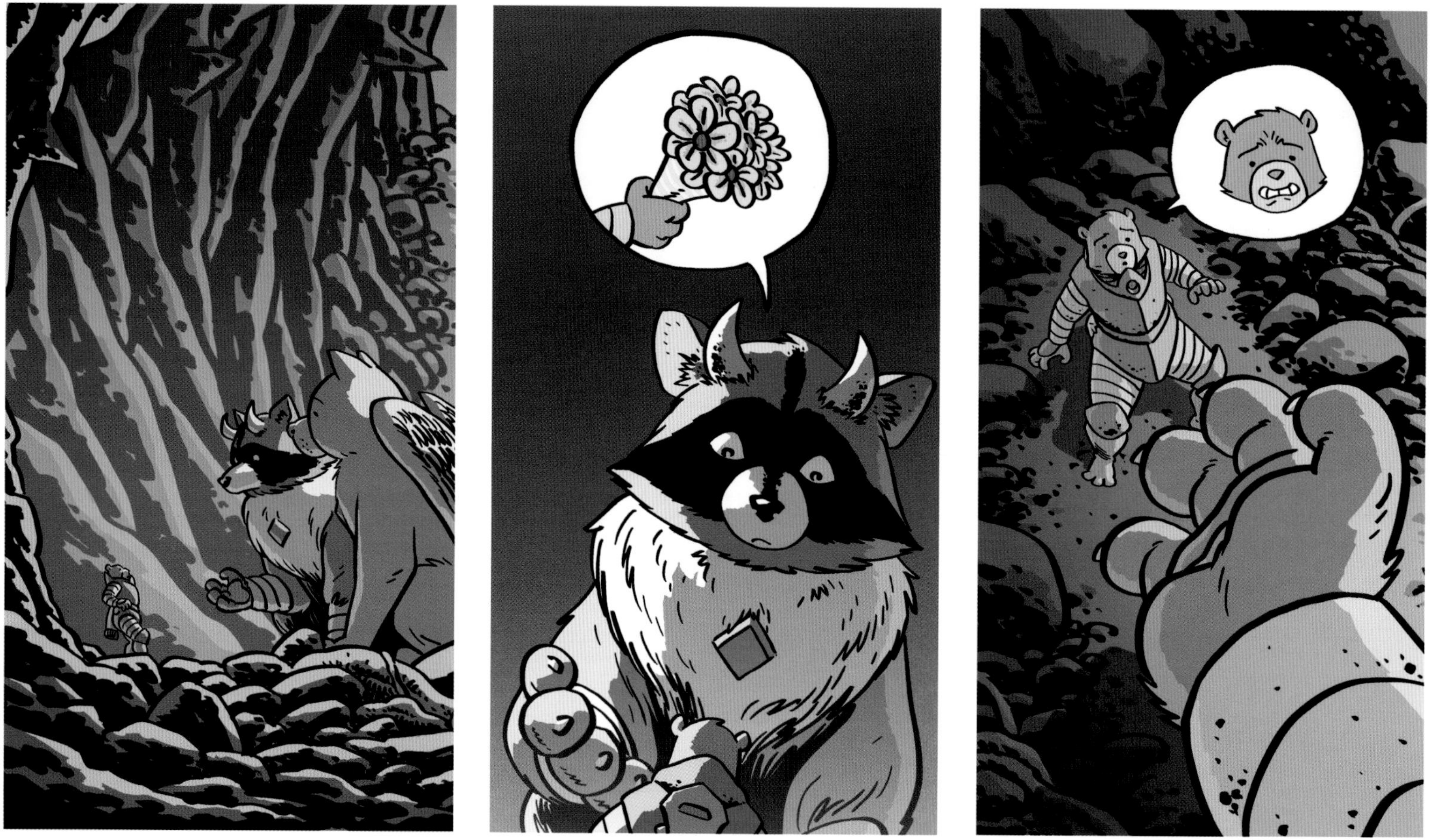

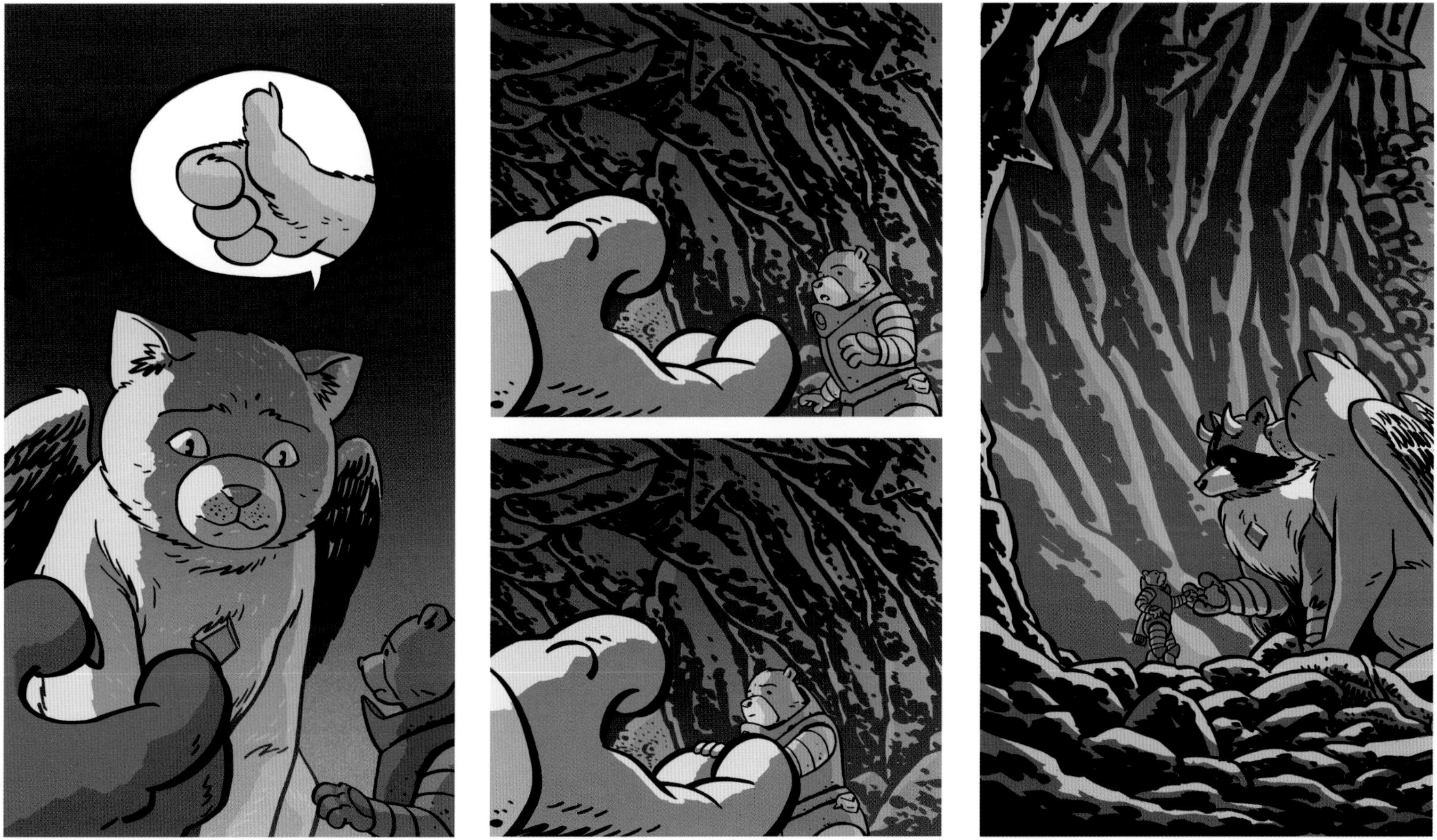

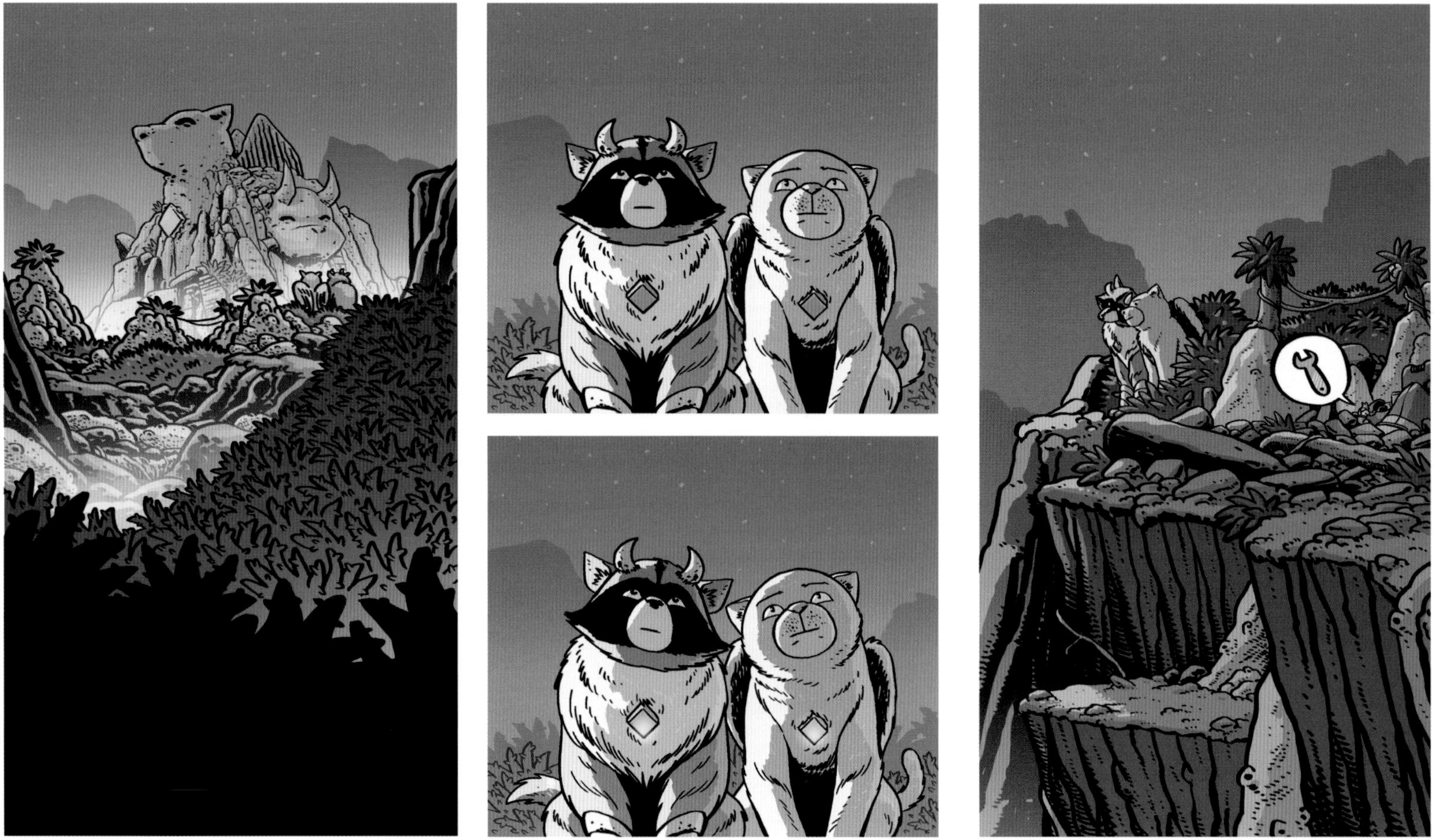

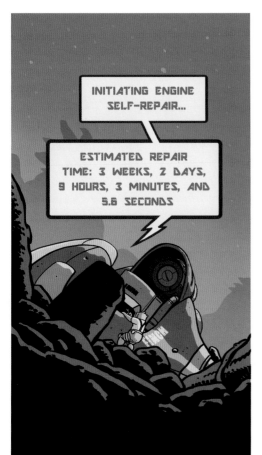

INITIATING ENGINE SELF-REPAIR...

ESTIMATED REPAIR TIME: 3 WEEKS, 2 DAYS, 9 HOURS, 3 MINUTES, AND 5.6 SECONDS

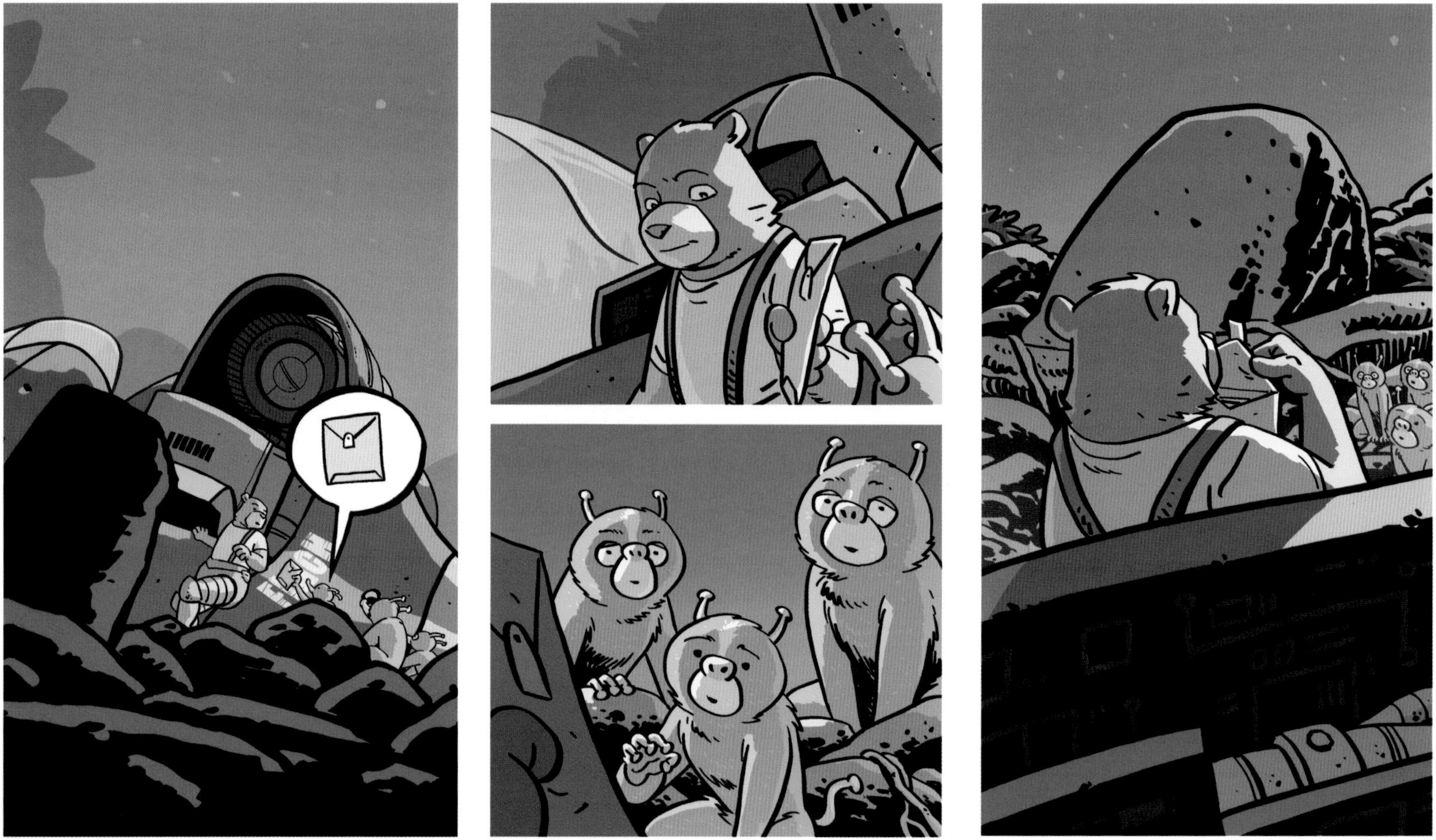

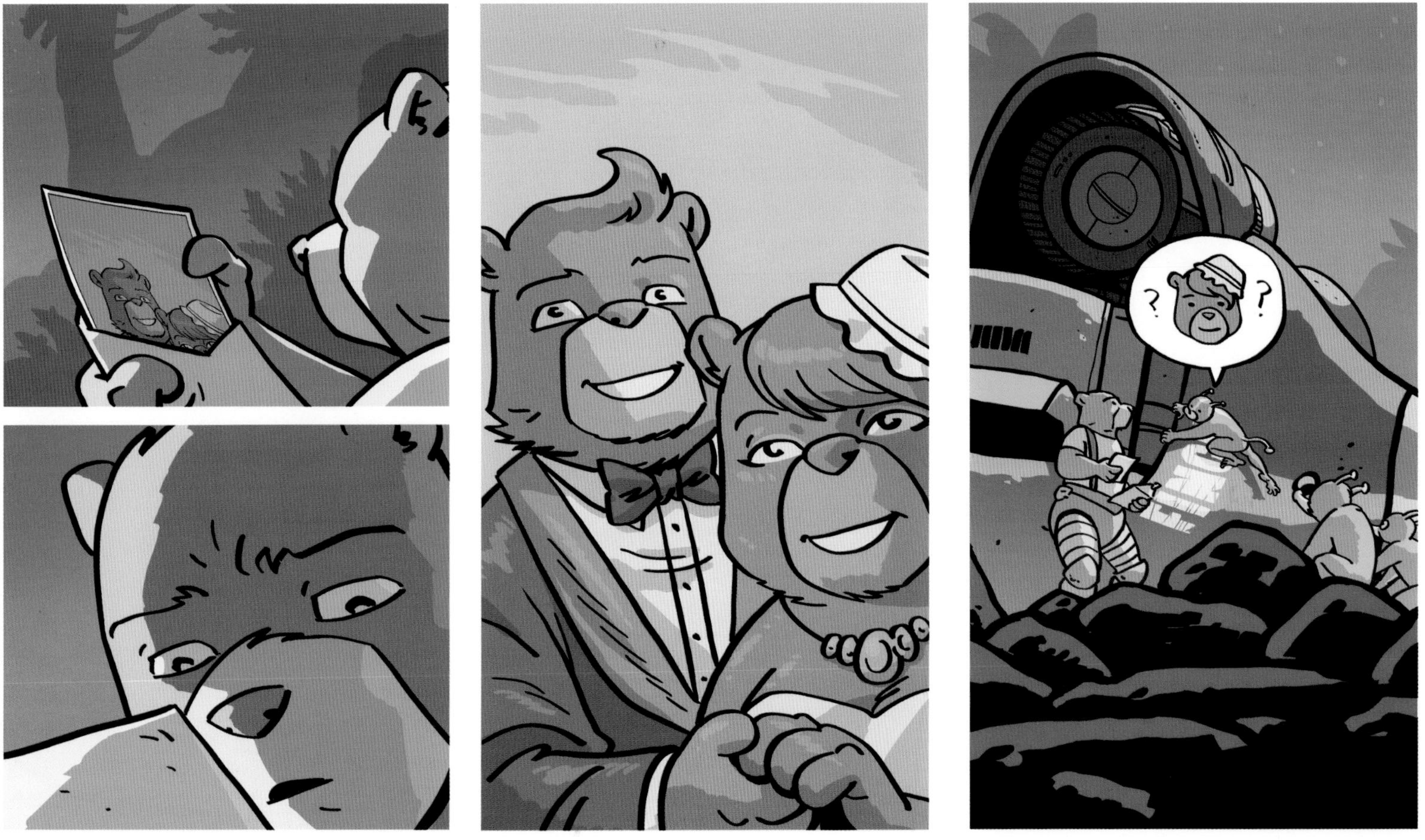
? ?

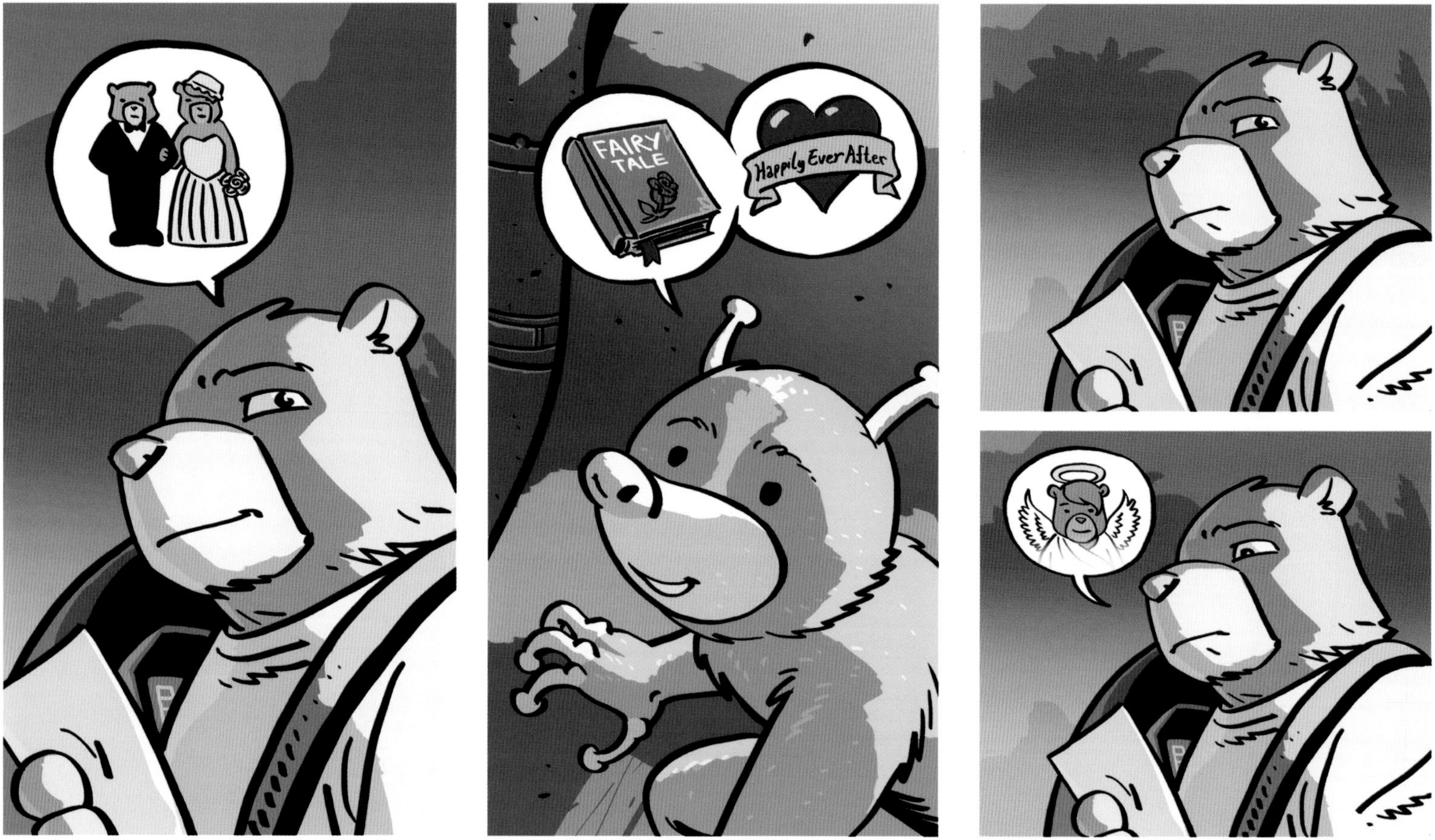
FAIRY TALE
Happily Ever After

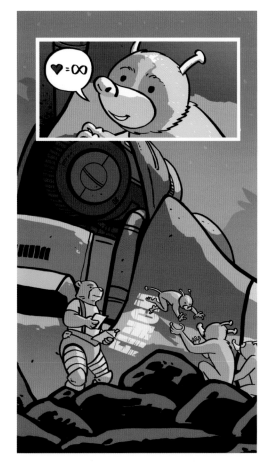

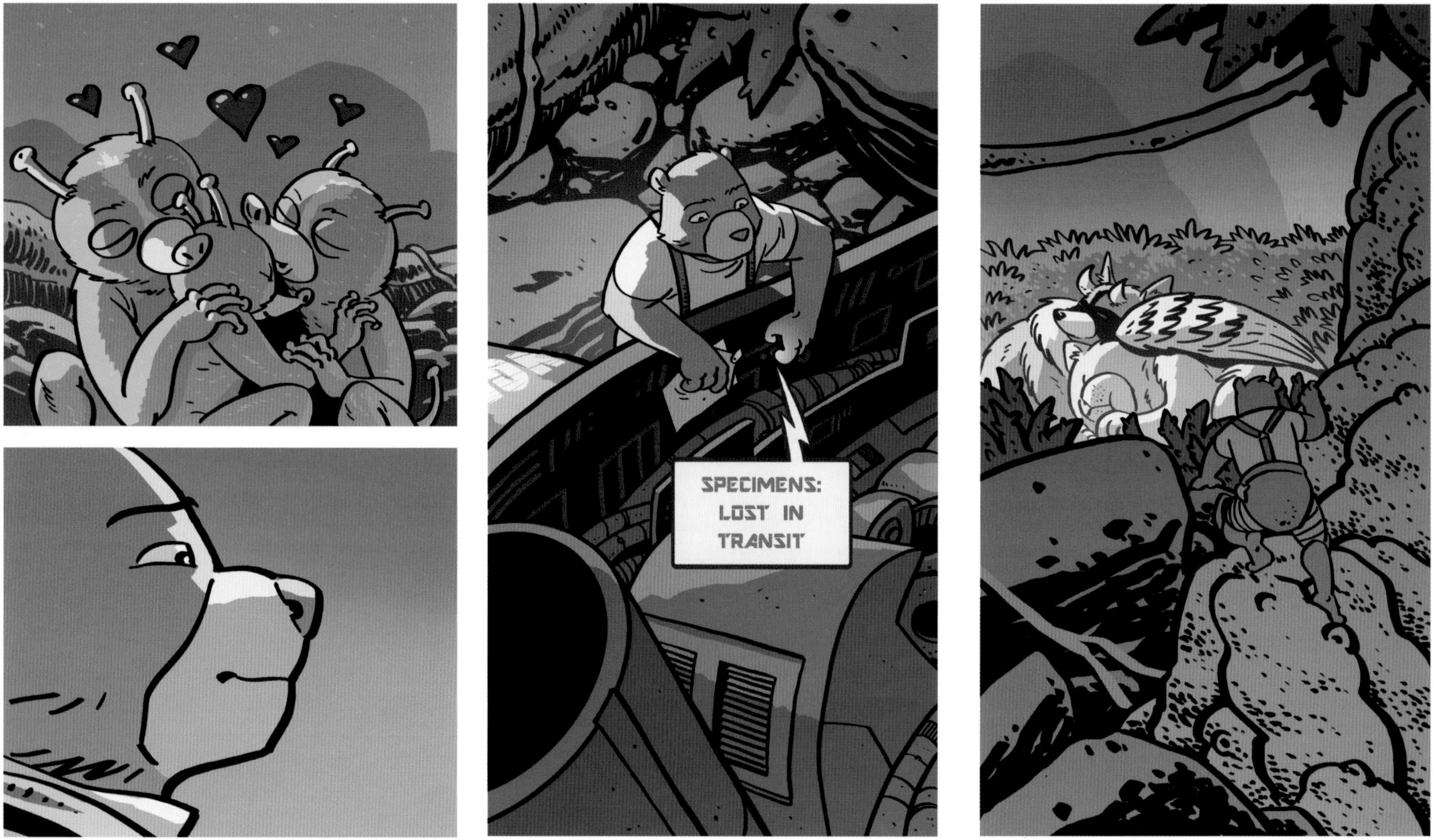
SPECIMENS: LOST IN TRANSIT

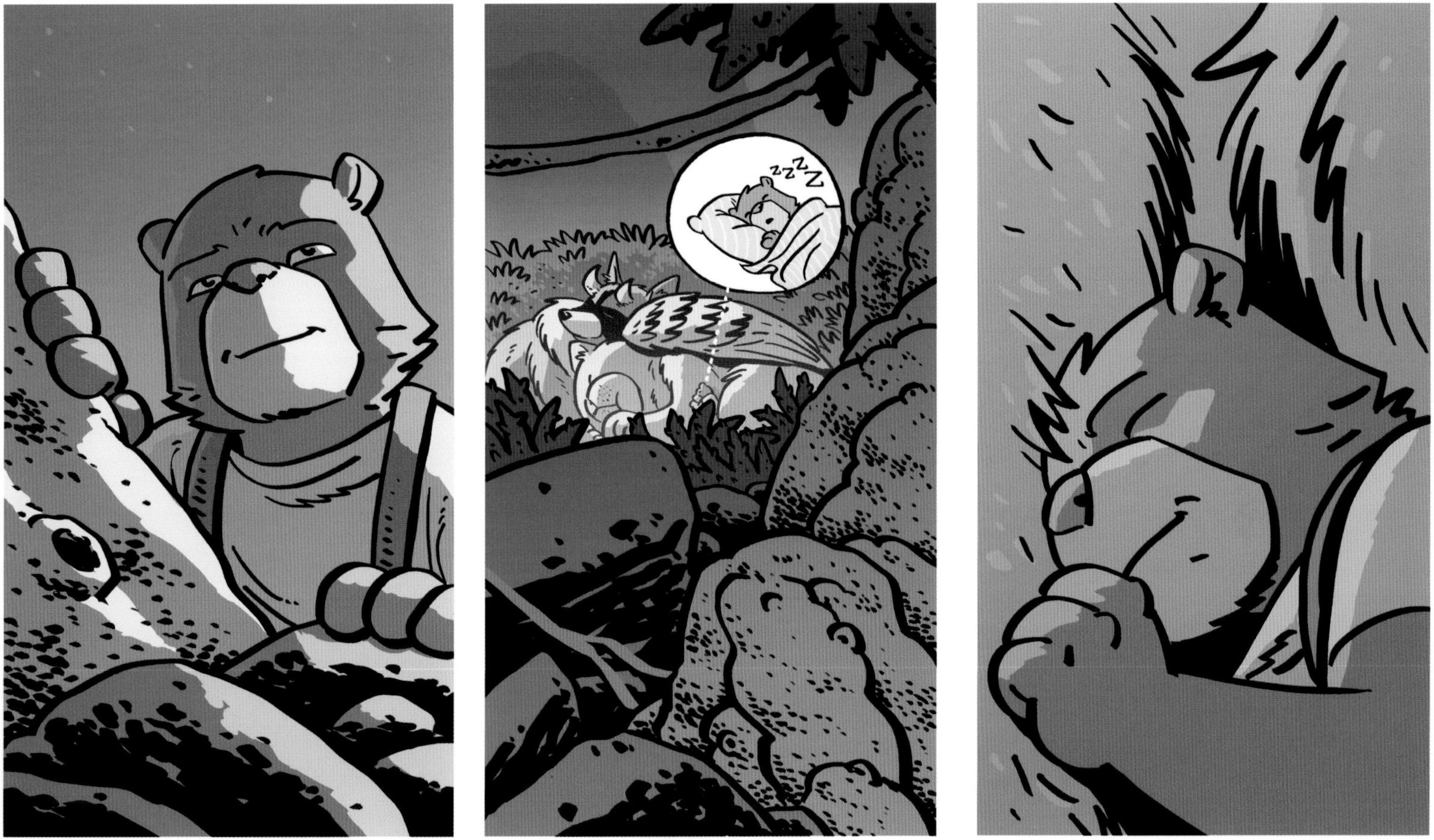
zzZZ

THE END

ETHAN YOUNG was born and raised in New York City. He is best known for *Nanjing: The Burning City*, winner of the 2016 Reuben Award for Best Graphic Novel. His other graphic novels include *The Battles of Bridget Lee* and *Life Between Panels*. In addition to comic book work, Young is also a prolific freelance illustrator, and once served as a character designer on *Major Lazer* on FXX.

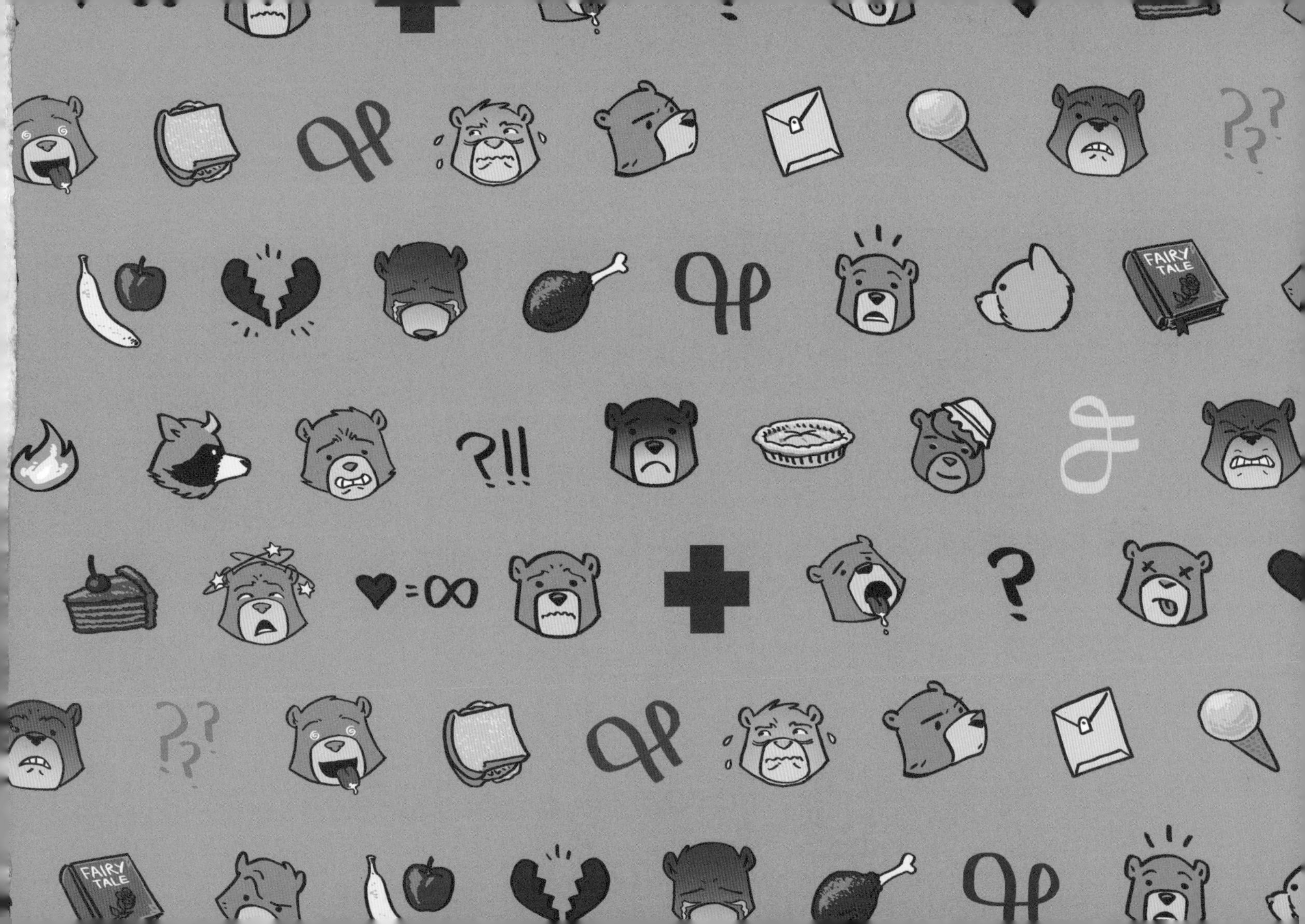
FAIRY TALE
FAIRY TALE

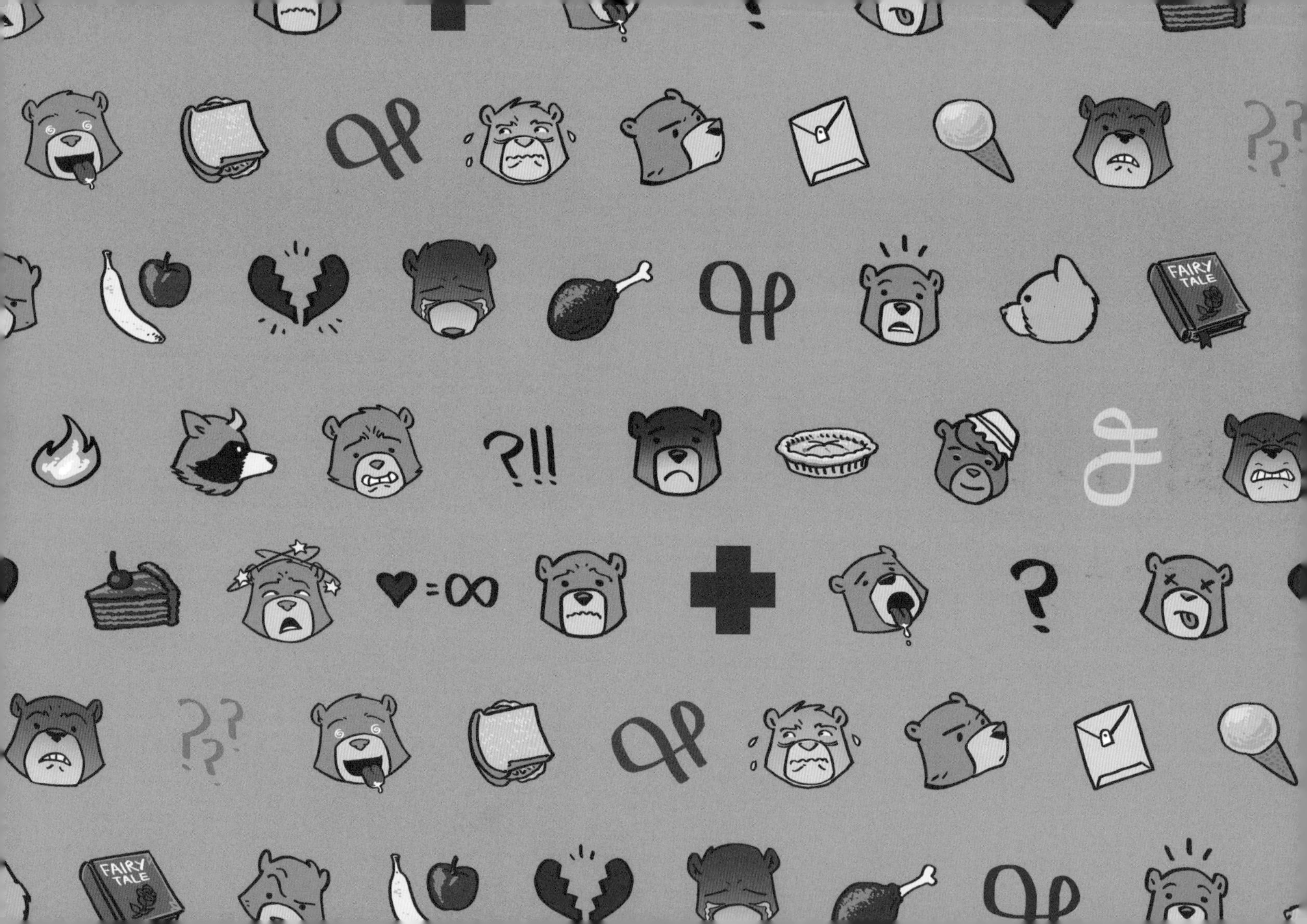
FAIRY TALE
?!!
FAIRY TALE